GRASSMAD

By

Bronwen Winter Phoenix

To Sam & Janice
Best wishes

Bronwen W Phoenix

Published by
Cauliay Publishing & Distribution
PO Box 12076
Aberdeen
AB16 9AL
www.cauliaybooks.com
First Edition

ISBN 978-0-9564624-9-7

Copyright © Bronwen Winter Phoenix

Dedicated to two men in my life; the one who hates drama, and the one who creates it. You know who you are.

Author Disclaimer:

My name is Bronwen Winter Phoenix; I am a teller of tall tales, and in no way should this novel be taken seriously. You are about to embark on a tall tale of a humorous, strange and quirky nature, sometimes saucy and sometimes scary, but most of all, for 'grown-ups'. It in no way reflects upon how things work in the real world, and I repeat, this novel is not to be taken seriously, but instead with an open mind and, if you like, an open heart. Thank you for reading and I hope you enjoy it.

Prologue

The rain fell heavily out of the dark Edinburgh sky. A lone female figure approached the building which stood tall ahead of her. Cool drops of water splashed over the smooth pale skin of her face, wetting her eyelashes, and slipping down off her black belted mac. She gave no expression as tiny black earphones, revealed only by her black hair pulled tight in a pony tail, blasted out heavy metal into her skull. In one leather-clad hand she carried a single black file. Her knee-high patent boots hardly made a sound as she approached the entrance. The letters displayed above read: Gatehouse Hotel. It was a five-star establishment, and already she knew exactly where to go. Her evasion technique in the past had never failed and she was able to stare straight ahead as she walked by reception and across the marble floor to the secure elevator. She entered the code quickly; aware that over her shoulder the watchman at the desk was eyeing her up, and probably about to speak even though he could no doubt hear the music which bled into the room from her mp3 player. As the doors swished closed behind her she allowed herself a small sigh of relief as she removed the torrent of harsh sounds and screams from her ears. She had always been more of a Sinatra fan, despite her appearance to the contrary.

The 3rd floor was reserved for those higher paying guests who wished not to be disturbed; especially in the early hours of the morning when things got a little... heavy. As she walked through the lush carpeted corridor, she ignored the sensations in her chest and made a controlled effort to slow down the pounding of her heart. When she was ready, she knocked at the door of Room 312, and listened for the reply of stunned silence she'd expected. The faintest hint of a smile passed her full lips as she pulled out the key from her hip pocket, and silently turned. Well, as silently as the old-style key allowed.

Unlike most hotels, the Gatehouse preferred to keep some traditional touches, such as proper old-fashioned locks instead of the simple electronic chip-on-a-chain 'keys'. Part of her felt glad for that; it kind of upped the suspense. As the door slowly swung forward, her curvaceous-but-toned figure was captured in the doorway and within, everything was as planned; she'd caught him in the act. She raised her left hand, and a camera flash highlighted the room. A pair of green eyes flashed wide in reminiscence of a feral cornered rat, and met with her icy cool response. She restrained her expression, although inside she didn't know whether she felt disgust or hilarity.

"Who – Who are you?" The old man cracked first.

"A friend," she replied, "Or perhaps an enemy - your choice." To the stranger in the room, her voice sounded smooth like the rain, and although so obviously foreign, it was at first hard for him to place. His voice, on the other hand, sounded frail and full of guilt as his puny pathetic body backed towards the corner. He reminded her of a worm, its soft pink underbelly exposed. The hair on his body was grey, unkempt and looked slightly sticky towards his nether regions. But he wasn't entirely exposed. He was wearing...

She turned away, disgusted; after all the camera had it captured.

"Wha-what do you want from me?"

"I have this... file. Evidence," she replied, "I have copies for the papers, too. Take a look at it, if you dare." His expression was one of fright, realisation, and then anger as he took a step forward. It was like watching a picture, or a frame-by-frame children's cartoon. He was almost spitting with rage.

"You ought to be ashamed of yourself," her voice was barely steady as she fought to remain icy cold. He held back no longer.

"You're one of them, aren't you? I should have known by the accent! What gives you the idea that you have the right to come here and threaten me? Filthy swine, should go back to where you belong! In the pig shit! Y-you won't get away with this!"

"Bribing bigoted bastard," she said, unable to disguise her hatred and disgust any longer, "You are the corrupt one; we simply want to perform as our family always has. We have the right, don't we? We have done nothing wrong and there is nothing you can do to stop us!" Eyes full of loathing now, his hand moved swiftly to reach for the file, knocking it into the air as he let out a low moan and grabbed his shrivelled chest, mouth open in shock and pain. "You're joking... right?"

Her voice held a hint of humour as she watched the show. But her smile soon faded as he slowly stumbled to the floor, and she realised it wasn't a performance. Nope; not a performance at all. His breathing came in loud, heaving whines and gasps as thoughts whirred round her mind. Could she let him die? No, because then that would make her an even greater monster than he was. Suddenly so vulnerable and unsure, she let the room key drop to the red-carpeted floor, pocketed the camera and calmly picked up the room's telephone, before uttering three simple words. She then turned swiftly and let the door swing open as she walked out of the room towards the fire stairs, exiting as quietly and deliberately as she'd entered.

From a safe distance, her watcher observed the dark foreboding of the hotel with a subtly building unease. The slim digits of his left hand wandered carefully down to the pocket of his brocade (cloth of kings) long-line jacket, and felt the reassuring presence of his mobile phone. It was yet to ring. It was the unpredictability that most unnerved him about these sorry affairs, mixed with a good hint of disgust and loathing for bringing his involvement to such crude matters. But, needs must. His own involvement was, for the moment anyway, minimal, and he most certainly preferred to keep it that way.

He kept an eye trained on the hotel entrance. All was quiet; much too quiet for his liking. Whenever a scene was as quiet as this one, it usually meant death or twisted dealings of some kind. He was sure of the latter, but not so certain of the former. After all, he put little trust in the morals of bourgeois performing whores. Whether she'd deliver the goods was almost certain, but at what price was anybody's guess. He pushed the thought that he could possibly have missed it to the back of his mind. Such a thought was ridiculous, after all, when he'd been watching since she'd entered the building. Feisty little thing, with more attitude than he cared to dwell on for any great length of time – at least not in public, at any rate.

The situation had turned serious, yet it was not his game to play, which is why he stood well back. The car was ready in case of an emergency, not that anyone would recognise him in such an out-of-place setting. Why he had to be there in the first place was really anyone's guess, but there he was, nevertheless. There, the door had opened and the female figure trotted like a dark fox out into the night. It had been done, for better or for worse. Too far away to tell the expression on her face, but close enough for discomfort, he narrowed his eyes. She was walking faster, edgier then when she'd entered the place. Something was most definitely up. He watched her disappear into the night, before reaching once more for his mobile and pushing speed dial.

"Are you still inside? It's out of the bag," he stated, still facing the front entrance of the hotel. A reply came from the other line.

"He's what? Are you sure?" He listened to the reply, his expression hard to read, partly because of the dark, and partly because he was very unreadable.

"Ah, well. He didn't want my help. He was lost to us, anyway. And you've got it? Thank God for small favours, at least. Goodness, what a mess... going to have to take care of things myself," he muttered over the sound of approaching sirens. It was all a dreadful inconvenience, but now it was in his hands.

"No... For God's sake, no. I hate cats, they give me

allergies... oh, what does it matter? Now, I'm getting out of here and I suggest you do the same."

"No, it's not what we planned. It's better," he growled, before rather aggressively pressing the 'end call' button on his touch-phone and retreating back to his car.

1

"It's not that you have to see it to believe it; on the contrary, you have to believe it to see it." – Elizabeth Wurzel

Winnie Hobbes

Far, far away from the darkened city, a small girl sat under a papaya tree, partially shielded from the hot African sun. She wore a burgundy vest and matching shorts as she waited in her temporary resting place. Her long black hair did not blow in the wind, for there was no wind today; yet she was accustomed to the heat. She would shiver if it got cold. An albino red-billed hornbill watched over the girl from atop the same tree, whilst viewing the surrounding splendour of the Ghana jungle. Although the bird was very rare and seldom seen, it was at home in the quietened jungle, and felt safe in the girl's company. In fact, it was fair to say the girl had drawn the bird there, simply with her very nature of being. If the bird could have talked, it would have said the girl was special. But the bird could not talk, and was not at all bothered by this thought. After all, the bird was simply a bird. A rustling of leaves signalled the approach of another, causing the bird to abruptly take wing, which in turn caused the girl to look up beyond the tree. She smiled a wide and genuine smile. In the near distance and beyond the trees, came the familiar figure of an elderly woman in a cream safari suit and matching hat. She walked slowly, with a cane to steady herself, yet she walked with the assurance and grace of age and true wisdom. The woman was Winnie Hobbes.

Stopping for a moment, Winnie viewed the surrounding area of the jungle with good humour and kindness, before raising an arm and waving in the direction of the girl, whose smile could be seen even with Winnie's old eyes. It was their usual meeting place, and Winnie had walked the distance from her makeshift camp every day ever since she had first laid eyes on the girl. The girl was a mystery to Winnie. All the other children had run into her arms and welcomed her with trusting smiles, confident words and many, many questions. Yet the girl had not been like the others. Instead she had not spoken a word, and had a permanent faraway look in her dark, soulful eyes. She was indeed beautiful, with a ghost of a smile on her lips and skin so dark it looked almost the colour of pure ebony. No, the girl had not exactly come to Winnie, but instead had quietly followed on, always a few steps behind the others. And when they had come to the jungle, the girl had followed but would only go so far as the very tree she sat under now. So Winnie walked the extra distance every day, no matter what and always the girl would be there, waiting.

"Granny, Granny!" called a young boy called Gift. He began running down the hill behind her, through the thick growth of the trees. All the children called her 'Granny', as for some reason it was the name she felt most comfortable with. It was the name she was always given back home, in Ireland, and it would remind her of that home every day. The boy handed her a small pink flower, and grinned.

"Why, thank you, Gift," Winnie said, her smile creasing the corners of her face with genuine joy at seeing the boy's smile. The boy turned and ran, still shy at her presence, and she carefully pocketed the flower, with consideration of the effort the boy taken to find it for her. As she approached the tree, the girl gave Winnie a smaller, sadder smile, which Winnie was still thankful for. Slowly and silently, she found a place to sit next to the girl, who appeared to be calm and totally at ease with her, as always.

"Hello there, Magdalena," Winnie said, her voice deliberately steady and friendly. The girl nodded, still silent.

"I brought you some food, and water," said Winnie,

noticing the bottle of water the girl carried was almost empty. Of course, she could always get more from the stream, but Winnie brought it to her anyway. Carefully she placed it down, cautious not to get too close as to startle the girl. There was something very profound about her, something that Winnie could not quite place her finger on. Perhaps a deep sadness had stopped her words, as Winnie was certain the girl knew how to speak. She just refused to. Nevertheless, Winnie felt a great comfort in her company, and instinct told her that one day, the girl would need her.

Some of the village children had told Winnie the girl's name was Magdalena, and so far she had responded when Winnie had addressed her as such. Apart from her name, Winnie knew that Magdalena had been orphaned at a young age, and had been brought up by a woman on the outskirts of Ghana, called Markarite. The woman had since passed away and Magdalena mostly kept herself to herself, a small scavenger yet to find a new home. Winnie had a feeling that particular story was only the tip of the iceberg; she still had much to learn about Magdalena. But she at least hoped there would be plenty of time for them to get there. She hoped that one day, the small, skinny little girl would finally trust her enough to open her mouth and utter those important first words. Until then, she was happy to soak in her company, and although not a lot was said, Winnie took a great deal of enjoyment simply from being there next to Magdalena.

They would sit for a while under the tree, quietly taking in each other's company as the day stealthily passed them by. Time seemed to pass a lot quicker for Winnie these days, and she had begun to notice that there were far fewer days ahead than she'd left in the past. Time was precious, but well spent on these hot afternoons. They invigorated her, energised her in a way, as her old bones settled under the tree. And in that time Winnie's mind would wander back to Ireland. She had left a family there, a family she would one day return back to. Her son, Ambrose, would be waiting for her with welcoming arms. She sent postcards and sometimes even got replies, although she moved around a lot. She'd always thought postcards were a wonderful thing. And although she had many loved ones back in Ireland, her thoughts would more often than not be drawn to just one; her grandson. Living in Edinburgh, he was sometimes troubled, a quiet soul who had seemed to suffer more in his heart than others she had known throughout her life in the small town where she was born. There was something in his eyes, so bright and blue yet at the same time concealing something much stronger, deeper. Yet he wasn't entirely different from Winnie herself. No, he was more like her than she could have guessed. And just like her, he had flown the nest to travel less further afield to Scotland's capital.

Her grandson's name was Stanley.

2

"Have you noticed there is never a third act in a nightmare? They bring you to a climax of terror and then leave you there. They are a work of poor dramatists." – Sir Max Beerbohm.

Stanley Hobbes

Stanley Hobbes had a tie in his collection for every occasion; pinks, blacks, blues, spotted, striped, woven, hand-woven, silk, nylon, cotton blends; ones for weddings, funerals, holidays, meetings, work, play; ones for Mondays, Tuesdays, Fridays... Many people collected many things. He was a collector of ties.

As the lift took him up the various floors to the Edinburgh Times office, his hand unconsciously wandered to the blue silk affair he wore today. It happened to be light blue to match his shirt, and this made him feel curiously at ease.

People often got excited when he told them he worked for the paper, but their faces quickly turned to indifference when they learned of his job title. Being an obituary writer, it had never bothered Stanley - in fact he had almost come to expect it. It never really occurred to him that he craved something more than writing stories about the recently deceased, but then he hadn't been thinking very much at all lately, except perhaps about the weather.

Today would be the same as any other day; the same blue coffee mug he kept on his desk, the clickety-click of his slightly discoloured keyboard and the faraway whirring noise of the printer churning out exciting scoops of the living and lively. *Alive and kicking.*

Stanley had no need to print off anything. He wrote about dead people, alone in a small, dull room with only Clive

17

for company; quiet, vampire-like Clive, who seemed to dislike sunlight, and closed all the blinds in his vicinity without exception.

Because of the size of the room, Clive's vicinity also happened to be Stanley's vicinity, but he didn't mind too much. Health and safety regulations meant the light was bright enough to prevent eye strain, and who was Stanley to block out Clive's eccentricities when he revelled in his own on a daily basis.

The elevator finally swished open and Stanley took a few cautious steps forward. But when he looked up the view didn't look quite right. Instead of the brown carpet and beige walls, the corridor seemed to stretch out for miles in deep, smooth walls of blue and a floor that looked like black marble. His feet echoed on the hard surface, and before he could check what floor he was on, he felt a shift in the air. Turning, he saw there was no elevator behind him anymore, only more corridors that seemed to go on forever. Hesitantly, he started to walk forward again, trying to make out something – anything – in the distance, but the expanse seemed to fade into black, as if it would suddenly stop and become nothing. His heart sank as the realisation of the dream hit him – always late. It would be any minute now and although he knew it was coming, it would nevertheless make him jump. He halted abruptly. In the distance in front of him a figure dressed entirely in white dashed from one side of the corridor to the other.

"Make it stop," he whispered. His heart started beating faster in his chest, and with trepidation he slowly started to walk, then run, to the spot where it had crossed. He had no choice; the way it always felt in this particular dream. The corridor came to a crossing and he turned right, the way he had seen her – and he knew it was her – sprint in her bare feet. It looked empty and exhausting. Silently he waited for a noise, his intuition telling him there would be a clue he didn't really want to hear. A high-pitched, yet faraway moan came through the hall and made the hairs on the back of his neck stand on end. Shakily

18

he pushed forward, almost unwilling to look. He knew what was coming. The noise steadily grew louder, until he was standing outside one solitary blue door, almost invisible in the wall. It was all exactly the same. He could imagine her behind the door, pressed up against it, beckoning for his warmth and waiting, always waiting. But that was ridiculous because he knew the first thing he'd see was her eyes; always those eyes craving warmth that her body could no longer provide. Taking a deep breath, his hand reached for the handle and turned it without making a sound. It yielded, and the door slowly opened. She stood before him, her white dress flowing in the odd indoor breeze, every strand of her long, blonde hair perfect as it had always been in his mind. Time seemed to move slowly. He didn't want to look, but he knew he had no choice and suddenly there they were, piercing straight into his soul. Her eyes were dead eyes, out of focus with one pupil significantly larger than the other, but somehow they managed to see him anyway. Her face reacted and an ugly smile spread across her lips. Her red lipstick had long ago rubbed off, leaving a painted red crust along the outer rim of her lower lip. Her name was Lorraine.

Before the nightmare could go any further, he managed to find himself and he turned, stumbling for the door as he heard her laugh pierce the air behind him, closer than he had expected. He imagined her staring eyes and red encrusted lips were right against the nape of his neck. He shivered as he felt her cold fingers on his back, and that was all he needed to run. The corridors spread out into eternity and he kept running, turning corners and trying to somehow find a way out of this nightmare but the maze continued to elude him. He couldn't help panicking as he heard her feet faintly echoing behind him. *How could someone that looked so dead be so quick on their toes?* Her laugh began to grow again as somehow she gained on him. Dread filled his whole body as he came to an abrupt halt, not daring to go another step further.

"Stanley! Stanley... Let's play a different game now,

huh?" She called to him in a playful voice that wasn't quite hers; it was dead and thick as if her vocal cords weren't quite attached properly anymore... it sounded like broken glass to his ears. All the energy flooded out of his system and he found himself sliding pathetically down the wall until he was in a crouching position. The dream seemed to be sliding into a confusion of chaos and, finding it harder to understand the situation, it was as if the air had started to thicken around him, making it hard to think. Where was she? Oddly, he could hear music, first faraway but slowly getting louder and he cursed it for blocking out her cold words – how would he be able to tell which way she was coming for him... did it even matter? A hand slowly reached around the corner in front of him and he watched helplessly as her blackened nails scratched across the wall, the veins on her hand stood out from the skin as if they had been starved of water, or blood. He could imagine those hands reaching out for him, so she could take his blood instead, that somehow she had turned into an evil monster – a vampire. The music gradually got louder as she almost fell into his view. The eyes had found him again and he was unable to move, paralysed in place as she inched forward towards him. Her weak body looked almost unable to support her and now her dress was ripped, showing her bare skin. Her ribs stood out as if she had been starved for months. The music bothered him – it sounded like noise, he couldn't figure out what was playing. At least it was blocking out Lorraine's voice. As she got closer, the marks on her neck resurfaced. They were bright red, as if she had worn a tight necklace of barbed wire. That was enough for him. He buried his head in his arms and tried to make it go away. It didn't take him long to realise he was leaning forwards, almost as if he had fallen to the ground.

He awoke with a start, his body jolting into the bed. The same music was playing, but as he cautiously looked up, he was relieved to see the familiar surroundings of his bedroom. He'd had another nightmare. His old radio had once again picked up

Edinburgh's Polish channel, which explained why he couldn't understand the words. It sounded like heavy metal. That was when he realised the time. 08:43. Surely not… he was due into work at nine. "Shit," he muttered, switching the radio off with a rather abrupt smack. Quickly pulling himself out of bed he stumbled, clutching his arm which had seized with pins and needles, whilst trying to find a clean shirt in his wardrobe and attempting to brush his dark, unkempt hair into something almost resembling neatness. He looked over to the bed, where Jasper the cat stared at him with contempt for his rude awakening. His small Persian grey face looked less than pleased.

"What?" he asked the cat, "You should be used to the routine by now." The room had a certain minimalist charm. He reached out for a shirt in the alphabetised closet and for a second it was just like any other Monday. Then he turned towards the tie rack. Stanley Hobbes did indeed have a tie for every occasion, a little quirk that had followed from his early tie-collecting days. But something stopped him from selecting one from the rack as the dream came back to him, coldness trickling down his spine. Almost a year ago, Lorraine had used one of his ties to hang herself.

3

"I don't believe in hatred anymore, I hate to think of how I felt before." – Edie Bricknell

She was in his head again, like a dark shadow over his whole day. Lorraine had used to tell him off for being a 'neat freak' but since the accident that was never really an accident, things had gotten almost out of control. Sometimes he showered three times in one day, as if trying to scrub away the memory from his slim body, yet never feeling completely... clean wasn't quite the word. It was more like clear – he never felt completely clear of the past, the memories. But then, who does? Luckily by the time he left for work he'd managed to get a grip of things again and the sun shone brightly as he made it out the door at two minutes to nine.

He wore a casual dark blue jacket, a light blue shirt (minus the tie), black trousers and smart shoes. He left his apartment alone and he would walk to work, alone. And when he got in at night, he would still be alone. Luckily for him, his day would be padded out with a nice big helping of death - other people's death, of course. There were many different types of obituaries in Stanley's typical day: dull obituaries, sad obituaries, amusing obituaries, and interesting obituaries. Those last ones depressed him the most. Those were the types who had crammed their lives so full of colour, travels, awards, relationships, family… everything that he currently did not have. Stanley didn't like the constant reminder that one day—and say that day was today—his time would run out and all he'd have was; obituary writer, rented a flat in Edinburgh at the age of 27, had a cat called Jasper to whom he left all of his worldly belongings, and occasionally bought the Big Issue. Not because he particularly wanted to read it, but because he felt sorry for the person selling it. At least he always recycled.

Stepping into the elevator felt like stepping back into his dream; it had seemed so real – then again, it always did. It was a dream that he had every so often, but one that was, thankfully, starting to fade in his mind. Eventually swishing open to reveal a usual everyday scene, Stanley relaxed as he stepped out of the elevator, and forward into the usual brown carpet and beige walls of the Edinburgh Times office. It was as usual, quite busy, and promptly at 9.30am the editors would commence their daily meeting. It was unlikely that Stanley would be called to these meetings, but every so often he was invited to take a seat to offer his opinion on the obituary pages. This suited Stanley, as he mostly preferred to avoid the editor, Rory MacDuff. Stanley found Rory intimidating, as he constantly paced around with ruddy red cheeks whilst looking positively stressed. Everyone knew he kept a bottle of vodka in a secret drawer hidden under his desk, next to the obligatory bottle of whisky every Scottish news editor was required to keep handy for emergencies. Often Stanley would hear his shouts from across the office, sharply followed by a slamming door. His friend Gill had been in tears on countless occasions, wondering why Rory did not understand her, or even give her a chance on a decent story. That was enough for Stanley to remain in his office on most days, even in the stifling summer months, writing the obits and staying well clear of the Edinburgh Times editor.

The office was looking particularly bright as he walked into the busy newsroom. He opened his mouth to say good morning to Alan Hunter, the resident senior sub, when a bunch of balloons hit him instead. Momentarily confused, he brushed them aside only to see the holder, Gill Gallagher, with the biggest grin on her face since she'd received a dozen red heart-shaped balloons on Valentine's day. Of course, he'd never let on they were from him, and just because he knew how much she loved balloons. "Hey, Stan! Aren't these great? It's Jenny's birthday!" she explained in a childlike manner only she could reserve for balloons of the helium (squeaky voiced) gas-filled variety.

"Oh, so that's what they're for," he replied, amused.

Jenny was the new junior reporter, who'd only started work two months earlier.

"Yes, I'm going to put them on her desk before she gets back from her job at the Pony Club, she's reporting on dressage, or something. It's her first job out by herself," Gill said, a slightly concerned look showing through, just for a second, before muttering; "Nah... she'll be fine." Stanley nodded, thinking of accident-prone Jenny and her questionable shorthand – she had already accidentally offended Duke Ford on a visit to his manor house with another reporter last month. She'd never live that one down. Stanley was on his way to his office, when he heard Gill call.

"Oh wait, Stan? I think Kev wants to talk to you," she called after him, before uttering the words he dreaded to hear, "Something's happened. Some politician or other..." Gill's voice faded into the background as she took the balloons to the far side of the news desk. He knew it. He thought there was an air of tension that wasn't usually around on a Monday morning, but he'd just put it down to Jenny's birthday. The girl was barely out of braces. How old was she anyway, twelve? Turning, he looked in the direction of Kev's desk, only to find it empty. Phew. "Oh, and don't forget, drinks at Red Eleven tonight!"

"Oh, great," he smiled to Gill before going in search Kevin Leonard, the news desk editor, only second to Mr MacDuff himself, who could be heard shouting at an unknown junior in his office: "Have you read it? Have you actually READ it? Take a seat back, relax, read it over and then open your fucking eyes and read it again!" Stanley smiled; it was evil, but he couldn't help himself. It didn't take long for him to find Kev, hunched over the desk of little Fair Summer, the tiny sub-editor who although pretty, like her name, couldn't harm a fly and was mostly quiet as a mouse, unnoticed among the hustle and bustle of the office. As Stanley approached, Kev looked up from the screen and Fair gave Stanley a relieved look, her cheeks slightly blushed. It was barely 9:20am and Kev was already gathering a sweat on his brow. His hair was an unkempt dirty blonde with just a hint of a receding hairline, his shirt of the crinkly (it was rumoured his wife had up and left him for the broadband installation man, but that was strictly office talk) blue and white check variety. "Ah, Stanley, just the man I need!" he exclaimed, his voice already showing levels of stress that sent Stanley on edge.

"Oh? Right, well what's been going on?" he asked with more than a slight trepidation. Kev looked at him blankly. "Don't you know?" he asked. Now it was Stanley's turn to look blank. "Haven't you heard the radio this morning, switched on the television?" Kev demanded; his small beady eyes focusing uncomfortably on Stanley as his paunch of a stomach showed under his crinkled, (clearly needing a woman's touch) white shirt.

"No sir, I... I'm afraid I slept in today," Kev sighed.

"Well, we'd better get you filled in. This is a major obituary and we're putting a lot of trust in you. How long have you been working at this illustrious newspaper now, young man?"

"Two years."

Kev looked taken aback, before lowering his head. Stanley noticed his knuckles were white as he gripped Fair's desk. Poor Fair was quietly trying to get on with her work, pretending not to notice.

"Really? Two years? God, it doesn't feel that long. Well, anyway. It's – alright, it's Jeremy Bogleur, he died early this morning, of heart failure."

"What? The politician?" Stanley asked, genuinely shocked.

"Yes, the MSP. He will be sorely missed, and the Fringe

25

will not be the same this year without its main supporter. He's done a lot for this year's festival. Without him, it might not even have gone ahead and with so many acts it's not a surprise that some were less than kosher. He really cleaned up. Plus there was that ridiculous tax charge and he... well, let's just say he's the unsung hero in all of this. But not for much longer; we have to change that."

"Right."

"No, not just 'right'. Rory wants this done just so, got it? He'll be wanting to hear the full report on this, he's already looked out the back articles about Jeremy's work for the festival. Now, you'd better give his family a call right away and find out what they have to say on... this tragic event." Stanley nodded, and started in the direction of the obits office he shared with Clive. "And Stanley? Remember what happened with Ozzie Hanservan? We can't have that happen here, okay?"

Now it was Stanley's turn to blush. The whole office had heard. And they all knew the Hanservan incident very well; even Jenny.

"Here, you better take this as well," Kev muttered, handing Stanley this morning's paper, "There's a small piece announcing his death, we managed to fit it into our later editions."

Stanley walked briskly into the small office and for once he was the one slamming the door as he tried to block out the murmuring voices and the repeated word of 'Hanservan'. He even scared Clive as he looked up from his notebook. Stanley was greeted by dark brown eyes, pale skin and the usual short, curly brown locks surrounded by the unnatural dull light that he'd come accustomed to each and every morning. Clive looked worried. "Hey, what's up... wait; did someone bring it up again? You know, the Han-

"Don't say that word to me Clive, I'm warning you," Stanley warned.

"Fair enough, so, apart from that, did they tell you about

Bogleur?"

"Yep, has his family been in touch yet?" Clive shook his head, and slowly went back to studying his eerily neat shorthand. His jumper was dark brown today, with a beige check shirt and brown tie underneath. He was wearing beige cords. Clive was 36, single and mostly lived on a diet of microwave lasagne. Stanley began the ritual of unfastening his jacket as he waited for his computer to slowly boot up, before sitting at his desk and wondering exactly how to word the phone call to Bogleur's wife. It was a job that required a lot of patience, sympathy and understanding – luckily Stanley's quiet manner could often be misunderstood as such, making his life a little easier. But it didn't stop him feeling awkward. Especially when *he* had to make the call.

Sighing, he opened the paper and studied the text on the page.

MSP DIES OF HEART FAILURE.

Well-respected MSP Jeremy Bogleur has unexpectedly passed away in the early hours of the morning, due to heart failure. Mr Bogleur was found dead by staff at the Gatehouse Hotel after an ambulance was called to his room. Bogleur, known for his recent work for the Edinburgh Fringe and also as a senior MSP, will be sorely missed in the local community. Police are keen to trace a female dressed in black seen leaving the hotel around the time of the call. The death is not being treated as suspicious.

A pretty standard death announcement, only two things stood out to Stanley as being a little odd.

"The Gatehouse Hotel... but doesn't Bogleur live in Morningside, surely that's only 20 minutes away? What would he be doing there in the early hours of the morning...?" Clive momentarily stopped typing, seemed to think on it, shrugged and continued with his work.

"And a female dressed in black... could be anybody I suppose, but that is curious they would mention that," he muttered, mostly to himself this time.

Usually his day would revolve around family members calling him, which wasn't quite as bad as him phoning them. All he had to do was listen and take down each word accurately. But not too accurately, as a lot of people, especially mottled with grief, could not consider spelling or grammar. Mostly Stanley had to be very careful when wording obituaries, as sometimes people would read between the lines and take offence at something he had written – for example 'humble' would be taken as tight with money, and 'tidy' as gay etc. – at least if you were a Rangers supporter from Greenock called Kenny – apparently it was a veritable mine field. And then there was the Hanservan case... really, how was he supposed to know there was more than one Ozzie Hanservan, and one of them had been a celebrated Nazi? He knew he was delaying things. So did Clive, who was pretending not to be curious by playing with the cuticles on his fingernails and fidgeting.

"This is the part of the job I really hate," Stanley muttered.

"It's easy, you've done it so many times before; just explain who you are and why you're calling and... look, do you want me to do it?" Clive asked.

"Nah, it's just... nah," Stanley shrugged. Clive turned back to his screen and started clicking away at the keys again, already in full swing of the day. Stanley eyed the phone, reached out and –

"What time did you get in today, Clive?"

"7.30am, usual. Why?" Clive momentarily stopped clicking on the keys.

"Just wondered," Stanley replied. He whether Clive ever saw full sunlight if he could help it. Stanley pictured Rory MacDuff in full suit and impossibly shiny shoes, pacing around his office and waiting on the 'full report'. It gave him the chills.

Pushing that thought to the back of his mind, Stanley picked up the phone and dialled the numbers on the notepad in front of him. He took a deep breath and listened as it started to ring.

"Hello?" The voice of a woman came on the end of the phone.

"Good morning, is that Mrs Bogleur?"

"No, it is not."

"Well, err, may I please speak to Mrs Bogleur?"

"Who is this?" the voice said sharply down the end of the phone.

"My name is Stanley Hobbes and I'm calling from the Edinburgh Times office. It's about Mr Bogleur's obituary, you see we're hoping to devote a page to Mr Bogleur, his life and the work he's done recently for the festival." There was a pause, and Stanley could hear breathing as the woman decided what to do.

"Wait a moment," the voice rasped, before a heavy clunk made him jump. She'd obviously placed the phone down rather swiftly upon a hard surface. Stanley strained to hear what was being said, but it sounded more like good morning television than anything else. A few moments later, footsteps started getting louder.

"Hello? Is that the Edinburgh Times?"

"Err, yes, this is Stanley Hobbes on behalf of the Edinburgh Times. Is that... Mrs Bogleur?"

"It most certainly is. What do you want?"

"It's about Mr Bogleur's obituary, I" – and there was a sigh. "Oh God, that fucking man and what he's put me through! I'm sorry, what do you already know?"

"Well, not very much to be honest. I have a copy of this morning's paper, have you seen it?"

"Yes, I do. It's all quite correct."

"Ah, I see; and so on the obituary, is there anything particular you would like said?"

"I don't even want to think about it, really. I'm sorry,

29

I'm just not in the best of spirits after all this..."

"I can understand that, Mrs Bogleur, I speak to close friends and families all the time and I know how difficult it can be."

"Oh, I'm sure you do."

"Well, I do have a backlog of articles on all Mr Bogleur's work with the Fringe, and I'm sure I can look up the rest." She hesitated, seeming to want to say something else.

"Mrs Bogleur, there is one other thing that's troubling me."

"Yes, go on."

Stanley paused, aware that he was getting into unfamiliar territory. But something made him continue.

"Well... it says in the article that Mr Bogleur passed away at the Gatehouse Hotel. Surely that's only 20 minutes from your home; I just wondered what he was there for." There was a deep intake of breath from down the line, and Stanley waited for her response. When she finally gave it, her voice had changed tone from being rather abrupt and cold, to small and almost vulnerable.

"I suppose it had to come out. Well, why should I go hiding his disgusting little secret?

"I beg your pardon?"

Stanley listened as Bogleur's wife explained the situation surrounding his death, in explicit detail, including his less-than-squeaky-clean past.

"I've caught him out in the past, you know. That's why the police are calling for a 'woman in black' to come forward. Prostitute, I'll bet. Wouldn't be the first time," she said. Clive was watching this conversation take place, dropping his usual stance of pretending not to listen, instead full-on enthralled. His coffee had gone cold. He watched as Stanley's face took on a variety of unique expressions – quite an interesting day already.

"Wait... he was wearing WHAT?"

"That's right; sick, isn't it? The dirty old rat deserved

30

everything he got."

"Ermm, that's all very well Mrs Bogleur, but tell me this; are you at all familiar with the term 'exclusive'?"

*

When Stanley got off the phone a couple of minutes later, he was met with a pair of familiar brown eyes once more.

"What the hell, Stan?"

"I knew something was a bit off from the start. She didn't want to talk to me, but not only did she not want to talk to me, she sounded... angry. She used the 'f' word to describe Bogleur and... you really don't want to know the rest."

"Yes I do!"

"Not now... I've really got to go."

Clive pondered for a second, looked down at his hands and back up to Stanley again.

"What did you mean by 'exclusive'?" Clive asked, with minimal consideration.

"Hold on, I can't say, just need to figure out what to do," Stanley replied, looking down in awe at his slightly trembling hands. Clive's voice was the calm sea in the middle of a storm.

"Thought you were going?"

"I am."

"Who are you going to tell then, Rory?"

"I don't know!"

"This doesn't sound good."

"I know!"

"... Don't shout."

"I'm sorry, Clive."

"No worries."

Stanley sighed, head in hands as he dreaded his next steps. He knew he had to tell Rory; the story had huge potential, but also some big implications for a recently-deceased public figure. It was a tricky one. Just then the phone started to ring

31

next to him, shattering his thoughts and making him almost jump out of his skin.

4

"It is a common delusion that you make things better by talking about them." – Rose Macaulay.

"Hello, obits office?" Stanley said as he picked up the phone. He noted Clive was still listening, and not only was he listening, but peeling another damn orange. Oranges were Clive's little obsession, and most days the smell would distract Stanley from his shorthand notes. Once he ended up writing something very embarrassing while in a rush to finish on time. "Hi, are you working on the Bogleur story?" The woman on the end of the phone sounded young, the voice slightly broken as she spoke in whispered tones, but what struck him most of all was her accent. It was obviously foreign, velvety and utterly transfixing.

"Err, sort of. Who is this?"

"A friend."

"Right. Well I'm actually working on the story right now, what can I do for you?" Stanley asked, still confused at the mystery caller. There was silence on the other line.

"Hello?"

"Yes, I'm here. Look I... don't want anyone to track this call, but this is important." Alarm bells started to ring for Stanley as the room started spinning slightly in an almost movie-like slow motion. He had to swallow before he realised his mouth had gone completely dry.

"Look, I'm really confused here. What's going on and what does it have to do with Bogleur?"

"This story is going to get out of control. The file, do you have it?"

"No," Stanley replied, cautiously, "I don't know what you're talking about."

33

"Well, someone does, and it's not going to be pretty when it all comes out."

"Wait, what is this? What are you talking about?"

"Bogleur was corrupt. The police... Ask the police, they'll tell you."

"Just tell me what this is all about, please."

"Ask them for the file. It was in the room where he was found. You could say it's of... how do you say... public interest," the mysterious voice explained, remaining calm and cool as it cut through his whirring thoughts and baffled confusion.

"A file? Okay, but who are you?" There was a considered silence, before the line went dead.

*

The office was alive with raised voices, ringing telephones and general Monday morning madness that can only truly be found in a daily newsroom. There was always something happening as the team worked to stay on top of the latest stories and developments. There would usually be at least one rushed decision in a day – whether to print, whether to stash, whether to bin completely – but that was of course, Rory's decision. There was an in-house legal team there to help, but in the end, the editor had the final say on each paper that went to print. Rory could be summed up in one word; brave. A lot of people found him intimidating too. He had been making controversial decisions ever since he was made editor five years previously. So far it had paid off. Today was, hopefully, no different.

The sounds of Kev and Rory's argument could be heard over the general office noise. This time it was about what heiress and socialite Kandess Spencer had been up to on a night out at Scotland's capital when she was spied on by one of the Edinburgh Time's 'glamour girls', Sandra Newton.

Normally it wouldn't have been an issue but Kandess's publicist had since been on the phone explaining Kandess's fragile situation before threatening legal action if the story – and pictures – were ever to go to print. Rory thought to hell with it, but Kev was always more cautious and argued that she was only a C-list celeb anyway, what did it really matter? To Rory, it was a matter of principle.

Gill was vaguely listening to this argument whilst twisting strands of hair around her little finger in an almost girl-like manner, and studying her screen with pure hatred and contempt, before opening up her Twitter page (which was always a safe clickety-click of a tab away). The name of her account; GillGoGo. Normally it would have caused a hint of a smile to form in the corner of Stanley's mouth, but not today. He grabbed her by the arm, leaned down and said: "I need to talk to you; now." She shot him a surprised glance before reluctantly getting out of her seat. As she got up he started to walk swiftly towards the unisex toilets, and she had to struggle to keep up with him while some of the girls around her gave each other knowing looks. She was well aware that, in a matter of seconds, the pair of them had become the talk of the office.

"What the hell, Stan?"

"I need your help, this is bad; really bad." Stanley spoke quietly, the stress levels in his voice raising her suspicion even more. When they got to the toilets, a quick check gave them the all-clear and Stanley leaned back against the sink, trying to think where to begin.

"Stanley, you're really worrying me now, okay, what's wrong? Just tell me. It's not another Hanser-

"No, it's not. But Gill... the strangest thing just happened. There's potentially a big story in it, but I can't figure out how it makes any sense, or what to do."

"What do you mean, a story? Okay, start at the beginning." Gill had to try to calm herself as she searched his eyes for answers. He looked back at her in despair, then again down at the sink. And so he explained to her about Bogleur's death, the phonecall with Bogleur's wife and the 'corrupt' claims of the mysterious caller (not forgetting the way they found him) - all potentially ruining Bogleur's sparkly reputation in the public eye if it were ever to get out. Not that he'd mind anymore, of course.

"This is serious, Gill... Gill! Stop laughing!" Stanley was serious. What would the obit say now?

"Okay, I know it's serious. Those are some pretty serious allegations. But how is this file connected?"

"That's what I need to figure out," Stanley replied.

"Do you think the woman in black was a prostitute, like his wife implied? But that doesn't necessarily make it a matter for a newspaper... something about this just doesn't add up." Then she turned on him with what he liked to call her serious face. "The police would have told you to keep her on the phone, you know. That's what always happens in crime dramas on TV."

"Sorry I'm not an expert," he replied.

"Wait, do you think Bogleur was murdered?" Gill asked her eyes wide with intrigue. Stanley noticed he'd been washing his hands. He didn't know when he'd started, but the skin was starting to feel raw.

"Don't you think that's jumping to conclusions? I don't know. She didn't once say the word 'murder'. But how would she know there was a file in that room?"

"You need to tell this to Rory, not me," Gill replied, "and you need to tell him fast. This could have all sorts of legal implications for the paper." They both stared at the floor, thinking of Rory's reaction.

"Shit."

5

"If you can fill the unforgiving minute with sixty seconds worth of distance run yours is the Earth and everything that's in it, and you'll be a Man, my son!" – Rudyard Kipling

The walk to Rory MacDuff's office was a slow and painful one, as Stanley tried to work out what to say without sounding like a complete and utter twat. Stanley checked his watch; it was now 11:05am. He knew Clive had sensed he was on edge, but Stanley had fled the office before he could comment further. Stanley pretended he hadn't noticed his confused and inexplicably innocent face staring over the monitor as he'd slammed the door in his hurry to be somewhere else – anywhere else. God knows why he'd gone for a fag break. He didn't even smoke. Nevertheless, Martha, the 60-year-old typist had been standing outside the door at the usual time and place, and had been happy to provide him with one of her Marlboro Lights. Taking it in his slightly shaking fingers, she lit him up while saying, "Glad of the company, my dear boy." Stanley had smiled, before inhaling on his cancer stick and immediately coughing like he was on his last breath. At least feeling sick would momentarily take his mind off what was to come. Martha pretended not to notice his coughing fit, and remarked on the weather. The weather was fair, but still she clutched a tattered old umbrella in her left hand. It was an umbrella she had carried everywhere with her since she was forty-five and had to give up her child benefits. It had been a tough year, but that umbrella had seen her through the worst of it. She'd nicknamed it 'Todd'. Everyone knew the story.

"So are you going to tell me what's wrong, or are you going to keep me in suspense?" she asked.

"I thought I needed the... fresh air?" he replied, sheepishly. She gave him a knowing look, before taking another puff on her cigarette, savouring the smokey badness. Eventually she let out a satisfied sigh, making Stanley feel slightly uncomfortable. Todd seemed to look up at him, sympathetically.

"Perhaps you should go back inside where the air is conditioned." Martha made it sound as if she somehow knew everything, without having to ask.

"In a minute," he replied.

"Very well," she said, the hint of a smile crinkling up her face as her eyes narrowed on a junior administrator walking past in a stupidly short skirt and bare tanned legs.

"Todd, it's not polite to stare," she murmured, almost to herself. Quirky lady, Stanley thought. Suffice to say, he hadn't been able to stay out there long, and now, walking towards Rory's office, he could tell he smelled of cigarette smoke. Not the best impression he wanted to give to the editor at such a stressful time. He wasn't used to this. He was an obituary writer, and now he was completely lost. To make matters worse, he knew he should have told the police the second he'd come off the phone. He imagined going into Rory's office with the all-famous line; "There's been a murder." But that was ridiculous... had there been a murder? Gill seemed to think so. It was all so confusing. To make matters worse, he knew Rory would have wanted the obituary by now, and he hadn't even started it. The door beckoned him forwards, and nervously Stanley approached it with unease. All was quiet inside, which was either bad or good - he couldn't tell which. It was as if he wasn't actually in his own body but instead watching himself from above as his hand reached out and knocked upon the frosted glass door. The sign above read: **Rory G. MacDuff**. The 'G' stood for George. For a moment, nothing happened and Stanley was considering knocking a little harder, before the silence was interrupted by:

"Come in then, for fuck's sake!" Stanley turned the doorknob and entered the room. Rory G. MacDuff was sitting in his leather swivel chair with his back to the door, facing the window outside, which overlooked a small courtyard. Like a scene in a thriller movie, the chair turned swiftly to face Stanley. Stanley's bright blue eyes were met with Rory's hazely-green ones, his lips pursed under his grey-ish moustache; they seemed to be waiting for the punch-line. "Err, hope I'm not interrupting anything, Mr MacDuff," Stanley murmured.

"What? Come in, sit down, what do you want?"

"I need to talk to you; it's ummm... quite serious."

"Right, Stanford, is it? Make it quick," Rory replied sharply, putting Stanley even more on edge. He clasped his hands together.

"Ummm... it's Stanley, actually," Stanley murmured, before seeing Rory's disapproving glance and continuing, "It's about the Bogleur obit."

Rory glanced at his watch, before saying, "Ah, yes, do you have it?"

"Well, err, that's what I need to talk to you about..." Rory sat still, eyebrow slightly raised as if waiting for a damn good reason why he didn't have his story yet. Stanley quickly sat down, took a deep breath, and told him everything. And when he'd finished, he had to stop and take another deep breath, unable to look into Mr MacDuff's face yet compelled to at the same time. Rory had listened to everything Stanley had to say with a poker face. It was, logically, the only thing to do in this sort of situation. As Stanley spoke, the words registered slowly until he thought he had a feel for the story the lad was nervously trying to portray. Rory also noticed the smell of his favourite Marlboro Lights and recognised Stanley as a fellow smoker – his type of chap. And then Stanley said something else which made Rory's gut flip over with excitement, confusion, alarm and confusion; all in one. He simply smiled, and said: "Wait a minute... he was wearing WHAT?"

"You heard, sir," Stanley lowered his head as he said it.

"Well," Rory said, "that IS news."

He seemed to ponder for a moment, weighing everything up while Stanley's mind raced at the possible outcomes.

"Sir? What should we do?" Stanley blurted out the question he couldn't keep in any longer.

"Weeeell... it's not as if this 'lady' has told us anything specific, is it? It could easily be a hoax. What do YOU think we should do, Stanley?" Rory almost looked as if he was enjoying himself.

"I think maybe we should contact the police," Stanley answered, honestly. Rory made a face, as if brushing off the suggestion.

"For what? It'd be a waste of their time, I'll bet they wouldn't be able to track the call, and there's absolutely no straight facts here." Rory paused in thought, his slightly chubby fingers tapping on his desk as Stanley practically heard the turning of cogs working in his mind.

"This is very interesting..." Rory muttered, almost as if talking to himself, before eventually saying, "I'll get back to you on it – in the meantime carry on with a small standard obit. It'll go into the paper as if you know nothing different, at least until we can get our facts straight. If there's been a cover-up, as our lady suggests, then we'll find out. In the meantime I'm sure Mrs Bogleur will keep quiet, thanks to you."

Stanley stood up, not daring to question Rory's decision as he quickly backed out of the office, unsure whether he should be leaving things the way they were.

"Leave it to me. But, nice work, Stanley - nice work." Rory gave Stanley a toothy, unsettling grin as he carefully closed the door behind him. Stanley left the office even more confused than when he'd gone in. He was in fact, so lost in thought that he almost bumped into Fair Summer at the water fountain.

"Oh, I'm sorry – didn't see you there," he said absentmindedly. Fair turned to face him, her short blonde wisps of hair soft around her face made her look almost pixie-like under the harsh lights of the office. But there was nothing harsh about her. Her soft features, high cheekbones and pale skin with a slight scattering of freckles on her small nose made him momentarily forget about the phone call and Rory's strange reaction. Her ears were tiny and pink, also like a pixie. He noticed her eyes were pale cornflower blue as she gave him an odd look, almost non-existent eyebrows raised then knotted in an elegant but good-humoured dance.

"Oh, hello. Is everything all right?" she asked him. He liked Fair; her voice was always sincere and open. Her tiny frame was almost dwarfed in a dark woollen pinafore, layered over a long-sleeved purple top, and teamed with dark skinny jeans tucked into black knee-high boots with a tiny heel. Still, she was only about 5ft tall.

"Yes, I'm fine. Just a typical day at the office," he replied, feeling awkward and silly in front of someone so serene and calm.

"Oh, I wouldn't call it typical, but yes, I know what you mean," said Fair.

"So, are you coming to Jenny's birthday drinks tonight?"

"I don't think so, no. But thank you for asking." Stanley smiled, unable to think of what to say next.

"Are you sure you're all right?" Fair asked, concern in her eyes, "you look a touch... red."

"Nothing I can't handle... just Clive with his cheap tricks again," Stanley laughed, and Fair smiled sweetly.

"Well, I must get back to work. See you later, I'm sure," Fair left the fountain leaving behind a sweet scent that Stanley couldn't quite name, her uneven hem entirely in place with her usual, enchanting style. Stanley stopped to fill a plastic cup with ice cool water that slipped down his throat and made him feel a lot better.

*

41

Rory MacDuff sat still in his office, quietly impressed with Stanley Hobbes. Of course, the Bogleur story was quite a revelation. Betrayed by his own wife, and then prostitutes, indeed. Yes, he realised there could be a story there.

Although this was all well and good, what he hadn't told Stanley were his own suspicions. But, could he trust the lad on this one? Sure, he was an honest-looking boy that he hadn't really bothered about before. Always showed up on time, polite manner – and the familiar smell of his favourite cigarettes had indeed shed a new light upon young Stanley. Just then, there was a knock at the door.

"You wanted to see me, Rory?" It was Pamela, from HR.

"Yes, it's about Mr Hobbes."

"You mean Stanley?" Pamela asked, looking confused.

"That's right. Give the lad a job in the newsroom – I want him working on the festival this year, chasing some proper stories, some real grit," Rory said.

"You mean, you want to take him of the obits office?" Her surprised face said it all, really.

"Are you thick? Of course, out of the obits office! He's been in with that recluse – what's his name - Clive, for too long. I have other plans for him. Get him set up as a reporter, and fast."

"Right, I'll get on to it," said Pamela, unsurely.

"Oh, and could you get me a latte? Thanks."

6

"Only enemies speak the truth; friends and lovers lie endlessly, caught in the web of duty." – Stephen King, (Roland, The Gunsligner)

"You're an attractive guy, you don't need to have all this 'neat to the point of OCD' bullshit."

Stanley sighed, his hands poised over the bar in an attempt not to leave before he was properly drunk, but Gill was making it hard for him. After all, he didn't want to go home in a sober state, not with all the ties, staring at him in that accusing way only ties can manage.

"I. Don't."

Gill raised her cosmopolitan and tried to do the same with her eyebrow, failed miserably, and ended up looking even more drunk - which only confirmed Stanley's suspicions that he should disregard anything she said, however personal she allowed it to get.

"That's bullshit," she replied, and he stopped her, mouth poised in an observational epiphany that he was sure he wouldn't want to hear.

"I'm trying to get over all that. You don't know what it's like, Gill, and," he paused for a second, her eyes meeting his with a slightly surprised yet knowing look, he told her, "You're drunk."

"Who else do you know that irons their socks, for fuck's sake? You waste your time doing every menial thing so that you don't have to think about anything that actually matters. You should at least buy a dishwasher, I mean, whatever happened to that novel you were going to write?" Stanley lowered his head, pretending to be more offended about the socks than he actually

43

was. He felt her warm hand on his arm, her long, auburn hair falling out of place and tumbling over her slightly tanned skin; an achievement she was proud of. He could smell her breath; a mixture of cocktails, brandy and vodka shakers. He was surprised at her lucidity; how was she still making any sense at all?

"Look, I know everything that happened with Lorraine, but that was almost a year ago, Stan. She only knew you for four months, there was nothing you could have done to stop it."

He turned towards her again, and saw a twinkling of a tear just below her left eye. He knew he'd probably have to get her home soon. After all, it was him that should be doing the crying, not her. She was waiting for him to say something, anything, to recognise the fact that his ex girlfriend had killed herself. But what was there to say? She was right - it was almost a year ago, so what was the point?

"The worst part is when I try to think about her. I spend most of the time avoiding it, but when I do try and face it, I can't remember her face. Just those marks on her neck..." he continued.

"The only time I remember is when I dream, but when I wake it's gone again." He smiled now, a sad but truthful smile that eventually seemed to satisfy her in some way. He had been honest, it was how he really felt and he hated to say it. At least it was enough for her to try and remove herself from the stool. He reached out as she tumbled to the floor, helping her support herself on the bar.

"Well... you need to get over it. See a psychiatrist or something." He laughed, and gestured to the men's before leaving Gill to collect her things. The music was beating in his head, and the crowded atmosphere didn't do much to clear his thoughts. It was Jenny's after work drinks that had turned into a full-on party on a Monday night.

Luckily, Kev had the 'work hard, party hard' attitude and was dancing on one of the tables, his hair ruffled and tie over his shoulder. He was dancing with Jenny, who had changed into a little purple dress. She looked more than tipsy and was constantly pulling up the straps on her dress. Stanley was sure she'd regret dancing with Kev in the morning. The poor girl would never live it down.

The toilets were cooler, calmer, and he paused as he caught his reflection in the mirror. Gill was right - he wasn't entirely unattractive. His bright blue eyes – Irish eyes – still managed to sparkle at one in the morning, his pale skin and prominent cheekbones made him feel a bit like a skeleton but at least he ate well, and his hair was dark almost to the point of black. It was mussed, a little on the long side but he liked it that way. He smiled. It looked natural enough. He washed his hands for the 59th time that day, noticing his skin was smooth compared to his rough, bitten fingernails – not so neat there. Maybe that small, human flaw gave him some hope as he soon under the bright, unforgiving lights. The peaceful moment was broken by the sound of someone throwing up in the cubicle behind him. The spell gone, he returned to the bar. Gill was downing another shot and had somehow managed to get back up on her stool. He'd lost all inclination to drink any more.

"Come on, we've got work tomorrow. Let's get you home."

"Wait, you haven't even thrown any shapes on the dance floor, yet! Come on, do your famous Thom Yorke impression – Lotus Flower!"

"Fuck off, we're going home!"

"No!" she cried above the loud music, "Just one more, come on, you've got to try this, it's bloody amazing!" He glanced dubiously at the shot she'd bought him. He downed it, grabbed her handbag and walked towards the door without turning around. Outside the street was crowded with smokers enjoying the competitive sport of 'smirting' – the combination of smoking and flirting that had become popular after the smoking ban came into force. To Stanley it was a reminder of

45

the incident with Martha earlier that day, and he smiled as he waited for his friend to catch up. He heard Gill's moans behind him, and knew she'd thank him in the morning, even if she would be a wreck. He tried to give her back her bag, but she pushed it away."You can carry it!"

"But I'll look like a goon," he smiled, the conversation already much lighter. He didn't mind really, he was happy to carry her bag – she was having enough trouble just walking straight in her heels.

"You already look like a goon," she replied as she held onto his arm for support, her hair blowing in the cool summer wind.

"Come on, I'll walk you home."

The pair walked through Rose Street, the night surprisingly refreshing. It was Tuesday, and he knew he'd probably sleep in again, but he didn't really care.

"So, Kandess Spencer," Gill said, as if urging him to continue the sentence.

"I heard she caused a bit of a stir, right enough. I'm not really interested, to be honest," Stanley replied, sensibly. He didn't really buy into all that celeb culture. After all, why should he?

"But you find her attractive though?" she asked, playfully. He turned to her, questioningly.

"Should I?"

"Nah... she looks a bit 'identikit' for my liking," Gill said, before turning to him. "You know, how all the Hollywood celebs go for the same sort of nose, the same Botox etc, they all start to look a bit... samey," she shrugged.

"Right so," he replied, in good humour.

They were silent for a time, a contented silence that they'd mastered to an art, without being at all awkward. She liked that about Stanley. She liked the way they were together.

"Why are you looking at me like that?" he asked, amused at her drunken stare. There was something else in there

46

too, but he couldn't figure out what.

"Nothing," she replied, the tone in her voice hiding a playful secret. They returned to silence, but he broke it by uttering a thought:

"I had the dream again."

"Oh. So that's why."

He nodded.

"I wondered where your tie was today," she said, the faintest smile still on her lips. The lipstick had rubbed off hours ago but a trace remained.

"Well, do you want to know what I dreamt? I dreamt I was watching Coronation Street, and David Platt got eaten by a horse," she said.

He laughed, but she was right; the ridiculousness of the situation suddenly hit him like a thunderbolt. How pathetic! It was just a stupid fucking tie, what was the big deal? Why even wear them, when most people in the office didn't even bother?

"Gill, you're right," he told her, catching her attention. She gave him a confused look as she tried to find her keys inside her bag.

"Maybe I do need help." She burst out laughing as she dropped the keys onto the pavement, lost her footing and stumbled to pick them up off the ground. She seemed to find that even funnier, and he tried to steady her before she was lying next to them. He was in hysterics himself by that time. He helped her up, put both hands on her shoulders and said: "Look, I'm serious. Thank you, from the heart, for saving my life."

"No! Noooo!" she cried, before remembering that it was a Monday night and most people were in bed.

"I wasn't serious!" She hushed her tones, "do you want to come in for a coffee?"

"I think I'm going to have to," he said.

They walked upstairs to Gill's flat as quietly as possible, until they finally reached her front room and she fumbled for the light switch. Her place was always stylish, colourful and immaculate. It was cute, and very unlike his. A fuzzy but shiny pink rug lay in the middle of the floor next to turquoise green couches and a cute brown coffee table. The walls were orange. She stumbled into the kitchen and switched on the kettle, moaning as she looked at the microwave clock.

"Can you believe we've got to be at work in a few hours?"

"No," he called to her. He liked looking at her fish tank. It was very blue, and pretty, and colourful. Her fish, Larry, Moe and Rebus were swimming around happily.

As she was making the coffee, Gill's voice called from the kitchen, "You know, you can learn to do this thing called full lucidity; means you can learn to be aware you're in a dream and actually control it to go however you want it to. Just say you're being chased by a giant monster, you can focus and turn it into a cuddly big lump of floating candy floss!"

"Sounds like something out of Harry Potter," he commented.

"Maybe I'll look it up, sometime," Stanley said. As Gill came out of the kitchen with two mugs in hand, he turned to her and noticed she'd taken off her shoes and was now about four inches shorter. He realised he liked looking at her too, almost for the same reasons as he liked the fish – only she was not very blue at all. She sat close to him, sipping her coffee before setting it down on a lime green coaster. Her eyes were big and brown, like Bambi eyes. Her long eyelashes had no need for mascara, and she smiled at him with those eyes.

"So," she said.

"So," he replied. Her eyes continued to smile at him, although how, he couldn't really figure out. She didn't look as drunk now as she had been at the bar. He liked her dress. It looked almost like a fairy's; the skirt had a deliberate ripped effect that showed the bare skin of her legs. She moved her hand on to his thigh, and it sent an internal shiver down his spine. It felt good. Her scent was sweet with perfume, her features delicate as she searched his face for what he wanted. And suddenly, he knew what he wanted. He kissed her without knowing whether it was the right thing to do. It felt even better. She kissed back eagerly, and suddenly he just wanted to lose himself in her touch. It became passionate, their bodies barely touching next to each other as they sat on the couch. He could feel her small, pert breasts light against his chest and he resisted the urge to pull her closer, instead running his fingers through her soft, long hair. Her lips were sweet and she tasted of black coffee. She began to get up from the couch, pulling him up with her and as he was beginning to find his feet he realised they were heading towards the bedroom. But it was Gill, his friend, his work mate, the only one he could really talk to about his problems; and they had been drinking. The coffee tasted bittersweet as her lips pressed against his, their bodies unable to resist each other any longer. It was almost like a dream and he was kissing her through thick air, as if under water but somehow he was able to breathe at the same time. For just a moment there was nothing else, and it all made sense. It was the right thing to do. His hands moved over her perfect body and he was lost in her scent, her taste, her long hair, soft to the touch. Then it hit him, and suddenly it wasn't right at all. They were almost through the door when he pulled back.

"I'm sorry... I can't," he whispered. With that, he broke free from her hands and took a few steps back from her. It was wrong, all wrong... her Bambi eyes asking him why yet she didn't utter a word. Instead she seemed to gather her self-esteem from the floor and with a sigh, closed the bedroom door. He was able to make it back to his own flat without the full horror hitting home of what he'd just done. He splashed cold water onto his face, this time avoiding the mirror.

Jasper was in the corridor, playing with one of the small brown caterpillars that had recently appeared in his flat. It had curled up into a ball and was either dead or just appearing that way to trick the little cat. Whether it was dead or not, Jasper ate it.

"I think someone needs to be fed," Stanley said, causing the feline to look up with the usual expectation. Quickly, he followed Stanley to the kitchen. When Jasper had eaten his fill, Stanley brushed his teeth, washed his hands (again) and changed into his pyjamas. He dropped his work clothes onto the floor, before remembering about the caterpillars and instead transferred them to his chair.

Too tired to do any more, he found his way through the dark to his bed where he collapsed for the night and immediately slipped into slumber.

7

"You look like the perfect fit, for a girl in need of a tourniquet."
– Aimee Mann

His feet were echoing down the dream corridor once again; strange, how he always seemed to be wearing the same shoes and completely dressed for work. Even down to the tie. As each footstep hit the cold hard floor, he knew exactly what to expect. This was getting ridiculous; it was too soon. He'd had the same dream the day before. But as he continued down the path to his old friend dread, Stanley remembered one small thing. Actually, it was more like two words; *full lucidity*. Could it work? He'd dismissed it at the time, but then, it's funny how in dreams things come back to you and make more sense than they did in the waking world. Suddenly it became a very real option.

Making involuntary fists with his hands, in and out, in and out, he moved forwards almost forcefully, like the air was thickening around him; almost like a protest to his actions. He struggled to keep his breath even, and now it came in short bursts. Could this mean he was already altering the dream? *Come on, get it over with*, he thought. He knew at any moment she'd dash along the corridor... but wasn't he closer now, much too close? Just as he'd expected, she rushed past in a swirl of white so close he could almost feel the air shift, and with almost fluid movement he surprised himself. He reached out for her and with what seemed like solid luck, gripped the hem of her dress. But to his shock, the dress came away from her in his hand and with inhuman speed she was gone again; he was left holding nothing but the ripped white material. This did not bode well. Finally gathering the courage to look around the corner, he saw nothing but blue walls as far as the eye could see. This was the part where he was supposed to search for her, but without the dress, he wasn't sure if he wanted to. He let the dress fall to the floor, and it was funny how he could even feel the lumps of the material under his shoe as he walked over it. That was far too real for his liking.

Looking back as if to avoid the evil garment, he stepped away slowly and reluctantly braced himself for the next part of the dream. But her usual moan did not come; instead it was eerily silent as he crossed the corridor, eyes fixing on the same blue door that he'd come face-to-face with in the past. Only this time he imagined her pressed up against the door naked, the dress he'd torn from her skinny, almost deformed body still lying ominously on the floor far behind him. That somehow made the dream more sexual, and that was horrific... he imagined her trying to climb maliciously on top of him, her bones so tight against her skin, scratching against him, seeking warmth. Those eyes would be staring into his soul. That was enough to make him realise the dream wasn't actually going his way; he had lost control. He didn't want to reach for the door, but there he was, watching his hand grasp the handle and turn it soundlessly. The door slowly started to open. She was closer than before and looked just as he'd imagined; naked and starved of a decent meal for far too long. She looked ravenous, and again there were those eyes staring and somehow searching even though dead. Her hair was mussed and fell partly over her face, knotted and stuck to her lips, hiding the crusted lipstick marks. But even though they were hidden, he knew they were there. She looked vulnerable yet utterly horrible at the same time. The marks were standing out on her neck again. She stumbled forward and he knew he had to run, like he always did, but this time he couldn't quite pick up his feet. She was getting closer, her blackened nails reached out for him, and still he couldn't move. How in hell she still managed to walk, to support herself on such a wasted frame, he didn't even want to know. Somehow, he knew anyway; hate was a powerful emotion. It drains its host, yet fuels wars. *Wake up, for god's sake wake up*, he told himself as if almost outside of the dream. But he couldn't move. He recoiled as he waited for the moment where her nails would scratch, her withered but somehow inhumanly strong hands would grab, her teeth would bite, hungry for fresh blood...

As if someone had turned on a loud speaker, the music blasted through the corridors, finally waking him up from his sleep. Yet his eyes were closed tight, and he could actually feel her nails just lightly scraping his chest. How could it be? Was the nightmare not over, had it somehow crossed into the real world? Heart racing in his chest, he opened his eyes to come face-to-face with a pair of wide grey cat eyes. Jasper the cat was lying on his chest, exercising his claws the way cats do, and looking at him with a rather unpleasant just-woken-up face. The alarm was yet again pounding what sounded like Polish heavy metal through the room. Stanley gently pushed the offending cat from his person and reached over to disable the alarm. Feeling strangely energised if not a little spooked, he made his way to the shower, only glancing once at the time. It read 08:23am. In the mirror, he looked pale and more than a little dishevelled, and he needed a shave. It was then he remembered last night's events.

"Bollocks, what was I thinking?" he muttered as he stumbled into the shower, savouring the feeling of warmth and protection it gave him. By the time he'd stepped out, most of the dream had become a distant, faded memory and Jasper was desperately seeking attention in order to receive breakfast. Still, he hesitated in choosing a tie. In the end he chose a silk purple affair with the faintest hint of a pattern. While he was putting it on in his usual well-practised manner, he thought about Gill. Hopefully it would be just another day, and the events of the night before would be completely forgotten about. At worst, a minor blip on the radar, or a ghost remaining forever unsaid between the two of them.

8

"I haven't had coffee yet. I could literally marry a puma right now." – Rich Fulcher

Later that morning when Stanley strolled (on time) into the newsroom, he was slightly disheartened to see Gill's empty desk. Walking towards the obits office, he hoped she wasn't too upset over the night before, but he didn't have much more than a moment to contemplate the matter further as his eyes settled on Kev marching straight in his direction.

"Stanley, your new desk's over here," Kev gestured to the far left corner of the newsroom, next to the door to Rory's office. Stanley looked. There was indeed a desk set up there.

"Sorry?" he asked, momentarily confused.

"I thought Rory talked to you yesterday? You'll be working in the newsroom for now," Kev replied, nonplussed.

"Oh, right, yeah... how could I forget?" Stanley said, awkwardly. Well, it was definitely an improvement on his last desk; it was one of those larger-style modern jobs with three drawers instead of two, complete with a shiny new PC and bigger monitor, too. It even had in-trays and a stationary set, kindly left there by some considerate member of the admin team. Not too shabby, only what the hell was he doing in the newsroom?

"Oh and don't forget, once you get settled, Rory wants to see you in his office," said Kev, before wandering back to his desk. Kev's wander was really more of an uptight amble; the kind that looked like he meant business, and in Stanley's opinion, also like he had a stick up his arse.

"Ah, right so," he muttered as he dropped his bag into the spacious drawer to his right. As he removed his jacket, he noticed some of the reporters casting him some odd glances, and tried to smile.

Probably just feeling threatened; nobody likes change, you know, he thought. *I mean, what's the weird obit guy doing here I ask you? Come to think of it, what AM I doing here?* He wished Gill was there, at least then the situation would be slightly more bearable, maybe even fun. But he could see her desk; still empty. There was only one thing for it. He took a deep breath, and strolled up to Rory's door, hesitated briefly, before knocking politely. The door opened straight away, and standing right in front of him was the man himself, Mr MacDuff. He looked more than amused and it seemed even his hazel eyes were smiling. This disturbed Stanley.

"Hello there, I've been expecting you, son," said Rory, gesturing for him to come inside, "take a seat and I'll explain everything." Stanley took a seat. He was starting to think Rory was enjoying himself. In fact, of course he was; it was written all over his face.

"So, I'll bet you're wondering what's going on," Rory continued. It wasn't a question, more of a statement.

"That's right, sir," Stanley replied coolly, crossing his hands together over his waist and trying not to look worried.

"Well, there's been a few developments since our last conversation, and I'd like you down near the action," Rory told him.

Stanley raised an eyebrow, "The action, sir?"

"Yes, the action. Now, I'm putting a lot of trust in you, boy. Don't let me down, alright?"

"Right, sure."

Rory looked back to the assortment of morning papers he was studying, as if Stanley had been silently dismissed.

"But can I just ask you..."

Rory's head snapped up again, "Yes, what?"

"Why have I been moved to the newsroom?"

The look on Rory's face said it all: "Look son, I'm

55

trying to do you a favour here. It's not very often I trust someone new to take on the main Fringe reports, but I'm asking you. So get on it! I've got you all the tickets you need right here and if you want some guidance I'm sure some of the team will be happy to help, I'll make sure of it."

"You're sending me to the Fringe?" Stanley asked, the shock only just registering on his face.

"Yes, and I won't pretend it's not because of what you know about Bogleur. I want you to do some digging and I've highlighted some of the acts he was personally monitoring. I'm not asking for miracles but find out what you can, alright? If you need to get further tickets to get in where you can, you can claim expenses. We need reviews from the Fringe, so why not kill two stones with one bird, look inconspicuous, like."

"Yes sir," Stanley replied, trying to find the words and not quite coming up with the right thing to say. In the end he settled with, "I'm not really sure what to say apart from, thank you and I'll do my best."

Rory nodded and Stanley got to his feet, feeling slightly daunted at the prospect of doing the job he was actually trained for, reporting, but nevertheless was that a hint of excitement in his chest or simply trepidation?

"Well, you won't mind starting tonight then? I'll send you along with Lionel, he's been our Fringe photographer the past three years now so he generally knows who's who," Rory replied casually. Stanley nodded; he knew Lionel well enough.

"Oh, and Stanley?"

"Yes sir?"

"Don't forget to have some fun with it."

When Stanley walked out of the office awkwardly clutching Rory's notes, the official Edinburgh Fringe brochure and tickets to several shows, he noticed all eyes were on him. He smiled, feeling just slightly self-conscious. It was a brief, almost unnoticeable moment yet he felt the slight shift in atmosphere, before people turned away and got on with their individual work. Again, he noted he missed Gill. She'd know what to do in this situation... he'd noticed most of the tickets were in pairs, maybe she'd even go to a few shows with him. Although he did indeed miss his friend, he'd also noted it wasn't in a relationship sort of way. He'd often thought about their friendship and it might make sense for them to hook up as a couple, but Gill was his friend, and a good one at that. No, he wouldn't jeopardise their friendship and it pained him to think of the night before and what he might have lost. He hoped it wasn't too late.

As he sat down to his desk he saw he'd already had an email from Lionel, entitled 'Captain-Consul McBeard'. And judging by tonight's tickets, that was indeed the name of the show they'd be going to see. Lionel was visiting a few shows that night to try and capture the general Fringe atmosphere, but he'd been looking forward to this particular show as 'McBeard' was rather controversial. Especially regarding his views towards women and donkeys whilst travelling in Egypt (but that's another story entirely, mainly regarding the time McBeard's pirate ship got stranded on the sand, apparently). He'd also had an email from Clive, letting him know he'd take care of all the outstanding obits. Stanley didn't quite know how to respond to that one, so he left it for now. Instead he started to research the Edinburgh Fringe's background for his first article, which was an introduction to the wide range of acts showcased at this year's festival. Along with the other material he'd been given from Rory, Kev had dumped a load of press releases on Stanley's desk and he flicked through these now. The acts sounded diverse to say the least. The names varied from the mysterious 'Lurman Incorporated' and 'Bearback Mob' to the comedic 'Neville's Ballet Shoes' to the downright silly 'Pink Custard Hotdogs'. He made a note of the latter, as it sounded interesting. Picking up a press release for 'Captain-Consul McBeard', Stanley read:

Parrot Blend #41!

Come along to see Captain-Consul McBeard in a sea of misfit ideas and hilarious seafaring conceptions, with a plethora of magic, mayhem and just downright parroting fun!
McBeard is funny, witty and sometimes just plain disgusting! As this year's theme, as always, is pirates, so beware of the seamen jokes, keep clear of the hooks and have a laugh at other people's expense!

10:15pm in the White Belly!

Stanley carefully placed the press release back on his desk. It was going to be an interesting night.

9

"I wish I was a crocodile." – Noel Fielding

That evening the air felt hot and humid as Stanley made his way up the Royal Mile. The street was terribly alive with crowds of people, performers and unavoidable scouts handing out leaflets to so many different shows it was impossible to keep track. He'd arranged to meet Lionel the photographer at the Smirnoff Underbelly, the venue for 'Captain-Consul McBeard', which he was supposed to be writing up for the paper. Stanley was slightly nervous at this prospect, as he imagined a cross between a sea-faring overt Captain Birdseye and the scary octopus beard character from the Pirates of the Caribbean sequel. Fighting his way through the many brightly-dressed and colourful festival revellers just proved that his usual aversion to crowds was well-deserved.

"Hello, man! Fancy seeing one of the most controversial shows to hit the Fringe this year?" Shouted a rather tall man with long black dreadlocks and a jester's hat, as yet another flyer was pushed out in front of him. Stanley took it, and nodded sheepishly.

"Thanks dude! See you there!" Stanley hoped not. He looked at the leaflet; the title of the show was called 'One Vagina, Two Million Pairs of Glasses'.

Moving on, Stanley was nearly at the turning for the Underbelly and would be thankful, if a little nervous, to go inside. Luckily Lionel was already there, waiting at the entrance. He waved at Stanley who had just swerved a rather large lady with a parasol, dressed in a pink taffeta Victorian-era costume, complete with a bustle and devil horns atop her head.

Lionel was a 42-year-old photographer who worked freelance, mostly for the Edinburgh Times, and was an experienced Fringe photographer. He had thin (balding) wispy dark blonde hair and was a sort of ordinary-looking bloke's bloke, slim build with grey-blue eyes, a slightly pointed nose and thin lips that formed an easy, pleasant smile.

"Alright, Stan?" Lionel said, "Nice night for it. Have you been to the Underbelly before?"

"Actually no," Stanley replied, "I've not really spent much time at the Fringe at all." Lionel laughed as he gestured Stanley through the entrance and down the steps.

"You're kidding, mate? You're in for one hell of a shock tonight then! Thrown you in at the deep end, haven't they?"

"Have they?" Stanley replied, suddenly more nervous than he had been to start with. Lionel seemed to consider this for a moment, before replying: "Nah, you'll be alright mate, just stick with me, ya know? It'll be fine."

They had gone down a couple of flights of stairs by this point, and Stanley's eyes were attracted to the many different coloured posters covering the walls. There was a slight smell that reminded him of potatoes recently dug up from the ground. The smell of dirt, however, only added to the atmosphere and yet more people were lining up to see the shows. Some of the entrances had names, and signs pointed to the location of even more venues. There was the 'White Belly', 'Jelly Belly', 'Big Belly', 'Belly Button' and so on and so forth and suchlike. It was the strangest place Stanley had ever been, and he said so.

"How come I never even knew this place existed?" He asked, partly to Lionel and partly to himself. Lionel shrugged. Stanley had started to relax again as they entered the main bar; it was an unusual place but it had a certain charm about it. By the time Lionel had ordered them a couple of pints, Stanley felt quite at home among the many Underbelly revellers. An odd mix of people seemed to gather in-between shows; there were the generally normal-looking ones, people in bright and odd costumes, some in large hats and plenty of others. It was hard to feel out of place, really.

A pretty girl in a purple tutu, black gothic hat and velvet jacket sat to his left. She had long white hair that looked sort of messy but somehow elegant at the same time. A man on his right was propping up the bar dressed in odd-looking red tartan trousers with tassels, giant black leather boots that looked almost comical, and a thin black top. Most impressive was his hair, which stuck out about two feet in a bright red Mohican style. An announcement came over the tannoy: "This is a call for Captain-Consul McBeard at the White Belly, please queue to the left of the bar if you're here to see Captain Consul McBeard'.

"That's us!" exclaimed Lionel as he grabbed his plastic pint glass and rather enthusiastically made his way towards the start of the queue. Stanley struggled to keep up with him. Before they knew it a huge line of people had formed behind them, all muttering between each other.

"Wow, this must be quite a popular show," Stanley remarked.

"You could say that," Lionel replied, a curious smile forming on his face. The bar was starting to get hot and Stanley removed his jacket, being careful not to crease it. Lionel was fiddling with his camera. When they were finally called up, they ascended the stairs to White Belly and handed over their tickets before entering a rather dark corridor that again smelled of potatoes, before following the people in front of them to a larger room with many metal seats all joined together. Background music was playing and on top of each metal seat was a leaflet. On the leaflet was a large cartoon bearded face with demented eyes surrounded by lots of pink, yellow and green doodles. It had to be the good Captain himself. Lionel began to choose a seat near the front, despite Stanley's insistence it might be better to sit further from the stage.

"Nah, you want a good seat, mate," Lionel said, "and

besides, I need to get some good shots so it'd be better if I sat off to the side on the front row."

"Alright, go on then," Stanley replied, trying to hide his anxiety at being so close to the 'Captain'.

It didn't take long before everyone was sitting, and Stanley noted the doors to White Belly being shut. The lights dimmed, and facing forward to the stage they could see a brilliant white spotlight. The background music stopped; the atmosphere thick with anticipation and expectation. A loud recorded drum roll began and rolling out very slowly onto the stage, a large dark pirate ship complete with cannons and ripped sails. Blue smoke gathered onto the stage and looked almost like a foggy, misty, fantastical sea. The drums continued up to a climaxing 'thump' as a large chubby pirate character with a massive unruly purple beard jumped on to the stage. He was wearing a navy jacket with gold embellishments and a large fake parrot perched on his shoulder.

"And now for the moment you have all been waiting for," the pirate announced in a thick Cornwall accent, "Ladies and Gentleman, get ready for some real magic beyond your wildest parrot, it's Captain-Consul McBeard!" Sure enough, as the fat pirate stepped off stage, he was replaced by possibly the most unusual man Stanley had ever seen in his life.

10

"There is a pleasure in madness, which none but madmen know." – Armando Iannucci.

Captain-Consul McBeard was not just a pirate, but every pirate that Stanley had ever imagined. He stood before the audience in his red pirate's jacket, smooth and elegant, yet a little rough around the edges with intricate gold brocade tapered along the sleeves and hem. His shirt was nothing special; ruffled and once pure white it now looked slightly off-colour and had the lived-in look. His trousers were flared and torn yet McBeard stood tall, and very tall indeed! Stanley reckoned to himself that the pirate stood about at least 6'7" tall. His shoes were almost like a clown's shoes, large and curled upwards at the toes, only McBeard's shoes were dark and worn, like a pirate's shoes should be.

On his head he wore a hat of the black variety with fancy white stitching along the trim. It was indeed a pirate's hat if ever Stanley saw one. But it was his face that really got Stanley's attention; his hair was a vibrant but natural-enough-looking gingery red and there was plenty of it. From his well-structured gelled moustache that hung down over his long and almost magnificent beard, to his thick yet structured sideburns, it practically stole the show. He had a large crooked nose that seemed to almost demand a third of his face (the visible part) and was so pointed at the end Stanley could imagine him as a big ginger crow. His eyebrows tweaked upwards in either jest or pure suggestion, and he winked at Stanley, making him do a double-take.

"Is that him?" Stanley whispered. But of course it was. Lionel ignored the question, photographer's fingers instead poised on the camera. A pair of big wide eyes so pale they almost looked silvery-white stared out at the crowd and seemed to look almost directly at Stanley. There was no eye patch; at least that was something. His body was slender yet not girlish. No, not girlish at all. Despite his curious attire, the man's demeanour seemed to be one of sophistication and true grace.

At a guess he looked at least 44, but it was hard to tell under the beard and general weirdness that he projected with his every fibre of being. Saying that, he moved in a most unusual gait, almost in a limp but not quite a limp, as if his body was lopsided and needed to be corrected with each amble the good Captain took. All eyes were on McBeard now and although an entire minute had gone past, he hadn't said a word. The room was silent in that ever-growing anticipation that made Stanley feel slightly sick. Instead, he motioned with one hook poking out of his sleeve, and seemed to command a wave of blue smoke upwards around his person, before sidling to his table and heavily dropping the hook down on to it, revealing both of his original hands were intact. He raised them up and gave the crowd a most unusual smile.

"Alright there folks? Having a good time at this year's festival? Who's here to see me then?" the Captain exclaimed in a thick accent; a cross somewhere between Cockney and Cornish. The crowd cheered loudly, and only a few people looked baffled. Stanley included.

"Of course we're here to see him, we wouldn't be here otherwise," he muttered under his breath, causing Lionel to give him a sly look which Stanley read as 'shut up, mate'.

"Here's one you might appreciate in Edinburgh, what with most of you being Scottish and the like! What's a pirate's favourite socks, eh? Arrrrgyle!" McBeard shook his head, "Yeah, that one was terrible, wasn't it? Moving on, I hear there's a couple of journalists here tonight from the Edinburgh Times! Give them a big cheer ladies and gents, where are you two hacks?" The Captain exclaimed in an almost camp voice as he searched the audience. Lionel motioned over, drawing the Captain's attention, before shouting, "Over here, Captain!"

"Aww, look at you, with your snappy-snap! Feel free to get right in there with the camera; I'll do some little poses at certain points in the show just for you!" The Captain laughed, before noticing Stanley. "Is that the other one?" the Captain asked, before addressing Stanley himself.

"You going to give me a fabby write up for the paper then, eh?" Stanley smiled, trying not to look embarrassed.

"Whatever you say, Captain," he muttered.

"Right then! Who's up for seeing some REAL magic - pirate standard?" The crowd cheered again, and the spotlight focused on a small round table in the middle of the room. On the table, was a purple cloth disguising something bumpy. The Captain approached the table and pulled away the cloth in one fluid motion, to reveal a bird's cage containing a beautiful blue parrot.

"Wow, magic huh? This, my friends, is Horace, and he's my assistant, isn't he... Horace, you plank! I told you to put the hat on!" The Captain sighed, and Stanley noticed the pirate's hat on the bottom of the cage.

"Oh well, never mind, you've already messed up the show! Birds eh, who needs 'em? Got a joke to tell you about that actually, hold on, let me get comfortable and I'll tell ye!"

"A rather tragic experience happened to my mate, you see. I hadn't seen him in a while, and he came into the pub one day wearing an eye patch, a hook for a hand and a wooden leg!

"So I said to him, I said, 'hey, what's up bruv, haven't seen you in a while, what the hell happened? You look like a bag of shit!' Well, he didn't quite look that bad but he looked bloody awful, he did! He replied, 'what do you mean, I feel alright', so I asked him about his leg. And he was like 'well, we were in a battle with Big Joe's pirate ship, and I got hit with a cannon ball but it's alright now, I'm fine.' So I looked him up and down and I said, 'well that's bad luck, mate, what about the hook?' And he looked down and said 'oh yeah, forgot about that, well what happened was when I boarded Big Joe's ship I got into a sword fight, you see. But it's fine now, I'm alright, innit.' So I had to ask about the eye patch, didn't I? I said, 'so what happened with your eye then, son? Was it Big Joe, did he gouge out your eye with his 'ook?' and he said 'oh that old thing, nah one day we were trying to train a new bunch of parrots and they were all circling the ship. I looked up and one of them did a shit right in my eye!' and taken aback, of course, I was like 'Really? Right in your eye? I didn't know you could go blind from bird shit!' And he looked at me, and I could tell he was pissed off, but he just looked at me, and eventually he said: 'Nah mate, it was my first day with the hook' and that was that was that!" The crowd laughed, including Lionel, who laughed like a hyena on speed. The next few minutes involved the Captain dancing around and performing a few joke shop tricks with the parrot, who was obviously a born entertainer. He stopped a couple of times in deliberate poses for Lionel, getting a few laughs from the audience and deliberately providing some great pictures for the paper at the same time. Turning, the Captain seemed to pause in thought for a second, before continuing: "What's next? Ah yes, mind games!"

The Captain continued to amble around the stage with the parrot on his shoulder before he continued with the 'mind games' theme. "I'm walking myself into preparation, you see?" the Captain explained, before he addressed the audience. "Now, as we come to mind games, can I just ask some of you what you think about them? 'Four' instance, I mean, like, guessing numbers, thoughts, places, 'forethoughts', even appearing to contact dead relatives," the Captain explained, before pointing to one guy in the crowd, "Yes, you sir! What have you to say 'four' me?"

"I think it's a load of bollocks," the man said almost proudly.

"Well, that's your opinion, sire, you're entitled to that!

I'd like you to guess a number between one and ten, and don't tell anyone, and hold it in your mind, just four yourself, okay?"

"Alright, got it," the man replied, nonplussed.

"And you there, the lady with the pink top, how are you two night? Are you going two the after show later, might see you there, eh? I'm going two ask you two guess a number for me two, darling, alright? Think on it now, between one and ten please, two."

"Ermm... okay, I have it," the lady replied.

The Captain wandered to the back of the stage and pulled out a pirate's hat made out of what appeared to be tinfoil, before promptly sticking it on his head. He looked ridiculous. As what seemed to be an afterthought, he said, "Helps me to channel your thoughts, of course. In fact, to make this a little harder for me, I want all of you to think of different numbers in your head, whatever you like." The parrot flew out to both audience members and gave them each a white piece of paper and a pen.

"Everyone got their numbers? Right, you two please write down the number you originally thought and here I go," and indeed there he did go, as he closed his eyes, turned around and began making an almost chanting moan, like 'uuummmmm'. To Stanley the whole thing seemed ridiculous. The blue smoke was back, purely for effect, of course. After a small pause, the Captain asked, "Are the numbers written down?" The response was positive. The Captain sharply turned around and pointed first at the gentleman, and almost as if he was shooting the number out, he shouted, "Four!" He then turned to the lady - who looked slightly scared - pointed, and shouted, "Two!" He took the hat off, as if it pained him to keep it in any longer, and asked, "Am I right?" The whole crowd turned to look at the two, and both of them were nodding. The man looked flabbergasted. "But how... how did you know?" he asked.

"Ah, you really want to know? It was a TRICK of the

MIND! My friend, when I was talking to you, you must have at least subconsciously heard me bring the word 'four' into the conversation various times right before I asked you to pick a number. And so you had no choice but to pick four! No choice, ahahah!"

"You're kidding me? That actually works? That's amazing, I'm totally lost for words, mate," the man replied, looking disgusted with himself for falling for such a cheap trick.

"Same with you, madam," the Captain continued. "For you I said the word 'two' a lot and then asked you to pick a number. You didn't pick up on that, not just a bit? Just a tiny bit? Nah, you wouldn't, would you?"

"Great," muttered Stanley, "Could see that one coming a mile off." The Captain ambled full circle around the stage, knotting his hands together and generally looking anxious and somehow good-humoured at the same time. "Just a little mind fuck, ladies and gents, I'll be doing that for the rest of the show if you don't mind!" Suddenly looking serious, he turned to face the crowd.

"But really, there's a lot the human mind can sustain. I'd like to call up two people from the audience for this next trick. To balance it out again, let's make it a man and a woman – a man and a woman who aren't afraid of a bit of blood!" A few people raised their hands, and were chosen by the Captain to come up on stage. Meanwhile, the Captain began to remove his jacket and rolled up his ruffly off-white sleeves. From somewhere beyond Stanley's point of view, the Captain grabbed two shiny things that at first looked out of place, before Stanley realised they were hooks. They were indeed long, thin, sharp hooks and looked extremely pointy. The Captain gave one to both and man and the woman audience member, and asked for them to confirm their sharpness. Once everyone was convinced, the pirate asked the female, who looked a little bit unsure, to pierce his skin with the hook.

"Come on love, it's easy! Look, I'll get you started," the

Captain said, and he grabbed the hook and pushed it firmly through the flesh of his upper arm. The crowd gasped and the woman, in her mid-twenties, went a little pale. So did Stanley. "Now, push it right through for me, there you go," he said as she slowly took the hook and gently pushed it. "The faster you do it love, the less faint I'll feel, so just push it in, hurry up!" And so she pushed it until the shiny blade was poking through the other side of the Captain's arm. "There you go, now sir, I'll ask you to do the same." The man did as he was told, and soon enough both hooks were protruding through the pirate's upper arms. "That's what we like! Now, each of you grab the hook end if that's not too much trouble, use the cloths so you won't get any blood on your hands, that's it, and now pull in time to the music," the Captain laughed, as pirate-style music began to play out through the speakers. The couple looked at him as if he must be mad, but both of them made a half-hearted attempt to pull his arms and the Captain slumped down like a puppet as Horace flew around the stage in circles. The music stopped and he jerked back up to attention.

"Right, now I might need your help getting these out again," he said, "you still feeling okay? No? Don't worry, this is the easy part." Stanley could hardly watch as the hooks came out, but he did anyway. There was a little bit of blood, but luckily it looked like nothing had struck a main artery. He sighed in relief and was only glad he hadn't been the one to pull them out. Again he wondered why this guy was so popular.

"But seriously now people, these are my trusty hooks! Can't tell you how handy these came in when travelling in Egypt! But that's another story, one involving donkeys and women and one that I got slated for last time I was here! But anyway, how does a pirate like me make his money? By hook or by crook! Get it? Ahahahah," the audience moaned.

"Moving on... Horace, you were supposed to get the balloon you useless bird! Never mind," the pirate sighed, "I'll get it myself. Does anyone like balloons?" Lionel leaned over and whispered in Stanley's ear, "This is the best bit; he half inflates it, puts it up one nostril and down the other and then transfers the air from one side to the other, then puts it in his mouth and forms an animal out of it with his tongue."

"Oh for fucks sake..." Stanley sighed. He wanted the show to be over before he really started to feel queasy. The good Captain did indeed use the balloon to transfer air from one nostril to the other, and at that point Stanley zoned out in a bid to take his mind from what was actually happening. In the end he found himself doodling over his shorthand; a stick figure in a pirate's hat with a hook through the heart and crossed out eyes. By the time McBeard had done a couple of poses with the balloon firmly up both nostrils, told another joke, made a joke dog out of the balloon with his tongue, rinsed it and had subsequently given it to a member of the audience as a keepsake, the fat pirate had rolled another table onto the stage.

"I thank ye good sir," said the Captain, as he yanked off the purple cloth to reveal an ordinary-looking blender.

"Alright then Horace, I've decided it's that time of the night when I've just about had it (he pronounced it 'add it') with you! So if you please, get into the blender me 'old son." The Captain had Stanley's full attention again as Horace the parrot obediently got into the open blender, before the Captain closed the lid. "Some of the more faint-hearted of you may want to close your eyes at this part!" And so the Captain said a brief prayer under his breath, finger hovering over the 'start' button on the blender; Stanley could hear a murmur through the audience.

"He's not going to actually..." whispered Stanley, but Lionel didn't even look his way. Oh, but he was. And then he did. The blender suddenly filled with colours, mainly red, and the gasp of the crowd could be heard – just – over the noise of the blender.

"Ah, that's better, isn't it? No more good-for-nothing bird to mess up me' act," McBeard smiled, before sauntering around the table in a circle. Stanley realised he was still holding his breath, and looking around so were a lot of others.

"But that's not all folks..." the Captain approached the table again, pulling out the cloth covering the table, revealing the table was actually a cabinet. The audience watched as the good Captain quickly opened the small doors and let out Horace, who flew out in a flap of bright blue wings, before making his rounds across the audience.

"You didn't really think I'd top me best mate, did you now? Come on, people! Have a heart!" ('ave a eart!') The parrot joined McBeard and perched on his shoulder as joined by the fat pirate, he took a bow to the audience, who clapped and cheered. The show was over.

"Don't forget myself and Captain Shanksforth here will be at the after party tonight; should you care to join us, it'll be a laugh!"

11

"In the 1960s people took acid to make the world weird. Now the world's weird and people take Prozac to make it normal." – Damon Albarn.

The Underbelly 'after party' was awash with lights and loud music, and the two journalists stood around the bar taking in the atmosphere.

"Alright guvnors, did you enjoy the show?" came a familiar roar from behind Stanley's left ear. It was McBeard, looking more than a little drunk. It'd only been around an hour since his show had finished. Lionel shouted, "Heeey, how are you, mate? Enjoying yourself? Show was first rate, got some great shots!" "Shots? I'll have one if you are, ahaha-ah! Alright mate?" he asked Stanley.

"Yeah, great! Congratulations on the show!" Stanley replied, indeed feeling much more relaxed in the knowledge that it was over.

"Right mate, I'm off, need to get to the next show in time to take some more happy snaps," Lionel said.

"You're going? But..."

"Listen here, we're all adrift in the same great pond of life, so grab onto a lily pad and call yourself algae, like the rest of us. It'll be all right. Have fun."

Stanley watched him leave through the crowd as if he belonged there like a fish did water – or algae did a pond. With one small wave, Lionel disappeared among a crowd of dancing hippies. And then, he really was gone.

Stanley stayed and watched as revellers surrounded him and danced casually; normally it would have bothered him, but despite McBeard's show he still had the

Fringe feeling. He felt quite happy to stay and party, in the name of journalism and all, and most interesting it was.

McBeard had been explaining his theories on sexual attraction, at length, while downing shots of tequila.

"These hooks here, will definitely attract the ladies tonight," he explained, and Stanley noticed he still had the hooks hanging from his ripped trousers.

"I'll bet you anything. Because the ladies, you see, are always just slightly on the perverted side, really! They'll do anything to add a bit of kink, spice things up a bit, you know whar'I'mean?" He slurred the last few words out. Stanley just nodded and looked around at the many girls dancing in the crowd; all of them ignoring himself and McBeard. There were again a good mix of people in the crowd and some of the girls were very pretty and unusual – which made them interesting to Stanley, yet he knew that's as far as it would go.

Then something – or rather someone – caught his eye in the crowd. A woman dressed in black leather which hugged her curves in just the right way as she moved in almost perfect synergy with the people around her. She was almost catlike. Her dark hair (he couldn't tell exactly whether it was black or very dark brown) was tied in an odd way at either side of her head which - inexplicably - only added to her elegance and sexual prowess. Her skin was the colour of milk and looked ridiculously smooth and luminous under the lights, but he struggled to keep her in his line of sight, and then she was gone.

No, he wasn't interested in picking anyone up, not after the mess he'd made with Gill the night before. He wasn't even sure the latter would forgive him. Besides, he was technically still here for work purposes, which brought him back to his current dilemma. How was he supposed to find out any relevant information or 'dirt' as Rory called it, in amongst all the chaos of the festival? And what a festival it was. The Captain interrupted his thoughts with his Cockney/Cornish pirate voice.

"'Ave you got a girlfriend, Stan? You don't, do you, I

can tell. Why not, eh?" the Captain continued. Stanley didn't really know what to say to that. Was it really that obvious he was single? "Well it's a long story, you know, wouldn't want to go into it tonight," he finally replied.

The Captain lowered his voice and got closer than comfort for Stanley, his lips close to Stanley's ear. He said: "Look, you're a journalist son, keep your eyes peeled around here. There's something not quite right, I can feel it. Heck, I've seen..." The Captain's eyes seemed to dart as they shifted their gaze around the room, almost as if he thought he was being followed, and murmured under his breath something Stanley didn't quite understand; something about a jade frog being the sign of danger. Of course, he didn't actually tell Stanley he was being followed, but Stanley would remember that thought later along with McBeard's darting, nervous, shifting eyes.

In the mean time, and slightly taken aback, Stanley just nodded, and just as suddenly the Captain moved away again and was speaking in his normal pirate manner.

"Alrighty-ho then mate, why don't we try finding you one then, eh, what do you say?"

"No thanks, but you go ahead, I'm up for a laugh any day of the week," Stanley said, in as good humour as he could muster considering what the Captain had just told him.

"A laugh, is it? Gotta love the Irish!"

The Captain started to stand, before handing Stanley one of his hooks, "You look after that lad, I'm off to the swannie." Before Stanley could protest, he was holding the bright shiny metal hook with his fingertips. Examining it, it was indeed a strong sharp hook, hopefully sterilised, and would probably serve as an effective weapon.

"Ooh, what's that?" A girl who appeared to be in her early twenties stood in front of him, looking curiously at the hook. Her hair was tied up in a messy pony tail and her angular, interesting face held big bright blue eyes, heavily framed with eyeliner and mascara. Her lips were shiny bubblegum pink and she wore a bright blue top slashed at one shoulder, and grey wet-look trousers.

"Oh, this? It's not mine, I'm just looking after it for a friend," he heard himself utter the words and realised he sounded terribly guilty.

"Hahah," she girl laughed, "That's what they all say!"

"No, really, I..." Stanley felt a little lost.

"Minnie!" another girl shouted, with long black hair and fire engine lips, "What are you having? Oh hello, what do we have here?"

"I'm not quite sure, but isn't it cute?"

"Very cute; but you have to watch out for the cute ones, especially when they've got weapons that size!" They both found it hysterically funny.

"What's your name, then?"

"It's Stanley, and this isn't mine, it's a friend's," Stanley replied.

"Awww, he's Irish! Even cuter! Would you like a test tube shot, Stanley, blue or red?"

"Ermmm," Stanley realised he was going to turn into a pisshead if he didn't stop drinking. "Go on then, blue." He downed the shot and the two girls seemed to adopt him on the spot. Minnie, the one in the blue, reminded him a bit of a comic book eco-warrior while the other one, whose name was Lindsay, was more of a gothic ballerina right down to the black ballet shoes on her feet.

It took him a while to notice Captain McBeard had well and truly disappeared, and then he realised that rhymed, and burst into more laughter along with the girls who were by that time playing with his hair and buying him more test tubes. Surprisingly, he was all right about the hair part. He supposed that when a situation was out of his control it was more acceptable than it would have been otherwise. Not that he found the girls that incredibly attractive; and he knew that he was drunk... again.Music thumped in an odd beat and he couldn't place exactly what genre of music was playing. Sort of an odd mixture between electro and bass beat. People were dancing all around them by this time, and the girls got up a few times to do a giggly dance around the table. Stanley didn't join them, at least until they physically pulled him up and by that time he was too far gone to care. He even attempted his Thom Yorke impression. It went down well.

A large fish costume seemed to have replaced the DJ, and lots of people in shiny clothes seemed to reflect off its bright scales. The fish raised a fin in the air and the music went from being really sort of general, to extremely trippy.

There seemed to be more people in the bar than ever before, and a lot of them starting jumping to the music, including Minnie and Lindsay. That's when he realised he couldn't just feel the strong beat of the music, he could also feel his head throbbing, although at first it was hard to distinguish which was which. He needed fresh air, but he couldn't remember the best way out – was it up or down? People were all around him, and suddenly the bar seemed a lot smaller than he remembered. Not that he was claustrophobic – heavens no, as if he needed any more problems. L and M were dancing dangerously closely to him, which didn't help him steady his feet. What were their names? L was Lindsay, what about M? Then he thought 'mouse' and remembered her name was Minnie. Lights were flashing around the room and for a moment he couldn't make up his mind whether they were real or just in his head; he'd had migraines before which sometimes brought flashes of light, but none so extravagant as this. The lights danced off Minnie's shiny blue top with the slash at the shoulder, and that brought Stanley's mind back to the real world. As he tried to find his way back to the table – the crowd must have slowly caused him to migrate towards the decks – he noticed the state of his notepad. Someone had spilled what looked like a pint over it and now it was wet and brown and sticky. *Just great*, he thought.

He had no idea what the time was, but he had the notion that the Underbelly was not just a simple venue, instead a conscious bubble in which time seemed to stand still. He thought he saw the pirate, what was his name? McBeard - that was it. He caught a glimpse of a pirate hat up ahead, and tried to push his way towards the front of the gyrating crowd, but again he was lost in the sea of people. Suddenly Stanley was feeling more than a little claustrophobic. Surely it was impossible that the crowd were slowly turning into one big sea, ready to swallow him up into its depths and down to Davey Jones's locker? The Captain's words echoed in his mind, 'something's not right here'.

A hand grabbed his shoulder, and spinning around Stanley was relieved to see Lionel. He looked slightly worse for wear but nothing compared to how Stanley was feeling. Lionel was mouthing something over the music, but Stanley couldn't figure out what it was. "Sorry?"

"I said you almost had my eye out with that damn hook! Come on, I think you've had enough for one night!"

"Let's get out of here," Stanley replied.

12

"Has anyone ever loved you so much that they tried to kill you, or perhaps sucked you down into a hole so that you had to kill them to get away? Yeah, me neither." – Maynard James Keenan.

The Captain

The music in the Underbelly blared out over the large speakers as a large fish-costumed host took over the decks. The Captain (real name Dennis Fotheringham Ford the Third) had been swerving the crowd since leaving Stanley's table only a minute before. Aware of the fact he was being followed, this seemed like the right move to make – although who in their right mind would follow him, and why, still eluded Dennis. Telling the young Irish lad also made him feel slightly more at ease, as if he'd dispensed a dark cloud from his mind. Saying it out loud had also made it suddenly more real, and really, what could a hopeless boy like that do about it? Something was going to happen tonight; Dennis could feel it in his bones. It was not a good thing – neither was it a good feeling.

Shifting his gaze around the many revellers, trying to find a suspicious eye that would meet his, he found none. But that didn't mean it was safe. Dennis had watched his fair share of crime detective shows on television, and he knew that feeling safe was a very bad sign indeed. He knew that just as the victim had the slightest inkling that the danger was over with (for example, the beloved cat had made the noise and oh look, I left the window open by mistake, silly me – that's when the killer comes from behind with a large kitchen knife and slits their throat like a... well like slicing through butter, really), that was indeed when the danger would always strike. He hadn't lied to the lad – he did need to go for a slash, and that's where he was heading now. Without turning his back even once more, he made a B-line for the men's and quickly entered through the door to the left of the bar. All was quiet, and a quick check of the cubicles confirmed to the 'Captain' that he was alone. Feeling more than a bit tipsy, he absentmindedly he took the other hook from his belt and hung it over one of the cubicle doors, so as not to forget it, before making his way to the cubicle at the far end of the room.

Feeling vulnerable in his pirate costume, he was grateful for the privacy of the cubicle if only for a few minutes. He took the time to reflect upon his situation. Who in their right mind would want to follow him, anyway? His doctor had after all suggested he should lay off the Ritalin. Or if not that, then the joints he smoked on regular occasion. Thinking this, he didn't even bat an eyelid when he heard the door of the men's opening quietly, and the flush of the toilet disguised any sound of metal scraping against a hard surface.

Before venturing out, he quietly laughed at himself for being such a paranoid drunken wreck, and as he stood in front of the mirror washing his hands, he saw each individual wrinkle on his well-seasoned face and appreciated his age for the very first time. Of course, he didn't feel any older than twenty-five, but the truth was he was pushing fifty and perhaps it was time to give up the pirate comedian game for a more mature one. He did look rather dashing in his costume though, and the ruffled shirt hid the pot-belly that was starting to develop after years of abusing his metabolism with pork pies and beer. He dried off his hands and as he turned to throw the paper towel in the bin (his mother had always told him it was more hygienic to use paper towels rather than hand-driers, which only re-circulated filthy air around the room) he did a double-take in the mirror. Something was missing from the picture and a rising feeling of dread hit Dennis as he figured out just what it was. The hook that he'd carefully hung over the first cubicle had vanished. He hadn't heard the door to the men's close again, but nor had he heard the hook being taken from its hanging place. But it wasn't just the sight of the missing hook that had made the Captain's blood turn cold. There was another object in the room, staring at him with its little beady eyes. Despite his shaking hands, the Captain spun around and quickly, noisily, checked the cubicles one by one. All empty. That was all right – maybe someone had taken it as a joke, or simply saw the hook and claimed it as their own. But in the space of two minutes, the Captain wondered how likely that really was. And it didn't explain the *other* thing. The music outside could still be heard in the men's room, and the Captain slowly gathered his nerves from the floor as he readied himself to go out again. Yes, it'd be better to stick with the crowd; perhaps he could find young Stanley with the Irish eyes again and have a banter about the quality of this year's fringe. As he opened the door and cautiously peered out, everything looked exactly the same as he'd left it. The fish was flipping its fins to the music that pumped out over the speakers, and plenty of young drunk festival-goers were dancing and generally 'having a laugh' as he should have been. Yes, he was much inclined to 'have a laugh' with the best of them. But now the Captain didn't feel much like laughing at all. He started to make his way through the many faces in the crowd, not knowing who or what to look for in the blur. And it was blurry, because he was still drunk, despite the sobering experience in the gentleman's loos. A hand touched his shoulder, but as he swung round he realised it was just a young guy in a yellow and pink t-shirt, stumbling through with his mates in tow. Every eye seemed to catch the Captain's as he found his way through the crowd – probably because of the way he was suspiciously eyeing them, but he didn't think of that – and he realised it could be any one of them. From the minute he'd found the odd-looking jade frog on the dresser in his hotel room (he was sure it hadn't been there before); he knew that something was different this year.

His hotel room was cheap but cheerful, as always – anything was normally a nice change from his small London flat. Contemplating his years as a comedian, he'd decided to write an autobiography about all the things he'd witnessed along the way. But really, he hadn't got that far in terms of fame. He wasn't exactly taking it seriously, only had a few sheets of A4 paper so far, and most of those were covered in doodles where he'd got bored. It was on top of those sheets of paper that the frog had been placed. Whether it had any significance to the papers or not, he'd had no idea, but something about the frog and its sinister beady eyes gave him an uneasy feeling and he knew it was no ordinary paperweight. So he'd thrown it out the window without a second thought. When it appeared again three days later, he'd started to look over his shoulder while walking down the streets of Edinburgh. It was the very same frog that had been placed in the men's toilets when he'd gone to take a leak; he was sure of it. What did it all mean, was he indeed going mad? It couldn't be explained; not the hook or the frog. His heart was racing and so were the thoughts in his head as he tried to piece together the puzzle and again it hit him – it could be any one of them. He was started to feel very exposed, almost as if the crowd were closing in on him, suffocating him, and he realised what he needed was some fresh air. He removed his hat and weaved through the crowd, trying to come up with a plan before he saw the exit downstairs. There was beer down there, and plenty more people too, he'd bet. It'd help calm his nerves. As he descended the stairs he had to grab on to the banister for dear life; his legs felt like rubber that could give way any second.

"Aye aye, Captain!" shouted one guy in his mid-twenties, who passed him on the stairwell, almost making him jump out of his skin.

"You alright?" a young girl asked who had followed on

81

behind the shouter.

"Yes thanks, just need some fresh air," the Captain replied. Saying it out loud made it somehow easier to believe. Soon he was out in the warm humid air of the 'outer belly', as he called it. There were indeed people around, sitting at the tables and scattered around outside some of the belly doors, but not as many as the Captain would have liked. It was rather late, after all. Fumbling for his cigarettes, he looked around nervously. A group of youngsters had begun to gather their possessions from one of the wooden tables. As he lit up, he knew it wouldn't be long until the others cleared out and then he would be alone. That sparked an anxiety in the Captain which was most unusual. Perhaps it was crazy to think like that, but then again he had never felt quite so uncomfortable in his pirate's uniform as he did now. Still, he didn't want to go back inside as whoever – or even whatever – was probably still in there. No, he was safer to wait out here, to find his way back to the hotel from the back entrance. Some more people had finished smoking and were heading back inside; he moved to let them past. The cigarette had gone down fast. Dropping the butt on the ground he lit up another, and watched as the rest of the late-nighters either returned back inside or left by the back. The underbelly staff had closed the outside ticket office. The large doors were covered in brightly-coloured posters. He could still hear the music from inside bleeding out into the cobbled area, where his feet were currently planted. He realised he was going to be alone, and so began his walk towards the same exit the others had taken so as not to go back through the 'inner belly'. Which was ridiculous; he was one of the main acts there and would have to come back numerous times in the next two weeks for his shows. Still, he made his way across the cobbles, checking out of courtesy that the Belly had indeed been closed up for the night. He'd stopped to read a poster, when out of the corner of his eye he saw a door slowly open. It was a door that had always been shut before, probably for storage or perhaps cleaning purposes. Dennis hesitated, and something in his gut told him not to go to the door, to instead go back to his hotel room. But another part of him thought that he'd be giving in to an irrational (perhaps) fear, and as a performer working at the fringe it was partially his responsibility to maintain it. That decided him. He walked towards the cupboard and caught the door before it could softly hit the wall. Peering in, he saw that the cupboard was a lot larger than he'd first suspected – and darker, too. That caused him to hesitate a second time. Of course, he could easily turn around, close the door behind him and be on his merry way. But was that a shadow moving in the back there?

"Hello?" he called out. No response. It was like the stuff of horror movies, the kind where everyone knows never to enter the basement after hearing that odd noise, after all, how would you get out if the crazy axe murderer does happen to be down there? But Dennis couldn't help himself; it was as if he was watching himself on a TV screen, instead of having control over his actual body. Searching for a light, he took a step inside, letting curiosity get the better of him. Before he knew it, he was four steps into the – well, it was more like a small room than a cupboard, and still hadn't found a light. It was just blind luck that his hand came across what felt like a torch on one of the shelves. It was sturdy and not at all light; he reckoned it probably took those heavy duty batteries. Leaning over to grab it, he must have knocked over a broom or something equally large, because something fell to the floor with a loud startling crash. "Ah, shit," he muttered, as his hand closed around the torch and quickly switched it on. He hadn't noticed the door slowly swinging shut behind him, but the sudden blackness of the room made him turn around. Having second thoughts about venturing into the cupboard in the first place, he slowly began to make his way back towards where the door had been, as silently as possible, without causing any further disruptions that could alert a potential stalker as to his whereabouts. To further that thought, Dennis switched the torch off again. It was a complete surprise when, trying to find his way over some plastic buckets without knocking them over, a strong gloved hand came from behind him and closed over his mouth, muffling his startled cry for help. As he tried to spin around to see his attacker, it was even more of a surprise to Dennis when the other gloved hand punched him in the stomach, momentarily winding him and leaving him just vulnerable enough to let the hand grab him firmly around the waist and pull him even further back into the cupboard. But what really chilled his blood and made his heart pound quickly in his chest, was when he felt the hard metal of the missing hook against his back. In his head and muffled under the large gloved hand, Dennis screamed. He still had the heavy torch in his hand, and grasping it harder than ever he raised it as far back as possible and with force he hit... nothing. He tried again, and the second time the torch hit something hard; probably skull. His attacker gave an aggravated groan, and kicked Dennis hard. Pain shot up the back of his leg, as the muscles had been pulled taught, almost knocking him over. He let go of the torch and before he knew it he was falling through the air, almost as if it was happening in slow motion. He collided with the buckets and various cleaning apparatus that littered the floor. A white flash of pain swept through his head, and he realised that he'd been struck with the hook. Spinning around, he saw a large black shape in front of him, brandishing the hook, which somehow still managed to look shiny in the dark. The red dots in front of his vision made it harder for Dennis to make out any facial features on the man, but in horror he watched as the hook was raised up, and then brought down sharply. Then everything faded into fuzzy darkness.

13

"I dreamt last night I was chopping up carrots with the Grim Reaper: dicing with death." – Tim Vine.

Fair Summer

It just so happened that at exactly the same time as the world faded into fuzzy blackness for Dennis, Fair Summer, the tiny Edinburgh Times sub, awoke from her slumber with a start. She'd had another nightmare, and as she brushed her wispy blonde hair away from her delicate features and looked around sleepily to see the familiar surroundings of her tiny apartment, she heaved a small sigh of relief.

Fair sat up in bed and clasped both hands around her knees, as if trying to stay warm. The digital alarm clock by her bedside read 03:16 in bright red numerals. Tiny drops of rain tip-tapped on her rather large old window pane, which was framed perfectly by large thick beige curtains. On the windowsill sat a book entitled 'Nightswallow' and some crystals and odd little trinkets that Fair had collected over her years in the city of Edinburgh.

Fair hadn't always lived in Edinburgh, although she thought the city was beautiful; she was originally from Sweden. She now saw the Scottish capital as her home, having lived there for almost 10 years.

Her name wasn't particularly Swedish; her parents had been Abba-obsessed hippies. She didn't mind that much, however. The name was part of her. Fair lived alone and was quite happy like that, for most of the time at least. But now the nightmare hovered like a cloud over her thoughts as she sat in the darkness of her room. Tonight was not most of the time, as once again she pondered the frailty of human life. It was times like this she yearned for company in the form of old friends, new ones, or even past lovers; someone to keep the bed warm at night and offer her a listening ear when she couldn't find her way back to sleep.

Again she glanced at the clock; it was still early, yet the time would pass quickly and it wouldn't seem long before she'd have to give up the safety of her covers and haul herself out of bed. One thing she was sure of; she wouldn't be getting any more sleep tonight. The shower would soothe her mind and wake her up for the day, but she wasn't quite ready to leave her warm bed yet. Although she knew that even attempting sleep now would be useless.

She reached for the glass of water she often kept by her bed for occasions such as these, but the glass was extremely cold. Odd that someone should feel so cold in the height of summer, even if it was a Scottish summer; it wasn't all that bad. The boyish pyjamas she wore were supposed to keep her small frame snugly wrapped up and warm, yet the combination of vest top and baggy grey trousers was going to do no such thing on this night. She shivered and decided to make a cup of tea instead, hesitantly getting out of bed to carry the glass through to her small kitchenette. The memory of the dream flashed in her mind, and she had to stop herself from dropping the glass; she could just imagine it shattering all over the floor, and then who would have to clean up the mess? She pushed the memory to the back of her mind, and continued down the dark corridor.

She was comfortable in the dark; after all, it wasn't the dark that could harm her. Even though it was a separate room, it wasn't really what Fair would call a fully-sized kitchen, so kitchenette suited just fine. It was big enough for her to do all she needed to do in it, although if another person were ever to occupy the flat, it might seem all of a sudden far too small for her liking. After all, other people cluttered things, came in with their chaos and spread it around almost like a disease. It was the things they left behind that made sometimes made imprints only she could see. The crystals were supposed to have a purifying quality, but Fair wasn't so sure. After all, only hippies put their full trust in a few bits of rocks, and what good had they done her so far and if they had done any good? Fair would hate to imagine what would happen if she ever removed them. That thought was what kept the crystals where they were; on her bedroom windowsill, and one underneath her pillow. When the tea was made, she clutched it in both hands, enjoying the warmth it brought her. She didn't bother to switch on the light, as the kitchen was plenty bright enough. As she sipped the hot liquid goodness, she propped herself up at the large windowsill and peered out through the rain. She knew it hadn't happened very far away from her flatted dwelling, but how she knew that was inexplicable. And it had happened; she knew that somewhere in her heart of hearts. Mentally preparing herself for more flashes, she knew that they'd come as they often would; during the day, at times when she would least expect it. They often caught her off-guard, and put a dampener on events that would have otherwise made her quite happy. It was these dreams she hated the most, as there was absolutely nothing she could do to go back and change what had already been done. Fair shivered again. The thick texture of a glove, the sensation of falling, and a white flash of pain... it was all too much for her and again she forced it out of her mind using an imaginary mental building brick. The bricks would build a wall, and serve as a guard until she let it go. Still, the moment had been spoiled; she put down the mug and made her way to the shower, where she sat under its warm jets for almost a full hour, trying to wash away the blood from hands that didn't belong to her; to wash it from her mind. Wash it all away.

*

Fair was in the office by 8.30am, where she sat wide awake nursing a cup of green tea. She was waiting to hear the news, preparing for it, as she'd done in the past. She hoped that this time was different; that it'd just been a harmless dream. But that wasn't true and she wasn't fooling herself by thinking it. She'd taken the normal route to work, on her bike. It was far better than the bus, and it kept her mind occupied, swerving the many people on their way to work. Not many had much consideration for cyclists, although Edinburgh was supposed to be quite a health-conscious city.

It had still been slightly damp from the rain when she left her flat, and now small blotches of mud coloured her black skinny jeans, despite her efforts to wipe them down with a wet paper towel. The newsroom was already busy when Gill walked in full of the cold. She looked more than slightly like she'd been dragged through a hedge backwards, but was putting on a brave face for work. Gill announced her presence to the office. "Oh, for God's sake look at me, I'm such a mess! I've got a rip in my tights, my nose is redder than Rudolph's and it's nowhere near Christmas time yet - trust accident-prone little old me to get a cold in the height of summer!" She was indeed accident-prone. She obviously hadn't the energy to straighten her hair to the usual standard, so it looked half done. She looked truly miserable as she dumped her bag on her desk and removed her suit jacket, to reveal a slightly wrinkled purple shirt. Fair noted her heels were as high as always and didn't know how she managed to pull it off every day. Fair preferred to wear flats despite the fact that she was vertically-challenged, as she liked to put it.

"Hello Gill, are you quite all right? You didn't have to come in today, you know," Fair said, managing a small smile for Gill.

"Oh no, don't worry about me Fair, I'll be fine – I just like to have a little moan when I've actually got a valid reason to," Gill replied as she blew her nose again, loudly. She was probably the worst person to get a cold in the world, as it hung around her for weeks on end.

"If you're sure you're okay then," Fair said, and Gill nodded, before doing a double take in her direction.

"Are *you* all right? You look a bit off-colour," Gill asked. "Oh, that... I just had a bit of a rough night last night, nothing to worry about," now it was her turn to defend her health, and she'd do it with gusto.

"Fair... I never imagined you out late on a school night!" Gill laughed.

Fair smiled, "No, it's not exactly like that... just didn't get much sleep."

"Ah," Gill tapped her nose. "I see, say no more."

"No, it's not like that... oh never mind," Fair muttered. Gill had already turned to look at the new desk by Rory's office.

"Who's that for? I didn't know we had someone new?" she asked.

"Oh, you weren't here yesterday, were you? That's Stanley's new desk," Fair told her.

"Stanley!" Gill went a bit flushed, apart from her nose of course, which stayed bright red in defiance.

"Yes, Stanley; Rory's made him this year's honorary Fringe reporter," Fair replied, wondering exactly why the desk had caused such a reaction in Gill. It didn't take much calculating when she recalled them leaving Red Eleven together on Monday night. But hadn't they always been friends?

"Hmm, its twenty-five minutes to nine now, wonder where he is? Was he out at the Fringe last night then?" Fair went cold. Stanley had been at the Fringe last night; she'd heard that he went with Lionel to see that 'pirate' with the... hooks.

"I hope he's all right," Fair said, trying to look calm when really her heart was pounding in her chest.

"Are you sure *you're* all right, you look very pale? Maybe you're the one that should be going home," Gill commented. Fair started to reply, but the phone on Gill's desk started to ring, making her jump in her skin. Gill turned and picked up the phone.

"Hello, reporters?" she asked swiftly.

"Speak of the devil," a smile quickly formed on Gill's lips, "we were just talking about you and your fancy new desk... next to Rory's office and all!"

"Uh-huh... okay then, don't come in too late though, we need to have words. Alright, if anyone asks I'll just tell them you're out on a job. What? Oh thanks, very funny – I've got the cold, leave me alone!" With that, Gill placed the phone down again, still laughing. She seemed to have brightened up quite fast, although Fair really wasn't in a fit state to comment. Her heart started to slow back to its normal beat. Stanley was all right.

14

D.I Thompson.

Detective Inspector Thompson looked incredulously at the hand blocking the way of the door. The hand belonged to that of forensics assistant (still-in-training) Maggie Lockett.

"I wouldn't look at that if I were you," said Maggie. The words seemed to almost spill out of her mouth, dislocated and somehow lost, despite the sentence making perfectly good sense. Maggie's ginger-red hair spilled down over here shoulders in tiny curls, her uniform neatly ironed and shiny. At least, it was in one patch, where she'd had to wipe up her own vomit just ten minutes previously.

"Maggie, aren't you supposed to be in forensics?" Maggie nodded. "I'm new," she replied, defensively. Her big green eyes looked far too wide in comparison to Thompson's small blue shrewish ones. The D.I was beginning to lose patience. "And where on earth is everybody else?"

The building was practically deserted. Usually there'd be a whole team of forensics and unnecessary police officers bustling around with various pieces of recording equipment, i.e. Dictaphones, plastic bags, dusting kits, notepads, clipboards, pens... This just didn't feel right. There was most definitely something in the air, and the D.I didn't like it. Maggie mumbled something under her breath.

"Sorry, you're going to have to speak up, I didn't quite hear that."

"It's... ermmm... 'Donut Delirium' day back at HQ,"

91

Maggie repeated, averting her eyes.

"Donut what? Oh, for God's sake..." The D.I put her hand to her head. "And where's PC McMonaghan?"

"Think he's upstairs talking to the owners of the place," replied Maggie.

"Right. Well... I'm the one in charge here, I'm supposed to be investigating a crime scene and I need to look at the body. So I'm going to damn well look at the body!"

With that, the D.I moved Maggie's hand to the side and hesitated briefly despite herself. She took a deep breath and swung open the door. "Okay, let's take a look... oh shit."

"Told you." This would have almost sounded smug, if Maggie had not shrunk about ten inches into a standing-crouch position, hands in front of her eyes as if to shield herself from an onslaught of hailstones. The D.I paid no attention.

"Is that... shit."

"No, I think it's actually..."

"I'm going to throw up," the D.I said, matter-of-factly. Then, just like that, she did.

"Can I get you a glass of water, sir?"

D.I Thompson took a deep breath, and made her way back to the doorway. Maggie had resumed correct standing posture. "No, I'm fine. Boris!" D.I Thomson's new partner came jogging along, almost like a puppy, at the sound of her command. It would have been almost quite sweet, if he wasn't close to 16 stone and overall a bit dippy. Like a fat Labrador.

"Yes, Detective Inspector, sir?" Boris enquired. Maggie noticed his uniform was not ironed quite so well, and had the beginnings of a burn mark against the white of his shirt. One day, she was really going to 'make it' in forensics.

"Get off your iPhone and start cordoning off the front entrance to the public, would you!"

"Yes boss," replied Boris, who in turn looked like a scolded... well, puppy. Mouth agape, he pointed to the still (slightly) open door. "Wait, is that where the..."

"Where the body is? Yes, Boris."

"Can I take a look?"

"No. Now go and sort out the cordon, we don't want just anybody walking in here and ruining any vital clues as to who committed this crime," the D.I turned back to Maggie. "Do we know who found the body?"

"I did," a voice from behind her made the D.I jump.

"Oh, right," the D.I looked the small woman up-and-down. Pale, middle-aged, white-ish curly hair cut short, an apron. A cleaner. "Let's find a quiet place to sit and talk before we take you down to the station. Just routine, okay love? We'll get another cup of tea and we can start at the beginning," the D.I spoke in hushed tones as she gently put a hand on the shaken woman's shoulder.

"Do you mind if I make mine a gin, dear? Might as well start as I mean to go on."

15

"Almost everyone who has committed a murder knows that the business has its tragic side." – Robert Lynd.

Stanley Hobbes

Stanley hung up the phone to Gill and rolled over in bed. It was 08:51am and he had a massive head-throbbing hangover. It hadn't really helped matters when he awoke just a few minutes before to the sight of a shiny sharp metal object. He must have carelessly placed the pirate's hook on his bedside table as he'd fallen into bed the night before. Jasper the cat, in his efforts to wake Stanley, pounced on the bed before walking over the half-asleep lump and cautiously stepping onto the table to examine the hook for himself.

"You can leave that well alone, so you can," Stanley groaned, rubbing his eyes. His throat hurt, but he had to get up sooner or later. He'd already made his excuses to Gill about paying another visit to the Underbelly; after all, the Captain would require his hook back at the very least. It bothered him that he still hadn't found out any 'grit' for Rory, but then what did the man expect, miracles? Well, no, but he could at least hope his reporters could stay sober.

"Ugh, what was I thinking?" Stanley groaned again. It wasn't the first time this week he'd had that thought either. Jasper was looking at him curiously. Hunger does that.

"Okay, okay, I'm getting up!"

It was yet another peaceful day in the city; the sun was bright with barely a cloud in the sky. It was almost as if it were a holiday, except for the few people in suits that were scrambling to their cars in order to get into work on time. So it

94

was Stanley's holiday. Although not quite - he wasn't intending to take the whole day off; at least not when he first stepped out of the entry door to his rented flat on London Road.

It didn't take him long to get to the Royal Mile, as the Fringe was only just beginning to stir from the night before. Stanley savoured the quiet. He'd taken the hook, this time discreetly packed in a shoulder bag so that he didn't get any strange looks on his way back to the venue. When he got to the Underbelly, Stanley didn't take much notice of the police cars lined up around the corner. After all, he was an obituary writer and it'd been a long time since his journalism training. But after going down the first set of stairs and into the small room with the information desk, he'd had a feeling something wasn't as it should be. There was no-one there; the venue was silent and he was all alone. Stanley stood still and listened; a strong, definite silence. Surely that wasn't normal, even if it was early? Debating whether or not to go down another flight while reading a brightly coloured poster with a fox on the front, he noticed his apparently irrational fear of normal things had returned. After all, the Underbelly was a happy, friendly place – what was there to be anxious about? They were probably just setting things up downstairs. It was then he heard the footsteps and knew that he was not alone. Surely that was also a good thing, so why did he suddenly want to turn around and find his way back to fresh air? It was merely stuffy in the room; that was all - it had to be. The footsteps grew louder as they ascended the stairway to his right. And eventually he saw the person making them; a female police officer. "Sir, what are you doing here?"

"Uhh," Stanley replied, taken aback by her abruptness. Something was definitely wrong.

"I'm sorry, but you can't be here. The Underbelly's closed," the woman spoke quite firmly, but despite that Stanley noticed she looked slightly worn. She was in her thirties with shoulder-length blonde hair and tired blue eyes.

"Oh, I see. There was no sign or anything, so I just

assumed..." The woman stepped past him swiftly and checked up the steps leading to the main entrance of the Underbelly.

"Boris! Are you up there?" There came no reply. She looked back to Stanley.

"Well you assumed wrong, this is now a crime scene and I'm going to have to ask you to leave," she replied.

"It's just that I'm a journalist and I was here last night," Stanley said, "I only came back so I could hand this in to McBeard... you know, the Captain? It's part of his act, you see." Stanley removed the hook from his bag and the woman's eyes opened widely; there was a shift in her manner. "Where did you get that?"

"He gave it to me to look after while he went to the loo, only he never came back," Stanley replied, looking perplexed. He had a feeling something was very, very wrong.

"You were with him – McBeard – last night? Can I have your name, sir? Was anyone else with you?"

"Oh God... my name's Stanley Hobbes and I work for the Edinburgh Times - something's happened to him, hasn't it?" The woman paused in thought, seemingly unsure of what to say next; he could tell she was mentally torn. Stanley heard more footsteps ascending the stairs. A chubby male head appeared, followed closely by a chubby body and long legs. "Sorry, was bursting for the loo!"

"Well don't let it happen again. This is a murder scene, Williams, so next time you want to go to the 'loo' you'd better make sure there's someone there to cover for you. Weren't you taught these things when you went through your training?" Boris looked down at his feet, and nodded.

"Won't happen again, sir," he said, finding it difficult to keep a straight face. Stanley, not working out what was funny, was only just beginning to understand the severity of the situation. "Murder?" Stanley exclaimed, "is it McBeard? He's dead, isn't he?" The woman sighed and shook her head.

"Hobbes, is it... wait, *you're* Stanley Hobbes?" Her expression changed. This puzzled Stanley even more.

"I've spoken to you before; I know you. Don't you normally do the obituaries? Look, follow me downstairs, I feel... uncomfortable discussing this with you up here." As they began to walk, the officer continued.

"You're going to have to wait until we release an official statement and the body's identified, but off the record, we're pretty sure it's him." Stanley was aware she seemed to be watching his reactions very carefully, almost as if she was judging him, trying to work out if he was the murdering sort. Either that or he was paranoid. His legs felt weak, which is not a good thing to happen while descending concrete stairs to the Jelly Belly Bar. "But, but... if I'd only gone after him..."

"Did you see anything at all suspicious last night?"

"Not really, no," Stanley thought about it, "not at all."

"There were other people with you, people who saw you and can confirm where you were?"

"Yes, I'm... sure there are."

The woman continued to speak slowly, but firmly, and Stanley could hear the stress levels in her voice rising.

"I'm only telling you this now because it looks like you were one of the last people to see him. And we're going to have to take that... that *hook* as evidence."

"What relevance does the hook have?" Stanley asked, and immediately wished he hadn't. But the way she'd said *hook* gave it away.

"You don't want to know," the woman replied, "But you soon will anyway. It'll be all over the news so I might as well tell you, as long as you know it's strictly off-record until the statement is released."

"You're right, I'm not sure I want to know," Stanley replied.

"Let's just say he - the body - was found in a cleaning cupboard with one of those hooks embedded in his skull via the eyeball. It's one of the worst cases I've worked on, so you can understand if I'm a little shaken up."

"Oh God, I'm going to be sick," Stanley replied, his mind completely blank with the horror of the situation before him.

"I know that feeling, believe me," replied the police officer, who he later learned was named D.I Thompson. Stanley wondered why she was giving him this information so freely and why he had been granted the burden of knowing the gory details. The body was probably still... he stopped that thought dead, as it were.

"So the venue will be closed? What's safe to report?" He asked, trying to keep his voice steady.

"You can report the Underbelly will be closed, at least for the day, following an incident. But any more than that - please - wait for our official statement which will be released in the next couple of hours. We'll no doubt be launching an appeal for more information," the D.I. explained. "But I want you to know how serious this is, Stanley. Maybe you'll be able to help us with our investigations. Maybe you can help me." Stanley didn't really know what she meant. He hoped she wasn't coming onto him.

"I'll give them a head's up at work," Stanley replied, his mind already racing as he tried to remember any other details of the night, and failed.

"Before I go, do you mind if I just use the gents to freshen up? I feel a little... weak."

"Go ahead, but make sure you don't stick around here. I'll be in touch, you're going to have to come in for questioning as soon as we clear this mess up."

D.I Thompson gave him her card, took his details and again said she would be in touch for a more thorough interview. Her eyes seemed to meet his and again he felt nervous; which was entirely irrational.

In the toilets he made his way to the first sink and

splashed cold water on his face. He looked pale, but apart from that he was fine. His stomach had started to settle again, although it wasn't a particularly nice image that D.I Thompson had planted in his head. As he reached for a paper towel, he accidentally knocked something small and hard to the floor. Bending down to pick it up, it felt smooth beneath his fingertips. Examining it, Stanley felt a sudden chill down the back of his spine, although at first he couldn't place why. Staring back at him were the unusual beady eyes of a small jade frog. There was something about it that rang true to Stanley... something to do with last night. Standing up, he racked his brains as to why the small amphibian would be of any significance; and came up with nothing. As he stepped out of the door a couple of police officers walked through the room and down the stairs, and Stanley guiltily pocketed the frog. He made his way upstairs and took in the fresh air with eager lungs. Outside it seemed peaceful as the city went on unaware of what had happened in the bowels of the Underbelly. Apart from all the police that were now parked in front of the door, of course. Officer Boris Williams gave Stanley a nod and Stanley bowed under the tape that the police were using to close off the building, which was only just attracting attention from morning onlookers.

Stanley now had two options; he could head right, back to the office, and face the onslaught of questions from the newsroom. But he didn't much feel like that, so instead he turned left, into the Grassmarket.

The frog felt heavy in his pocket and he wondered if he'd done the right thing by taking it. He didn't even know why he'd pocketed it - he knew he should have given it to D.I Thompson - probably shouldn't have touched it - but there was something he really didn't like about it. He thought about the Captain as he made his way down the Grassmarket, passing many small and interesting shops along the way. He'd always liked this district of Edinburgh. What had McBeard said before leaving the table? He'd said something wasn't right, that Stanley should keep his eyes open. Stanley remembered the way he had looked around the room - had McBeard known he was being followed? But he'd mentioned something else too... what was it?

Still pondering that thought, he took his phone from his pocket and called Gill, who picked up the phone in her usual 'reporters' routine.

"Gill, it's Stanley," he said.

"What's wrong?" Gill asked, barely disguising the worry in her voice. She must have guessed from the way he'd answered the phone. He sighed. "It's not good. There was a murder at the Underbelly last night, they've found a body. The venue will be closed under investigation and the police will issue a statement in the next couple of hours."

"Oh my God, what happened? Do they know who it is?"

"Yeah, they're pretty sure it's McBeard but we'll have to wait for the statement. But Gill - I think I'm a little too close to this one. I was possibly one of the last people to see him alive."

"What do you mean? Stanley, what happened?"

"He – he got up and gave me one of his hooks last night, but that's not what's bothering me... he said something to me, something else..."

Despite the heat, Stanley felt a shiver down his spine. The Captain had muttered something about a jade frog... and danger. And hadn't he been going to the toilets when he'd left Stanley his hook?

"Stanley, you're not making any sense, tell me what's going on!"

"Sorry Gill, I've got to go. If you can, meet me for lunch at the usual place," Stanley replied.

"But I've got pilates-!" The rest of her sentence was cut off, as Stanley hung up the phone.

16

"I long ago came to the conclusion that nothing has ever been definitely proved about anything." – Noel Coward

It was exactly the right place for jade frogs. It had been across the street and face-to-face with Stanley when he'd hung up the phone. The sign read 'Trinkets and Trysts' and although Stanley had never noticed it before, he soon found himself across the street and standing in front of the window display. Littered on a bed of fake plastic grass were crystals, little Buddhas and other intriguing, but mostly useless - in Stanley's opinion - figures, some being of the jade variety. But no frogs as far as Stanley's eyes could see. Stanley took a deep breath and entered the store, setting off a small tinkling above his head. There was an interesting smell to the place; it smelled of the strong incense smell that he only associated with this type of shop, and lo and behold the shelves were covered in trinkets, candles, incense, a million different kinds of stones and a shelf of spiritualist books with titles to do with 'inner self' and 'spiritual healing'. It was a shop Lorraine would probably have loved. He didn't know exactly what he would prove by finding a jade frog exactly the same as his, but something about the frog didn't seem quite right. A quick browse of the shelves told him nothing, and although he'd found another (friendlier looking) jade frog, the one he was looking for was not in sight. Feeling silly and still none the wiser, he turned to leave and was confronted with a young shop assistant with a round, pleasant face and short dark hair tied back in a pink headscarf. Her brown eyes sparkled in the dim lighting of the store and complimented her embellished turquoise top. She wore an apron of blue and gold.

"Excuse me, but can I help you out at all?" the girl asked

with an Australian accent.

"Well, not really, but... you're going to think this is silly, there's really no point in asking..." Stanley muttered as he reached into his pocket for the frog.

"No, never silly, please go on," the girl replied, amiably.

"Okay, it's this frog. Have you seen one like this before? Only I found it and now I'm curious about it." The young shop assistant's eyes grew wide and she almost snatched the frog from Stanley's hands as she studied it with a careful gaze.

"*That*," she said, "is a bad frog. For starters, it's known as a Jungial Mata-Liana frog. I've travelled around Bali and East Asia and I've only seen a frog like that once before. They actually originated in Africa, and were carved out of wood or sometimes ivory. You see its eyes? They are supposed to be a window for evil to see the possessor and summon up bad juju on him or her. And then there's the creepy way it's sitting; it's crouched back so low, like it's about to pounce... gives me the shivers."

"Oh, well I don't really believe in all that stuff so... you've never sold these here?"

"No, I would never sell those... *things* in my shop. I never thought I'd see one of these in Edinburgh, they're actually quite rare," the assistant said as she examined the frog, a small frown appearing on her forehead.

"This is your shop? It's very nice, I've never been in here before," Stanley replied, taking the frog back. "Well, I best get going. Sorry to bring this in here, I'll get it out of your way."

"Wait, don't leave just yet. There's something else about that frog... I can feel there's something... evil attached to it. Call me crazy, but you'd be better off just throwing it away, right now." Something in her eyes told Stanley she was being deadly serious.

"Alright, well, thank you, errmm..."

"Amelia," she said.

"Thank you, Amelia. I'm Stanley, and I really must get

going... but thanks for the advice."

"Stanley?" Amelia called after him as he pulled open the door.

"Yes?"

"Please, take care," she said, as he turned his back to her and exited the store.

17

"Rudeness is annoying, but offended flouncing is worse, being so dreadfully conceited." – Alice Thomas Ellis.

He hadn't needed her opinion to know it was a bad frog. The way it stared at him as he drank his coffee outside the small cafe told him that he didn't like it. Didn't like it one bit. But that it could summon 'bad juju'? Surely it was just a frog, and that was that; not even a real frog. Incapable of conscious thought... but there was *something* about it he couldn't quite place. Perhaps McBeard had left it for him as a kind of clue, before... no, that was ridiculous. Besides, it anything the Captain had sounded fearful of the frog, although in the noise of the Underbelly it'd be easy to mistake fear for something else. He was still pondering what that something was, when a voice at the other table interrupted him.

"Nice day for it, don't you think?"

Stanley looked to his left, to see a familiar gentleman in a navy suit and colourful scarf looking in his direction, an amiable smile crinkling in the corners of his mature mouth. Steely blue eyes met Stanley's and at once Stanley knew why the face was familiar. Duke Edmund Ford's aged-but-regal features were framed by shoulder-length blonde hair, brushed back in an almost noble fashion and only slightly greying, despite the fact he had to be in his late fifties.

"You're Duke Ford! I knew I remembered the face, one of our junior reporters interviewed you for a story last month!"

"Oh, you're from the Edinburgh Times then, I presume," the Duke replied.

"Forgive me, yes, I'm Stanley Hobbes," Stanley said, remembering his duty to the paper, "I'm here reporting on the

Fringe."

"Oh, jolly good! That's why I'm here too actually... although perhaps not to report. I have a nephew called Will who quite fancies himself as a comedian," said the Duke.

"Oh, well if it's the Underbelly he's performing at, there's some bad news, I'm afraid; the venue will be closed for at least the rest of the day."

"Oh?" The Duke looked interested.

"Yes, I heard there's been an incident there... one of the performers."

"How terrible. Well now, Will is performing at one of the smaller venues, a free show, I'm afraid. It seems all the good places were taken up by the damn foreigners. Seems there's more and more of them every year. But perhaps you'd care to join me in a viewing this evening?"

"Well I should really check back with Rory..."

"What will Rory have to say about it? I've known that old dragon since university! Come, give me your business card and we'll arrange to meet outside the 'pub' where it's showing." The way he said 'pub' was almost comical.

"Oh, I don't have a card, but I'll try and make it if I can," Stanley replied, uneasily.

"Okay Stan, good enough for me; it's at the Black Belle in... wait, what have you got there?" The Duke asked, his eyes narrowing on the table. Stanley had forgotten about the frog entirely.

"Oh this?" he asked, lifting the frog and showing it to the Duke, "It's just something I found, that's all." The Duke glanced at his watch, and made a face as if he were late for a suit fitting, or something equally as riveting.

"Something you found, eh? Right, well, I'll be off then. Here's the flyer for William's show, if you decide you can spare the time." Stanley noticed his manner seemed to have changed from one of casual friendliness to one of complete detachment, like he was going to miss an appointment or something. He removed a small flyer from one of his pockets and Stanley watched as his fingers hovered curiously above the jade frog, and instead chose the menu to pin the promotion to the table, before leaving a five pound note on the saucer beside his half empty cup of Earl Grey. He didn't look Stanley in the eye once, yet it was something in his manner that made Stanley speak up.

"You know, I thought seeing people from different backgrounds and cultures was all part of the Fringe's appeal," he said. The Duke turned around, his fingers poised on leaving a miniscule tip at his table, his expression rather unreadable.

"What? I beg your pardon?"

"You called them 'damn foreigners', but really, isn't that why so many people go to the Fringe each year, for its diversity? If it were all Scottish or British performers with the same sort of acts, it'd be a bit samey and boring, don't you think?"

Whatever his expression was, he didn't look at all impressed. "Well, if you say so, Stanley. Maybe I'll catch you later, yes? Jolly good and jolly goodbye!"

Stanley watched as the Duke walked with a quickened pace in the direction of the Royal Mile. His shoes were bright pink and yellow check, yet were nevertheless very smart - an unusual combination with his otherwise normal attire. He was an eccentric fellow. But eccentric or not, what was it with some (not all) older people and their lingering racist attitudes and close-mindedness? Stanley sighed. He missed his Granny.

Granny Hobbes had been unlike any other grandmother in the small village of Douglas – a suburb of Cork. She'd been anything but racist, wore high heels everywhere she went and drove around in a Lamborghini that she'd purchased with her life savings – *"after all it's only money, you can't take it with you when you're gone!"*

Granny Hobbes wasn't in fact dead, but had instead left on a journey to the African jungle, and had never returned. That was almost three years ago and no-one had had word from

Granny Hobbes, apart from the occasional postcard; a picture of her with one of the African children, a different one each time. The last new 'friend' had been a seven-year-old girl called Magdalena, if he recalled.

The frog – inexplicably – made him feel closer to Granny Hobbes. It was a silly notion, and one he'd never have had if the shop keeper hadn't mentioned its African roots to him. Perhaps if she was around, Granny Hobbes would have known what to do with it. He imagined that she'd have said it was just a frog, it meant nothing, and maybe then he could easily just let it go. Still, the way in which the Duke seemed to suddenly change had Stanley once again wondering about this particular frog. What had the girl – Amelia – said it was called? A jungle mata... well, something he couldn't pronounce for starters.

'Trinkets and Trysts' was still in his line of sight, although only just, for the sun was blocking his vision as he sat watching the people of Edinburgh go about their daily business. He noticed there was a lot of young artsy types about, in tie-dye t-shirts and colourful attire. Some of them were now entering the shop and looking in the windows with what he imagined to be curious eyes. Stanley was sure if he went back to the shop and handed the frog in, the owner would gratefully take it and burn it for him, perhaps even muttering a sun charm or something to ensure her safety while she did it. But he didn't want to give the frog to anyone. Instead he'd hold on to it, at least until he figured out what it meant, and for whom. His thoughts were broken when a mobile phone started to ring on the table beside him, and he realised it was the Duke's.

18

"Time is an illusion. Lunchtime, doubly so." – Douglas Adams.

Stanley and Gill's usual place was an unusually small bistro off the Royal Mile, by the name of Scaly Tivets'. The curtains were thick red velvet and kept out the bright sun on a summer's day. It also kept out the busy festival goers who almost seemed to overlook the bistro entirely. With speciality sandwiches and light bites in an understated but sophisticated environment, it was the perfect place to have a quiet chat and forget the day of a lunchtime. At least, that's what the notice pinned on the window said. But it was the coffee that Stanley loved the most. Freshly ground and with a plethora of surprising flavours and textures, it was always a joy to experience a new brand shipped over from some exotic (or not-so-exotic) location.   The bistro's owner, Nigel, was a bit of a coffee fanatic, and always endeavoured to bring his latest new find to the bistro's customers. Sat in his favourite corner, Stanley sipped upon Nigel's latest offering, of Java Millennia coffee, fresh from Africa. It made him think of his Granny, who would perhaps have sampled the very same drink. Not that Granny Hobbes really liked coffee, but she was always up for sampling something new.

"Well, what do you think?" asked Nigel, who stood behind the counter, arms crossed in his usual blue and white printed apron. Although he was only in his mid-forties, his hair was entirely grey and curled at the ends. His nose formed almost a hook and he always carried an air of humour about him, as if the world was just one big joke. And who was Stanley to argue with that.

"It's... interesting," said Stanley.

"Oh, come on, you'll have to do better than that! Can you taste the slightest hint of orange peel in there? What about the guava?"

"It's not wine, Nigel... guava? Isn't that a tropical fruit? I thought this was from Africa?" Stanley asked. Nigel shrugged, before proclaiming, "To appreciate good coffee, is to truly live, my friend."

"Fruit in coffee just seems wrong... perhaps I just don't have the necessary tastes buds to distinguish the difference," Stanley said, smiling. Nigel opened his mouth, but quickly closed it again as the door swung open to reveal a flustered Gill, who quickly sneezed in a pre-prepared tissue.

"Hello there, Sneezy McRudolph," laughed Stanley.

"Oh, very funny – it's not my fault these tissues are so rough on my delicate skin!" Gill sat down opposite Stanley, and placed her Matthew Williamson bag on the table. It had butterflies on it.

"What can I get you today, Miss?" Nigel asked in his usual friendly manner.

"Oh, hi Nigel, can I just have a white coffee and a cheese and tomato Panini, please? Thanks."

"Are you sure I can't interest you in some Java Millennia coffee, straight from the heart of Africa? Stan can vouch for it, can't you, Stan?" Stanley raised his cup, and his eyebrow, and nodded.

"Oh, alright then Nige," Gill replied, rolling her eyes slightly, "So, what is the big deal, ruining my Pilates class, Mr Hobbes?"

"I need your advice," Stanley said, taking his eyes away from her gaze as memories from the other night came back to him, rather too vividly.

"Go on, spill," Gill said as she kindly accepted her Java Millennia from Nigel.

"Right... so I think I might be caught up in something here. We know McBeard's dead, right?"

"Do we?"

"Pretty much, yes. Can't confirm this, but they got him with one of his own hooks by the sounds of it. Right through the eyeball and into the brain." Gill put down her coffee, open-mouthed.

"They told you *that*??"

"Yes... it's funny, I must come across as someone to confide in, not like 'proper journalists' at all, really. They'd avoid you like swine flu."

"Thanks. Now get on with it, did you say you were one of the last people to actually see him alive?"

"Yes, he gave me his other hook, which I returned this morning, and the really strange thing is, before he left for the loo he was going on about jade frogs. And then, this morning, in the gents, I found this..." Stanley reached into his pocket and presented the frog to Gill.

"That is one ugly mofo," Gill commented, as she examined the frog, "So what about it?"

"Don't you think it's a bit of a coincidence? Plus the woman from that trinkets shop says it summons up bad juju... that it's got evil attached to it?" Gill shot him a serious glance, before carefully placing the frog back down on the table.

"So get rid of it," she said, "Wait, what does this have to do with anything? If McBeard was murdered, where do you fit into all of this?"

Stanley shrugged, "Maybe I don't. But it did occur to me that maybe McBeard left the frog in the toilets for a reason."

"Hmmm, maybe, but why? Can you remember what he said?"

"Not really, it didn't make much sense at the time. But the way he was looking around makes me think he might have known he was being followed." Gill seemed to ponder this for a second. "It's sad, why would anyone want to kill a comedian?"

"I don't know, but I have a feeling I might be called to the police station quite soon and then what do I say? Jade frogs, they'll think I'm a fruit loop," Stanley replied.

"You should have just handed it in when you found it," Gill said. "What made you keep it?"

"I honestly don't know - I just did. What do you think I should do?"

"Well, I take it Rory has you at the Fringe for a reason. I take it this is all because of Bogleur? Oh, thanks Nigel," Gill said, accepting her toasted Panini.

"He wanted me to dig up some dirt, kill two stones with one bird, apparently," Stanley sighed. "I don't think I'm cut out for this, Gill."

"Don't be silly," Gill replied, before an extraordinary look lit up her face, like a light bulb in those cartoons. "Wait! Do you think Bogleur and McBeard are connected?"

"Nah, now you're being silly. Those two are nothing to do with each other! A politician and a pirate comic? You're having a laugh." Gill stopped playing with the cheese from her Panini, and sat back in her chair, giving Stanley an odd look.

"Well McBeard certainly wasn't! I think given the situation, you should just keep doing what you're doing, and don't tell Rory about the frog just yet."

"Why not?"

"Just trust me on this one, kiddo," Gill said, mouth full of Panini. Stanley had barely touched his club sandwich. He just didn't feel that hungry about the whole McBeard scenario. Not hungry at all. Gill was playing with her long auburn hair and looking around the decor of the bistro. Her favourite painting was the one with the gold leaf frame, and showed a beautiful blue Japanese scene, with cherry blossoms contrasting perfectly with the blue sky. Nigel had been quite the traveller in his day, and had picked it up himself from Osaka.

"Fancy coming to a show later?" Stanley asked, interrupting the silence and changing the previous subject entirely.

"Sure! What are you taking me to see?"

"Just a free one, I'm afraid, but we can always go out for a drink afterwards," Stanley explained, only just remembering why it was a good idea *not* to have a drink while at the Fringe.

"Duke Ford's nephew is going to be at the Black Belle... let's have a look at the flyer," Stanley pulled out the folded up piece of paper given to him by the Duke.

It read:

Haberdashery Spinx Co.

A lively mix of comedy sketch and adventure with just a slightly hint of the absurd... raspberry flavour!

7.30pm at the Black Belle

"What an odd flyer," said Gill. Indeed it was. Black and covered in glittery gold, with bright yellow writing, with a simple raspberry in the corner. It certainly stood out.

"The Black Belle... that's in the Cowgate, isn't it?"

"Yeah, I was a bit surprised when Duke Ford told me about it. I think he's hoping I can review it for the paper, since it's his nephew and all... Will, I think his name is."

"Oh, there he is, there," Gill pointed to Will's picture. A fresh-faced blonde boy with messy hair and wearing a polo shirt smiled up from the shiny surface of the flyer. "See any resemblance? Well, if you're reviewing it, let's hope he's bloody good!"

"Hey, I'm not that harsh... you know when you went to meet Duke Ford with Jenny that time?"

"Yeees?" Gill asked, suspiciously.

"Did he seem... well, all right, to you?"

"Of course. He was very pleasant," Gill replied, eyes narrowing. "Why, what was he like with you?"

"I don't know, he just seemed a little... off. I mean, he was fine at first, but then he just seemed to change; left rather abruptly, really."

112

"Maybe he had an appointment or something," Gill said.

"You're probably right..."

"I'm always right," Gill interrupted. Stanley was relieved to see her smile. Even with her red nose, she was still the same old Gill. Nothing had changed.

"Yeah, but the only thing is, he left his mobile phone behind," Stanley continued, as he reached into his pocket for the mobile.

"Ooh, shiny," Gill said, taking the phone from Stanley.

"Look, it's one of those ultra expensive ones made out of platinum or something. Just give it back to him tonight when he's at the show."

"Yeah, that makes sense," Stanley said, eyebrows knotting together slightly. "He must have been in quite a hurry to forget it. Left his tea too..."

"Right, well I'd better be getting back to the office," she said, as she cleared her plate. Stanley noticed she'd left some of her coffee.

"Can I expect the pleasure of your company, you know, back at that place we call work, dear sir?"

"Why not, I should probably show my face just so they know I'm not skiving off *all* day," Stanley replied, jokingly. Gill smiled, picked up her bag moved towards the counter, where Nigel was slicing some cheese and pretending not to listen to their conversation. As they paid their bills, Stanley happened to look out the window to see a pair of familiar shoes crossing the street above. They were pink and yellow check. They looked to be in a hurry. For Stanley, it was a spur of the moment decision. "On second thoughts, I just remembered there's something I've got to do!"

"But... but wait! Where should I meet you tonight?"

"Just see you at the Belle!" Stanley called as he rushed out the door, leaving Gill to collect her change and wondering what had just happened. Shaking her head, she said to Nigel, "I don't know what's got into him lately."

113

19

"Everybody was up to something, especially, of course, those who were up to nothing." – Noel Coward.

The Duke was walking very fast indeed down the Royal Mile, and Stanley found it hard to keep up the pace amongst the crowd. "Duke Ford!" Stanley called over the noise, but his call went unheard, at least to its intended recipient. In the middle of the street, quite a crowd had gathered. A group of African performers dressed in loin cloths and odd-looking headgear were banging on drums of assorted sizes, and taking turns to dance energetically while a large crowd gathered around them in a circle. There was really no point in calling on the Duke, as nothing could be heard over the drums and general furore of the performance. One of the performers, a man of athletic build, had long dreadlocks and bare feet, and managed to flip over in mid air just as Stanley glanced over. Again he was reminded of Granny Hobbes; it seemed he was thinking about her a lot more these days. And although he'd only looked over at the dance act for a few seconds, when he looked back to the street, Duke Ford was gone.

"Shit," he muttered under his breath, not knowing what to do next. A little girl with curly brown hair smiled up at him from her standing place on top of one of the stone pillars, and waved her fairy wand at him.

"Hi," Stanley said. The girl waved more, and shyly covered her face with the wand. She must have been about four years old. Deciding that the Duke could not have gotten far, and would most likely have continued down the Royal Mile, Stanley once again set off in pursuit, only to be halted by a rather unique-looking gentleman with very slim legs, accentuated in black skinny jeans. His face was distinctive, with a noticeable mole or birth mark on his left cheek.

"Sir, would you care for a flyer? I'm a comedian, innit," the man pointed to the flyer. The flyer read 'Richard Coughlan', and the man's face had been transformed into a devil in the centre of a brilliant flame design. "Yeah look, that's me, half man, half magic wand!" the man said.

"Ermmm... no, I'm in rather a hurry at the moment..."

"Oh, come on, give me a break,mate!"

"I'm sorry, I really do have to..."

As Stanley walked off, he heard the screech of, "I'm Richard the Dick Coughlan, motherfucker! I'm on YouTube!"

As Stanley continued his search, he soon found that the Duke did not have very a distinguishable hairstyle, as twice he had picked out the Duke from the crowd, only to realise it was in fact someone else – the last woman gave him a very odd look indeed. From then on, Stanley decided to look strictly people's shoes. It paid off, as Stanley caught a glimpse of said shoes, confirmed by sight of the Duke himself, turning left into Cockburn Street. Crossing the road and turning into Cockburn Street himself, Stanley noticed the Duke seemed in even more of a hurry than before, and then he began to wonder exactly where the Duke and his pink and yellow shoes were headed. It then occurred to Stanley that he should not call out to Duke Ford right away, but to quietly observe – from a safe distance – exactly where he was going. As an experiment, he reasoned.

Suddenly feeling a little more exposed than when he was trying to be seen, Stanley moved closer to the shops so he was directly behind his 'target', but still far enough away not to be caught if the target were to take a swift glance around. Anything more than a swift glance and Stanley would stick out like a sore thumb. His heart was beginning to speed up slightly, although he didn't really know why – he wasn't used to the art of following people and whilst looking inconspicuous. He felt a bit like a spy on a television programme. Then the Duke did a strange thing, and turned right onto Fleshmarket Close. What could be down there – a shortcut, perhaps? Stanley decided he had to find out. It was ridiculous really, he thought, as he approached the corner so that the Duke would once again be in his line of sight. What was this going to achieve, exactly? He had pretty much made up his mind to abandon the silly act, when he peered around the corner and saw... nothing. The Duke had once again disappeared.

"Who does he think he is, Doctor Who...?" Stanley muttered under his breath. From his line of sight, Stanley could see right to the bottom of Fleshmarket Close, which meant the Duke must have entered one of the small restaurants/shops. There was only a couple of places the Duke could possibly have gone, including an odd little shop that Stanley had never noticed before. It didn't appear to have a name, but it seemed to be some form of antique shop specialising in silverware. Or there were also a couple of cafes lining the sides, but Stanley didn't think the Duke would have had time to reach either of those. But what would Duke Ford be doing in a silverware shop, especially since he'd been in such a rush to get somewhere obviously important? Just then a large man in both width and length brushed past Stanley. He was wearing a large dark coat (even though it was a rather warm day) with the collar up and dark glasses. On top of his head he wore a beret, also black. Stanley noticed he was carrying something in what appeared to be a dark green blanket, and he too entered the shop with no name. Feeling nervous now and starting to think he'd been mistaken, Stanley surveyed the area, feeling less like a spook and more of a spoon. After all, what was he thinking, following Duke Ford in the first place? He should have just caught up with him, handed back the phone and been done with it.

"Oi, you mate!" a woman called in a Cockney accent. Stanley turned, heart almost in his mouth, to see a rather pale, almost skeletal woman with long white hair, dressed in full goth gear. In fact, she reminded him a bit of Edward Scissorhands, but female and minus the scissors. She must have been at least six feet tall, and wore spiked heel knee high boots.

"Ermm, hello," Stanley replied, looking somewhat perplexed.

"Would you mind giving me a hand with this? I need to get it down these stairs," the woman continued. It was then Stanley noticed the coffin. It was big and black and seemed to be covered in leather. A leather coffin, with small metal studs around the edges and an off-black cross decorating the top – the leather coffin and leather Edwina were a bit of an odd sight to take in on a sunny Edinburgh afternoon. Stanley noticed four metal handles along the sides.

"Is that a...?"

"Coffin, yes love," Edwina Scissorhands replied.

"What are you going to do with that?"

"Never mind that now, just help me get it down the steps, will you?"

"All right," Stanley replied, noticing the four metal handles along the sides. He grabbed hold of the front two handles. "Nah, you better go at the back mate, you're shortest." It only took the strange pair a couple of minutes to carry the coffin to the bottom of the Close, and although they managed it quite fast, Stanley was a bit out of breath at the end of it. A couple of times he'd almost stumbled, which would have sent Edwina reeling backwards and possibly breaking her neck and severing her spinal cord – especially in those boots. Stanley didn't like to think about these things, but often couldn't help it.

"That was quite heavy," Stanley said, before a worried expression took over his face. "There was nothing... in there, was there?"

"Oh, don't be a silly! Thanks for helping though, I'll just have to wait around for Howard to bring the trolley. Thanks mate, I owe you one! Oi, what's your name?"

"Stanley," Stanley replied.

"I'm Alice, nice to meet ya."

Stanley smiled, and made his way back up the eerily quiet Close. It was always a place he could imagine murders and not-so-nice things happening in. Perhaps it was the name – Fleshmarket Close, what kind of name was that? It sounded rotten. In fact, hadn't Ian Rankin named one of his books after that very same place? But it was also quite a dark place to be. And then there was the stairs, and poor Edwina's severed spinal cord. *Stop thinking about that,* he thought, *it's over now.*

As he approached the top of the Close, the large man in the beret had obviously finished with his business (whatever that was) and exited the nameless shop. By that time, Stanley was beginning to feel slightly better, and pretty sure he'd been mistaken about the Duke. For comfort, he put his hand back into his pocket to feel the cool metal presence of the expensive phone. He'd just have to give it to him later. Although perhaps the Duke had gone into one of the cafes for a spot of lunch; perhaps even to meet someone.

Stanley had just about made up his mind to turn around and leave, when he saw the door to the unnamed shop open once again. Out stepped Duke Ford. Stanley's heart once again leapt in his chest, as completely exposed, he tried to figure out what to do with himself. His hands would never stay still in these situations, and still contemplating what to do with them, he almost bypassed what Duke Ford was carrying under his arm. A familiar green blanket, holding something Stanley could only guess at. Cutlery? Silverware? Drugs? Turning to face Cockburn Street, and hands decisively thrust into both pockets, Stanley tried to act casual. This proved pointless, as out of the corner of his eye, he knew he'd already been seen. Turning back swiftly to the 'target', Stanley tried to smile as Duke Ford approached looking particularly serious. "Hello again," Stanley said, trying to sound jovial.

"Stanley, what a surprise, fancy bumping into you again," the Duke replied. There was suspicion in his voice, but also something else... something Stanley could not quite place.

Stanley nervously eyed the blanket-covered something. Perhaps it had been a mistake to follow the Duke.

"Oh well, yes, I actually saw you come down this way and I thought I'd try to catch up with you, but when I finally made it onto the street you were nowhere to be seen!"

"Oh yes, and why would you want to do that, son?" The Duke asked, his steely blue eyes fixed on a struggling Stanley.

"Well sir," explained Stanley, feeling ever-so-slightly nervous, "earlier you forgot your phone, see?" He reached into his pocket and brought out the offending item. The Duke's expression changed at once, and his tightened shoulders seemed to relax into a more natural stance.

"Oh right, I see! Thank you, Stanley, thank you very much!" the Duke tittered, as he seemed almost back to his usual jovial self. "I'd forget my head if it wasn't screwed on tight!"

"Oh, no need to thank me, I would have returned it to you tonight anyway," Stanley said.

"Well, I'm glad. It was nice to see you again Stanley," the Duke replied, his lips forming a smile that seemed almost forced. "But now I really must be off. Don't go getting yourself into trouble, hear me? See you later, perhaps!"

"Yes, good afternoon!" Stanley called as the Duke began his quick step back up Cockburn Street. Stanley wondered why he had to walk so fast, and why he kept casting quick glances behind him. The Duke was certainly an odd chap.

20

"There are few hours in life more agreeable than the hour dedicated to the ceremony known as afternoon tea." - Henry James, 'The Portrait of a Lady'

Winnie Hobbes

The hot African sun beat down upon the frazzled dry grass and overhead a bird squawked. Some of the children were playing, running around with a piece of pale pink cloth that they held high above their heads as they passed it to one another, shouting. The smallest of the girls and the owner of the cloth, Johanna, was unable to reach it as the others taunted her in their native language; child's play and a scene that could be captured and translated time and time again in any country.

Winnie Hobbes was in one of the few wooden huts. Hair tied back in a messy bun, small flyaway white hairs framed her face almost elegantly. She sat on a patterned fabric cushion, and wore a Kente Kaftan of brilliant African colours; yellow, orange, brown and green. It did not match her Irish skin. Her feet were bare, and from the hut she could only make out a few select words from the rowdy children. But that was the least of her concerns. She had finished her tea, and was about to try out the art of tea leaf reading – an art she had established from one of the elders in the village. Winnie picked up the small metal cup, and began to swirl the leaves around while thinking of her family back home in Cork; for it was them rather than herself she most wanted to learn of. Able to filter out the noise outside the hut, she concentrated all of her thoughts instead on the cup, and as the leaves began to slow and rest, she closed her eyes and made a wish only she could know. And when she'd done that, she knew it was time to look. She opened one eye. The leaves had indeed stopped moving, waiting to be read. But it didn't make any sense; no pictures spoke out to her, no familiar forms told her a story, no feelings halted her thought pattern and made her jump up and shout, 'hallelujah, I have it!' No revelation at all. Eyes narrowing on the cup, she could make nothing out from the unusual scattering the leaves had formed. Reaching for her reading glasses, and placing them on her head one-handed, she looked even more closely at the leaves. Breathing a sigh of annoyance, Winnie was just about ready to put the mug down, when she saw something rather odd.

"Wait... it can't be. Is that...?"

"Granny! Granny Hobbes!" Johanna shouted as she ran into the small hut, accidentally knocking Winnie and causing her to drop the mug to the floor.

"No, Johanna, look what you've done!" Winnie sighed, before realising she'd probably frightened the girl who was now staring at her with wide brown eyes. "I'm sorry, I didn't mean to shout," Winnie said, "What's the matter?"

"No, I am sorry... Keenan and Gift have taken my fecking kuba cloth, and they won't fecking give it back to me," the girl said, small tears forming in her eyes. Johanna, another orphan, carried her cloth everywhere. It was the only thing she had left of her mother, who had died giving birth to Johanna eight years before. Her adopted use of the word 'fecking' might have been funny in other circumstances, as she and the other children had obviously been picking up on Winnie's Irish ways.

"Don't worry, you go on, I'll be with you in a minute," Winnie said, as she bent down to pick up the mug from the ground.

"Uh-huh," said the girl, before she quietly exited the hut. Winnie did not notice the steps of one child leaving, and another entering the hut.

The floor was lined with rough hand-woven fabric, and the small hut smelled of Goloka incense, a mixture of rare herbs, flowers and resins; a forest incense. It was pleasant, and Winnie felt safe there. She much preferred the small hut to her own tent. She looked at the mug with a sad sigh. The leaves had changed pattern once again, and still she could make no sense of them. It was as if the African Gods were trying to tell her something, to give up her silly quest for answers and to find things out for herself. But Winnie had no intention of leaving Ghana; there was still much more to do and although it saddened her, she was hopeful that one day – when time allowed it – she would find herself back in the arms of her family.

"Stanley is in trouble," a small voice, somehow sweeter than the other children's, spoke from over Winnie's shoulder. The words made her turn to ice, and slowly she turned around to see Magdalena standing innocently at her side. Bare feet and arms clasped behind her back, she carried the usual grace she held under her favourite tree, yet Winnie had never seen her come so close to the camp.

"What did you say?" Winnie asked, taken aback by the small girl with the serious face and big, round eyes.

"Stanley. There's trouble. We need to go to him," the girl spoke softly, gently, with an air of patience that almost carried a wisdom Winnie could not explain in one so young. It gave her the shivers, despite the heat of the day. She racked her brains to try and remember if she had mentioned her grandson to Magdalena on her many visits to the tree. How could she know his name? But she knew better than to question such things. The girl was talking, and that was enough for now. The girl was, after all, special. Winnie had yet to figure out why, but something in the hot afternoon air told her she'd find out all too soon.

"Would you like some tea?" Winnie asked. The girl nodded, and took a seat on one of the cushions opposite. A small smile formed on her lips, before it disappeared and once again her face was open. It was like looking into a sea of calm.

As day faded into night, and although she did not say another word, Magdalena's eyes spoke volumes.

21

"You want to lower your blood pressure? Slit your wrists, love." – Becky Fairhurst, Wife Swap

Fair Summer

It was something she had been dreading all day. Fair stared at the glaringly bright screen until the words in front of her stopped making sense. It was as if she could somehow disassemble them, stop them meaning something. She wished that could be true. Sadly, when her eyes focused once again on the screen, the words had not changed, nor had she expected them to. The story was for tomorrow's paper, and as a sub, it was her job to carefully read the text and make any corrections needed before the story went to print. But she didn't want to read it. She already knew what it said, every gory detail as it had happened, in full. The word screamed out from her screen. Murder. Reading the text over again would only bring back the horror of her nightmare; the dream that hadn't really been just a dream at all. Fair sighed, and played with the fine wisps of hair that framed her delicate features. The job would have to be done; saying that, she could afford to get a cup of coffee to help her with the task.

Kev was standing by the opening of the small canteen area. He looked more stressed than usual. A stressed Kev was usually a sight Fair would try to avoid, but needs must. And coffee was a need. Kev looked up. His tie was long gone and small sweat patches stood out under the arms of his pink shirt. His hair was ruffled. He would have been cute, if he wasn't quite so annoying. Well, he still was, as long as she could keep her distance. To Fair, all men were cute in a way. Not in the

124

attractive sense, but more of the little lost puppy sort of sense. And Kev definitely fitted that category. He could certainly do with a little bit of help, from somewhere at least.

"How's it going?" he asked, smiling slightly. "Not too bad," Fair replied, happily enough. She reached into the cupboard and brought out her personal jar of fair-trade coffee. Just a sniff from the jar would do her a world of good.

"Don't know how you drink that stuff," Kev commented, as she spooned out the coffee.

"Have you even tried it?" Fair asked, raising an eyebrow.

"Actually, yes," Kev replied, sounding indignant. "Much prefer the old Nescafe, at least then you know where you stand."

"There's nothing wrong with fair-trade coffee," Fair said, sounding slightly annoyed. "I don't think the taste is really that different."

"Maybe you're right," said Kev, giving in before slowly dawdling back to his desk in his scuffed brown leather shoes. She'd certainly told him. Even his walk got to her when she was in the wrong mood. "Men," she sighed before making the finishing touches to her coffee.

She quickly glanced at her watch, and saw it read 17:15; it would be a while before she was finished for the day, especially if she was going to insist on coffee breaks. Still, the story on her monitor awaited her return; it gave her the chills. In fact, she even felt a bit dizzy. When she returned to her desk, Gill was packing up to leave for the day. She looked a lot perkier than she had earlier, and Fair smiled and waved a goodbye.

"Hey," Gill said, "are you okay? Got much left to do?"

Fair nodded, sadly. "Wish I didn't, but it's the Underbelly murder," she said.

"Oh God, I hate stories like that. Andy wrote it, didn't he?"

"Yes, he did."

Andy Gardner, young hot shot of the century, got all the gory stories and most of the good headlines. Andy got all the awards. Andy got this, Andy got that, Andy got a fucking ice cream cone from Rory. Fair was beginning to feel more than slightly queasy, and she stifled a yawn.

"You know, you look a bit pale again," Gill said, a look of concern on her face, "You should give that to someone else to do and go home, get an early night."

"There's no-one else in," Fair replied, "And I can't get Kev."

Gill turned to look, and the two exchanged a knowing glance. Kev looked as if he was about to camp out at his desk for the night, and it would probably be at least 10pm before he left.

"Are you off somewhere, then?" Fair asked, feigning interest.

"Yes, actually, I'm off to see this free show with Stanley... Duke's Ford's nephew, or something. And yourself?"

"Ah, I'm not feeling so good, so like you said probably an early night for me," Fair replied, blinking.

"Well, hope you feel better soon, amigo," Gill waved as she left the office on her clickety-clackety heels. Fair could actually feel each step in her head, which was never a good sign. She yawned again. It was hard work, being a sub. Fair was solely responsible for the stories she checked, and if any errors got past her, it would be her fault. But she managed to live with that, and had slowly built up a very good reputation within the paper. Andy, star pupil that he was, barely made any errors, so the odds were good that the story was fine the way it was. Rory hadn't given her a limit, so the length was also fine. She sat there for all of a minute, before deducing that the story did not need to be subbed after all. Which was selfish, but even the coffee was not helping matters at that point. Her head felt heavy after the flashes she'd been suffering throughout the day; flashes of memories from the night before. They flashed bright white pain in her head and meant that whatever had gotten into her, she couldn't bear to read the words neatly placed on the screen in front of her. The images were too fresh in her mind, and sitting there with her coffee mug gripped tightly in both hands, she knew that tonight would be another restless night, lacking of decent sleep. Hopefully no dreams though, and that was all right by her. So with all this knowledge taken carefully into consideration, and against her better judgement, Fair decided to fire the story through to the editing suite, without checking it over first - an extremely unusual thing for her to do. But before she picked up her bag and sipped the last sip of her coffee, Fair did something else out of the ordinary, not to mention severely out of character. She quietly removed an object from her bag; checking no-one was looking in her direction, before walking over to Kev's empty desk. She carefully placed the object down and mostly out of sight behind some stationery, and smiled to herself, a small smile, before continuing out of the office and into the warm evening air. She wondered how long it would take before it was discovered, and whether it would make any difference either way.

22

"Oh, shut up, Baldrick. You'd laugh at a Shakespearean comedy." – Edmund Blackadder, Blackadder II

Stanley Hobbes

The Belle had already summoned up quite a crowd for the main act when Stanley arrived. Brightly lit for the festivities, it was one of the oldest of the Edinburgh venues, and had quite a dark but jovial atmosphere, with old wooden floors and a downstairs section which was only to be opened as a venue for the Fringe, and for the occasional private party.

He found Gill at the bar, and she beckoned him over. She was still in her suit from work, but she looked bright enough, despite all the germs she was harbouring from her cold.

"If it isn't the man of mystery himself," Gill said, "So where did you disappear to earlier, then?"

"Oh, that," Stanley replied, looking slightly sheepish. "I'll tell you about that later... have you seen Duke Ford around yet?"

"No, not yet," Gill said, looking even more perplexed at her friend's apparent secrecy. They were silent for a second, and Stanley ordered himself a Coke – he'd decided to be good tonight.

"Eccentric chap," Stanley muttered.

"Eccentric, yes, but not in a good way. Not in a Maynard James Keenan sort of way."

"A what?"

"Maynard James Keenan, you know, frontman for Tool and A Perfect Circle? Started up a new project called Puscifer..."

"Pussy fur?" Stanley asked, thinking he'd misheard.

Gill nodded. "Anyhow, the man is incredible. One of the best performances I've ever seen in my life, live at the Rimac Arena, California, back in 2000..." She realised Stanley was looking at her oddly. "You have some odd music tastes, you know," he said.

"And *you* just don't know what you're talking about," Gill retorted. She had begun playing with the small plastic straw in her drink. Suddenly she looked up at him, and he saw she had a question in her eyes.

"So... is everything all right? I mean, with us." Gill asked, unsurely.

"Of course it is... we're always all right," Stanley replied, dismissively.

"Are we?" Gill smiled, "Well that's alright then, isn't it?"

"Uh-huh," Stanley replied, before looking over Gill's shoulder, "Uh-oh."

"What?" Gill turned to look, only to see the familiar-slightly-eccentric figure of Duke Ford making his way into the bar. He hadn't spotted them yet, and she was surprised when Stanley tapped her on the shoulder and mouthed '*stop looking!*' Perplexed, she mouthed back, '*why?*' and he just shook his head. Something was most definitely going on. Gill's favourite question was often 'why' but she recognised (most of the time), as a good journalist should, when to keep her mouth shut. Stanley continued to keep a subtle eye on the Duke, and she watched him carefully. Then he got up.

"Where are you going?"

"Shit, he's gone into the lower hall. Why is he doing that?"

"What's the problem, Stan? He's probably just gone to see his nephew – he *is* in the show, isn't he?"

"Yeah, maybe..." Stanley didn't sound convinced. The Duke was still carrying that something from earlier, and there was something about his shifty glances that Stanley really didn't like. Maybe it was nothing... but hadn't Rory asked him to dig up some dirt? That made Stanley's mind up.

"Right, we've got to follow him," he said.

"What!"

"Then I'll go, you stay here," he said as he made his way towards the stairs.

"No, I'm coming too, God help me!" No-one noticed as they slipped past the cordoned-off sign that separated the upper level from the creaky stairs, leading to... what? The area would still be getting set up for the show, and surely there would be performers down there preparing? But all was silent. As Gill made her way down into the darker room, she almost jumped as Stanley grabbed her hand and led her into a small alcove on the right. It was a strangely-shaped room, with the obligatory chairs laid out rather scattily, so as to fit the largest amount of people in at one time. Off to the side, there was an old wooden barrier that served as a screen to separate the rest of the room. At first neither of them saw the Duke, until they heard a noise like metal against metal coming from that very part of the lounge. A blonde mass of hair bobbed up and it was obvious that he was crouching down. Then he took up one of the seats, and crossed one leg over the other. Luckily from the angle of the room, he didn't see either Stanley or Gill, and they were still alone in the lower lounge when the Duke's phone started to ring.

"Hello?" The Duke said, as he picked up the phone. "Look, I can't really talk now."

"Yes, no thanks to you," the Duke said, annoyance seeping into his voice. "I got it earlier. Unfortunately the organisers didn't take too well to my little 'offering', so we're going to have to go about this our own way."

"I really must go now, but keep me updated." He hung up the phone, and looked at his watch with a heavy sigh. Gill and Stanley looked at each other, but said nothing. A noise from the top of the stairs alerted them to the opening of the cordon, and a call for 'Haberdashery Spinx Co.' came from up above. They were trapped. People started to filter down the stairs one by one, and take up the seats first at the front, then towards the back of the room. No-one cast a second glance at Gill and Stanley. The Duke stayed in his chair, both legs and arms crossed, but as the room slowly filled up Stanley no longer had a clear view. A small young man with messy blonde hair came up to the stage, and started making remarks about the audience. Stanley guessed – at least from the picture - that this was Will, the Duke's nephew.

Some music had started to play in the background, and slowly the anticipation started to build within the audience.

"So how are we tonight, ladies and gentleman? By the way, this isn't the show, it's not started yet! But we're about to showcase to you, the mysterious and exquisitely formed, Haberdashery Spinx, ladies and gentleman, please!" His voice sounded like that of a public schoolboy's, and the intensity and volume slowly rose up until the please was more of a shout, and the audience cheered. They seemed to like Will already, but they could easily turn. And from what Stanley could see of the Duke, he looked slightly bemused by it all. Soon, more performers were jumping up on the stage and dancing rather stupidly to some beat box tunes. One boy, a particularly svelte athletic young man, stole the show by back-flipping onto the stage. Everyone clapped.

"Ladies and gentleman, as you may or may not be aware, this is a show about taking risks, about having a laugh, and of course a few raspberries too! My favourite flavour, and by the way; I'm Sketchy!"

"This is my man, Will," Sketchy pointed to Will, before gesturing to the other three boys, "and this is Morris, Kleaton, and Veggie! We will be your entertainment for the next hour!"

All the boys seemed roughly about the same age, in their early twenties. Stanley looked over at the Duke; he looked less than impressed. As the first part of the show commenced, all the boys jumped off stage apart from one, who had put on some comedy glasses and was sitting at a school desk. The show continued in much the same vein, and Stanley found himself more interested in the Duke's expressions than anything else. He wasn't laughing at the funny bits, or looking impressed at the energetic parts of the show. Then the lighting seemed to darken, and grow more serious, which made Stanley look back to the stage.

"And now, we're going to be moving on, to the riskier side of the show! Everyone, watch these tricks very, very carefully." Stanley, more out of habit now, glanced back at the Duke, but he had disappeared. Suspicious, but unnoticed amongst the many people, Stanley slowly stood and found himself moving along the edge of the room, towards the Duke's section. Feeling a tap behind him, he turned around swiftly, heart beating fast now in his chest. It was Gill.

"Where are you going?" she asked, barely audible over the background noise. Stanley shrugged. Looking around the corner now and dangerously close to the Duke's chair, he saw that Duke Ford had not vanished after all. Instead, he was bending down, and had opened the green parcel that he had taken from the shop earlier.

"What's he doing?" asked Gill. Stanley brought his fingers to his lips and made a 'shhh' action, motioning her to be quiet. The act was still going on, and one of the other boys was explaining the danger of some of the next stunts, and how not to try them at home. The Duke brought out something that looked shiny, and had begun to move the shiny things from the green parcel, to a waiting black bag. He took something from the bag, and placed it into the green parcel, and that was when he sat back on the chair again. It was then that the black bag was picked up by one of the performers, who gave the Duke a slight nod as he took it to the stage. It was an awkward nod, Stanley noticed. The young man with the bag – Stanley thought it was 'Veggie' - began to speak as a large board was brought out from behind the stage. It had targets on.

"Now this is what you've all been waiting for, ladies and gents!" Veggie brought out some rather sharp looking knives; a set of three.

"Can a couple of members of the audience please confirm that these are real knives? Thank you," Veggie said as he passed the knives to a couple of willing audience members. They nodded that they were happy, before passing the knives back to Veggie. Meanwhile, Sketchy was positioning himself against the board, with a target at either side of him and one eerily close to his head. Stanley began to feel on edge.

"Now, no camera flashes or sudden movements while this stunt is underway, please," Veggie said, sounding very authoritarian and serious for once. Will was left to set up the next act, as Sketchy took the audience's attention with his funny faces and jokes. Veggie was poised to throw the first knife. Whap. It landed right on target, to Sketchy's left. Veggie posed with the second knife, and seemed to look at the angle with much thought, before throwing it towards the target on Sketchy's right. Then seemingly without any thought whatsoever, Veggie threw the last knife, which landed, surprisingly enough, on the target above Sketchy's head. Even some of Sketchy's hair had got caught by the knife's blade, and Will had to help him get untangled.

"Now, you thought that was bad, people! Wait until you see our next stunt! Sketchy is a bit of a risk-taker, you see, and he will now attempt to catch one of these very knives with his bare hands! And then, if we're lucky... his teeth!" A small murmur seemed to grow within the audience, and Sketchy slapped some chalk on both hands in preparation for the stunt. He looked confident, but so far Stanley had been on edge just watching the previous trick. Sketchy motioned that he was ready, and Veggie took up the knife. The next part happened in slow motion. Stanley watched the Duke stand up; he looked nervously on, and was clasping his hands. Sketchy was making

133

more silly faces at the audience, before staring straight ahead in pure concentration. Veggie was poised with the knife, ready to throw to Sketchy. It looked like Sketchy was going to catch it at the pointy end. The Duke was watching the stage with intensity, but he still hadn't sat down. The audience was completely silent. Veggie threw the knife. At first it looked as it Sketchy had caught the knife, and Stanley was ready to breathe a sigh of relief, when he realised all was not well. Sketchy was staring down at his hand. The knife had gone straight through it. Stanley's heart was practically in his mouth. Then, he laughed. It was all just a trick. Sketchy pulled out the knife and some red tissue paper fell out. The audience cheered.

"And now, ladies and gents," Will continued, as Veggie pulled out a very different style of knife from the black bag, "is the most dangerous part of the show. Do not attempt to recreate any of these stunts at home, people."

"Yeah, it's very dangerous!" called Sketchy, wearing a pathetic grin on his face. Stanley, who had only just begun to relax, quickly sat up again. He had a bad feeling about that particular knife. It shone very brightly under the Belle's lighting set-up. Sketchy had taken his place against the board again, and did a silly little dance as if to prepare for the stunt. If Veggie was slightly apprehensive, he hid it well. He raised the knife. Sketchy looked like a stone statue, suddenly very serious and unmoving. He stood rigid against the board, mouth pursed before relaxing his jaw muscles.

"Oh my God. Is he really going to..." Gill whispered. Stanley ignored his friend. The next part, unlike the part before, all happened very quickly. Veggie leaned back in expert poise; the knife took off in a very fluid and graceful movement. The audience was deadly silent, and Stanley imagined he could hear the weapon (well, that's what it was) cut through the air towards Sketchy. And Sketchy... didn't exactly catch the knife. Stanley turned away in horror. The audience gasped and was deadly silent. Someone screamed. Gill moved sharply to his left, and he heard her say, "Stanley!"

He turned to look at the Duke, who had started to walk sharply towards the door, and was now staring at him with contempt. A look of realisation came over his face, and before Stanley could say anything, he'd pushed him out of the way and was making his way towards the exit. Others were rushing towards Sketchy who was gurgling in a very unnatural manner. Veggie was staring at his hand (the one that had thrown the knife) in shock. Will threw up. Stanley barely registered any of this.

"Duke Ford!" he called after the Duke, but it was no use. Taking a deep breath, Stanley pushed his way (carefully) past a few onlookers, as the very real shout of, '*somebody call an ambulance!*' echoed through the room. By the time he'd gotten to the bar area, there was no sign of the Duke. One of the bartenders brushed past him in a hurry to see what was going on downstairs.

"Sorry, mate," he called as he descended the stairs two at a time. Gill would be there, trying to find out what had gone wrong in the chaos. She could handle that herself. Instead, he made his way outside. It was much quieter and peaceful in the night air, slightly cooler than before but still plenty warm as to only warrant a shirt. Heart pounding, Stanley looked down at his jeans and plain white shirt. The shirt was simple enough, but with deliberately rough edges around the hems and collar. Gill called it his Shakespeare shirt. No tie needed – he could do casual rather well, when he tried. But wasn't the whole idea of casual *not* to try? Searching the area, there was still no trace of Duke Ford, and the same feeling crept into him as earlier. It made him uneasy as he walked up a fairly deserted road just off Nicolson Street. Of course, he had a few questions. What the hell was going on? Why did the Duke act like that? Had he really swapped the knives? If not, why did he leave? It didn't make any sense. What had he been doing down there on his own in the first place? Just then, Stanley heard the sound of metal scraping against metal, and a hand grabbed him from behind.

23

Shock and fear seized his body as he was pulled back almost to the ground, before finding his feet and choking; the grip around his shirt collar had been tight.

"Who are you? Get your hands off me!" he shouted. But as he turned, he recognised the man from the shop earlier, minus the beret. He was now holding the same green bundle as earlier, and Stanley now knew what was inside.

"You! I don't believe this... I can't believe the Duke thinks he can hide behind someone like you and get away with this!"

"I don't know what you're talking about," the man replied in a deep throaty Glaswegian growl. His eyes were a bright blue that held a certain piercing coldness. He was a lot taller than Stanley, and wore a black leather jacket.

"I'm not scared of you, or Ford!" the man laughed, and moved to punch Stanley, who quickly swerved out the way and miraculously landed a blow to the man's stomach. Undeterred, he grabbed Stanley's hand and twisted it painfully up his back. The green bundle fell to the ground, and its contents rolled onto the concrete. For a second Stanley laughed. It was unexpected, to see a bunch of marbles spill out over the pavement. No knives there. He'd quite literally lost his marbles. Then Stanley got a grip. He blindly kicked from behind, and luckily managed to hit his attacker hard in the gut, making him weaken his hold over Stanley's arm. Without turning back, Stanley ran. He didn't look back for a while. It was hard to believe what had just happened... it didn't make any sense. Nicolson Street was busier than usual, and he had to swerve out the way of a few people as he slowed down to a quick walk. He realised he was shaking, and a scratch had appeared on the back of his right hand.

Looking behind him, he could not see his attacker. That was a good thing. Now he just had to figure out what to do next. It felt like he was the one that had lost his marbles. He imagined the large man, minus the beret, knelt down on the pavement, daintily picking up the spilled marbles from the ground, which caused him to laugh again, quite loudly. This got a few looks from some passers-by, but that was the least of his concerns.

The Edinburgh Festival Theatre loomed up ahead, and quite a crowd had gathered outside its doors. For a moment he was still unsure whether he'd taken a knock to the head. Women in '80s electro circus dresses and ragdoll costumes stood with plain looking men in skinny drainpipe jeans and short spiked hair; quite a mixture. A normal-looking woman in a black jacket and jeans smiled at him. No-one else gave him a second look. That was what he wanted. But at the same time he needed to stay with the herd. So he joined the queue. Some music was playing in the background, and he lost his thoughts for a while.

When he eventually reached the ticket office, he couldn't believe he was paying £50 to see a show he couldn't even pronounce. The name was printed on the ticket in large, thick black print. It looked like Russian. The posters didn't give much away; a rather athletic-looking man and woman were posing in what almost looked like sci-fi costumes, with a background of flames and white noise behind them. As the crowd slowly filtered into the main hall, he joined the queue up the stairs and eventually found his seat, towards the middle of the theatre.

He still felt slightly on edge, and confused as to what had just gone on. What was he doing? Standing up to let a couple through to their seats, he checked the time. It was edging towards 9pm, which was presumably when the act was due to start. For now all was calm as more and more people moved to take their seats. The red curtain stood brightly in front of him.

So why did he still feel nervous? Not really sure how he should be feeling, he lightly touched the scrape on his hand. It stung slightly, and he bit his lower lip. It was dry. Angry; he should be feeling angry... outraged, even violated, perhaps. What right did this guy have to put the frights on him – if that's even what he'd been trying to do. Stanley didn't know anymore, but something very odd was going on. Then it hit him; he was in shock. That would explain the laughter, the confusion... the odd behaviour. Before he could contemplate this revelation further, the lights dimmed and the curtains were raised... Show time.

24

"And you want to travel with her, and you want to travel blind, and you know that she will trust you, for she's touched your perfect body with her mind." – Suzanne – Leonard Cohen

It literally started with a bang. A big blue bang to be precise, accompanied by a spectacular flash of light that illuminated even the furthest reaches of the old-style Edinburgh theatre. The audience gasped in anticipation as 12 svelte figures (the dancers) bounced onto the stage all at once, and the energy was instantly electric. For a moment there was silence as things almost seemed to move in slow motion, before dramatic music sealed the deal and the show really came to life.

Stanley felt in his pocket; his notebook was still there. He had a good feeling about this show. And he was right. While the dancers were talented, energetic and most definitely brave, the show was an odd mix of dance and electro circus. The dancers moved through the air with ease and determination, and at some points Stanley even caught himself holding his breath. As the stunts got dangerous, one performer in particular stood out to him above the rest. She tantalised on the trapeze, was taut on the tight rope, dazzled on the dance floor and shone throughout the whole show; if any of them could have been the star, it was her. Taking a quick look at the programme that was issued with his ticket he saw that her name was Marcella. Athletic yet curvaceous, she wore tight black leather and her even her hair was tied in an unusual way, to either side of her head. He couldn't quite place his finger on it, but there was something almost familiar about her. Her skin shone brightly under the curious blue lights, but he was too far away to get a good look at her face. It was when she took centre stage towards the middle of the fourth act that suddenly the atmosphere changed. Instead of the upbeat music, it became almost melancholy, the blue lights becoming even more intense.

Her grace could bring a tear to his eye, if he would let it. She was flimsy, yet precise, and utterly beautiful in each movement. And the way she danced somehow told a story... it suddenly became clear that this was her, and he could feel it, actually *feel* her every move as if she spoke of every story ever told. It was something else; almost like a dream. Then it was over, and the show continued as if nothing had ever changed. Still, the fitness levels of all the performers had to be admired – the stunts they could pull were astonishing, and at times Stanley's breath was caught in his throat as they fell through the sky with no foreseeable safety net to catch their fall. But each one landed with spectacular accuracy, on individual poles that had been waiting for them. Any other time, he wouldn't have believed how they could not be wearing harnesses. But they didn't need them; the atmosphere was taking hold over the whole audience. The stage suddenly lit up with a trance of colours; pink, green, yellow, orange, red, blue. The dancers almost melted in with the vibrant colours and their movements made it almost impossible to keep track of who was where. It was the perfect climax to a – as far as Stanley was concerned – perfect performance.

With the act finally over, the audience gave a standing ovation and Stanley felt compelled to join in. He left his seat still wondering what had just hit him, the incident from earlier not exactly forgotten, but for now, a much lesser concern in his mind. The bar was full, but nevertheless he ordered himself a Diet Coke and sat on what must have been the only empty stool in the room. He didn't pay attention to the loudness of the voices, the babble of the many people crowded around each other, the 'luvvies' and fans; he wanted to write down his feelings from the show while they were still fresh in his mind. He was already into sweeping statements such as 'pure chemistry' and 'electricity revolves around...' when suddenly he felt a tap on his shoulder.

"A journalist, do we have here a journalist?" A voice almost boomed from up above.

Stanley looked up, not entirely sure what to make of the man who had addressed him; he came face to face with bright green eyes, thick bushy eyebrows, more than a hint of receding hairline and above all, a moustache unlike any he'd seen in the past 10 years. "I'm Stanley, from the Edinburgh Times, nice to meet you," he replied.

"Edinburgh Times, is it! Well, excellent, we didn't reckon on any of your lot showing up tonight! Did you enjoy the show?"

"Oh yes, it was... unexpected. I thought it was unbelievable."

"I can assure you it is entirely believable," the man spoke with an air of confidence that had Stanley wondering exactly who he was speaking to. But he had turned to face the other way. "Ah, here comes our shining star now."

Stanley turned to look. All eyes were on the female figure as she ascended the steps to the bar, before making her way almost eccentrically through the room. The way she walked was almost hypnotising in itself, and Stanley was struck again by her beauty, this time up close. Her brown eyes sparkled under the soft lights of the bar, and she looked so at ease as she smiled at some of the guests. Then, he couldn't quite believe it, but she smiled at him. In fact, she was walking straight towards him.

"May I introduce you to the wonderfully talented, Marcella Dimitrieva!"

"Hello," Stanley heard himself utter.

"And this is Mr... ?" The moustache continued.

"Hobbes. I'm Stanley Hobbes, from the Edinburgh Times."

"Oh, a journalist. How nice to meet you," said Marcella,

an even larger smile forming on her lips, as she eyed his notepad. He noticed she spoke in a Russian accent, which fitted her name perfectly. Her voice was like velvet, her lips full and painted a dark mulberry. He fidgeted. For some reason, the moustachio man had left the two of them together at the small table. Marcella raised an eyebrow.

"And what have you been writing there, anything about me?" Before he could stop her, she'd grabbed the notepad from his slightly sweaty left hand and began to look intently at the page. Her brow furrowed, darkly painted lips parting in something that could only be described as a cross between shock and absolute horror.

"What is this - ancient hieroglyphics?"

"No actually, that's my shorthand," Stanley replied, amused.

"Oh, well that's no fun! I wanted to be able to read how beautiful you think I am," she grinned, and he realised she was joking.

"Well, in that case I think you're very beautiful," he replied, again hearing himself say the words but not knowing where they'd come from. He felt a slight blush on his cheeks that he was just going to have to ignore. She smiled, and the light danced in her eyes. It'd been worth it for her smile.

"So, the show's called Kaskadiori... what does it mean?" He asked, out of curiosity more than anything.

"It means 'risk takers' in Russian," she replied. It seemed to make sense. It sounded almost romantic, and he supposed their show matched that notion perfectly. Just then he saw something out of the corner of his eye which caused him to do a double-take. It was Glaswegian beret man, but-minus-the-beret. Marcella turned to look, and then quickly shot him a glance; it was hard to decipher the look on her face, but a slight change in the atmosphere told him it meant something.

"Chort! How about we get out of here now?" she said. It took him by surprise, but he was in no hurry to argue.

He nodded. "I think that sounds like a plan." In that moment, if she hadn't grabbed his hand and sparked something off in an almost unnoticeable way, spawning a chain reaction that would slowly enter his brain and play tricks with his mind, the next set of events could have taken an entirely different turn - or may not have even happened at all. But she did, and they happened like this: As they approached North Bridge, they didn't really know where they were going.

"So, Mr Journalist, is this my interview?"

"If you like," said Stanley. He couldn't help but smile; in fact, he was finding the whole situation rather amusing. Marcella had put on her leather jacket, and they looked like complete opposites.

"So what do you want to know?" she asked.

"Oh everything. Tell me everything, Miss Dimitrieva." She paused, her eyes looking dramatically up at the sky, her mouth open in an amused grin.

"Okay, I'll tell you everything, but we've got to think of this as just one never-ending interview, right?"

"Okay, I'll try. So, what do you know?" he asked her.

"Right... Well, I'm half Italian – on my mother's side, and half Russian, although my Russian side is probably the more dominant of the two. I love chocolate pudding, reading between the lines in obscure pornography plots, I'm really into Kalai... oh, and I have a huge admiration for Star Trek. In particular, Brent Spiner – you know, Data from The Next Generation? As a man he was beautiful – as an old man, also incredibly cute!"

Stanley laughed. "Right; and when you do your act, do you ever get scared? Have you ever hurt yourself really badly?"

"No, but I easily could. Maybe I should one day, just for the life experience?"

"Maybe, but not any time soon, because I'd prefer not to have to visit you in hospital for the rest of this interview."

"Deal," she replied. "You've stopped holding my hand."

"Correct. Where are you taking me, anyway?"

"I have no idea! You live here, not me... can't we just pretend we're in Dreamland, and go on some awesome adventure? But then we'd have to sing."

"Ermm, right, okay... I'm not very good at singing," he replied, a little more serious, now.

"Really, you have an interesting voice, though. You're not from here, are you?"

"Nope," he said, not really wanting to explain about his accent again. But she'd already let go of the subject, stopping to lean over the bridge, as if it were some old friend she'd forgotten about, her arms sweeping over it in almost dramatic fashion. It made him smile.

"I love Edinburgh, it's so pretty at night."

"Marcella, can I ask you something serious?"

"Go ahead," she replied, straight away.

"That guy at the bar, you saw him too? Who is he?"

She turned and with barely the flick of an eye, Stanley registered a change in her demeanour. She sighed, "Here there be monsters, kid."

"You've seen him before?" asked Stanley, slightly puzzled.

"Uh-huh... gives me the creeps. Don't ask me how I know, but I think his name's McAvoy. I swear he's been following me." She didn't meet his gaze.

"McAvoy... rings no bells. How do you know his name? And why would he follow you?"

"Okay, okay... I know, because when he wasn't looking I flicked through his wallet. As for why he would be following me, I don't know, all right?" She shivered, visibly.

"And he didn't notice you'd taken it?"

"Nope, I put it back again right after. You could say I'm skilled like that. You see, whenever I'm in a situation like that, I have to think to myself, W.W.D.D," she said, breezily.

"Pardon?" he asked, perplexed at the meaning.

145

"You know. What would Data do?"

"Data? Oh, Data... Star Trek," he said, finally understanding. She was a 'trekkie'.

"Yes, Star Trek."

Silently stunned, and unsure of his reasoning, he reached out for her hand, and together, they walked in silence for a while. She bit her lip, and he could tell she was thinking about something – the meaning of which obscured behind the veil of her dark eyes. Eventually, she spoke.

"You're pretty too," she stated.

"Thank you. You're cold, maybe we should get you home; where are you staying?" Stanley asked.

"Quite near here, but I don't want to go back there just yet," she said, brushing off the question as if it were a stray hair. Instead, she reached for his arm, and pulled it around her. He obliged.

"Well, where do you want to go?"

"How about... Arthur's Seat! Will you take me there?"

"Is it safe to be going up there at night? We won't be able to see a thing," he replied, confused at the prospect of stumbling up what is basically a combination of grass and rocks in the dark.

"We'll have the stars! What do you mean, safe? Aren't I safe with you?"

"Well, yes. But... you don't even know me; you'll be taking my word for it."

"I'm used to a lot more dangerous activities than climbing a hill with a stranger. I want to see the stars, come on, Stanley, let's go!" She was grinning now.

"Alright... but I'd better not regret this. What if you break an ankle or something?"

"I'll have you," she replied. He realised she was serious.

"Okay," he sighed, "But, if you fall off a cliff, I did warn you."

The walk did not seem like a long one. She had barely

stopped talking since they'd left the theatre; but her conversation was unstructured, each strand almost completely disconnected to the next. Some of it was personal – her chocolate addiction for instance, which she seemed to take ever so seriously – and the rest was merely conversation. It didn't seem to bother him in the slightest; he was completely taken in.

The moon shone brightly in the dark sky, and exhausted, Stanley finally stopped on the hill. Hill climbing was not an activity he'd pictured himself doing when he left the flat earlier; he was wearing the wrong shoes.

"Right, we're here, Arthur's Seat. Are you happy?"

"Happy? Do you think that's all it takes to make me happy? We're not even at the top!"

He looked at her. It was dark, but he could still see her smile. She took a playful step back, and then lay down upon the grass.

"Going to join me?"

"I don't know... is it wet?"

"No, just cool," she replied, calmly. She seemed to pause, as if she was about to say something else.

"Isn't this romantic?" she asked, her gaze never leaving the stars. Her eyes sparkled.

"It's definitely odd," he said, as he lay next to her on the grass. They were on a slight tilt, and it sort of felt like being back in childhood, after a game of football in the park.

"Do you really want to know everything?" she asked.

"Yes. Tell me everything," he said.

"In Russia, the winter's cold. Winter. And my life. It's tough out there. Nobody told me about the tigers. Why didn't anyone warn me there were tigers? Hahah," she laughed, before her face once again turned serious. In the darkness, she turned to him, her pale face in the light of the moon.

"You see, there's this thing, this... barrier, between us all. It stifles, stops us from saying, or doing what we want to do. And sometimes I feel it so much it kills me. Like now, can you feel it? It's there, and it shouldn't be... because deep down, really we're all the same. You know?"

He couldn't think of what to say, but he could tell from her eyes that she meant every word. And suddenly he could feel it. She was absolutely right. She held up her hand as if she was looking at something she'd never quite seen before. Then she smiled.

"It's funny – when I was younger, I used to look at my hand and feel surprised I was actually here, in this body - that I was actually alive. I was fascinated just looking at my hand and making it move, as if it was some kind of miracle. Do you know what that feels like?"

"Yes," he whispered. He opened his mouth to say something else, but then she did something he didn't quite expect. She placed her hand over his, and squeezed slightly. It was a good feeling, but unusual. Then the moment was over.

"Marcella... you're cold. Do you want to come back to mine for a coffee?"

She let go of his hand, and turned to face him, an incredulous look on her face. "A coffee, at yours; what kind of woman do you think I am, Mr Journalist?"

"I'm sorry... I..." he stammered.

Her grin widened. "You mean you don't even have hot chocolate?"

25

"The truth of the matter is that window management under X is not yet well understood." – The "Xlib Programming Manual"

Fair Summer

Across the city, Fair examined the candle as if it were an old friend. Of course, it was not, but since she'd lost Jack, she'd kept this particular candle closer to heart than most. Especially the small tea lights that she would buy in bulk, light once, then throw away; their short-lived beauty flickering away to nothing. She often fell asleep with them still lit, which made it a small miracle that she was not encompassed in smoke and flames in the middle of the night, choked in her slumber. Now, she struck a match and carefully lit the wick, once more gazing into the small magic flame. It was only magic because it reminded her of him – it was merely her imagination that made it seem more vibrant than the rest. Suddenly, she didn't feel quite so alone.

"Jack," she whispered. No reply. She turned to the mirror, and out of the corner of her eye, the curtain shifted.

"Jack?" She caught herself. That was silly, calling his name, when clearly he couldn't hear her. He was long gone, and only dead air remained. It had been nine years ago, just before she'd moved to Edinburgh; the accident. They'd been close. She'd never know whether he knew just how much she loved him, but she would forever remain his friend. She was there at the end. She saw the look in his eyes, and she knew that whatever was between them would pass silently into the night, as would he. She'd held his hand, tight, as she felt him slip away beneath her fingertips. She'd never cried, not for him. Silently, she watched the yellow-orange flame. The candle was old now, barely recognisable from the gift he'd once given her for her birthday. Back then, it had been mostly green with a hint of other colours showing through – it had been pretty. Now it was misshaped and drooping, forming a wide crevasse down the centre. It was not so pretty, but instead, unique. She'd never figured out why men thought girls loved candles so much, and she'd still been a girl back then; a silly little girl. She cautiously set the candle down on the open windowsill, at her bedside. It was still warm in her room; there was no breeze, no reason for the curtain to shift. She had a feeling that might change, but for now, she ignored it.

It had been a car; such a silly way for death to take her one true friend. It all happened in front of her eyes. Of course, she'd had counselling, but that only told her what she already knew. She didn't mention her dreams. What good would it do? She'd never dreamt about him; no dream had warned her, no dream had predicted her loss, and no dream since had featured him. She didn't know if that was a blessing. The thought of being able to save him often tortured her in the months after the accident. In the end she'd just let it go. Life went on. The world was still beautiful, its colours faded only slightly to her forlorn eyes. But in a way, it made her feel sympathetic to Stanley. After Lorraine... although really, it wasn't quite the same thing. She was glad Stanley was okay.

Maybe she felt she could relate to him because they'd both lost someone they'd been close to. But there was something about Stanley... something in him that she felt deep down within. It wasn't love – no, she was sure of that. That wasn't to say she wasn't fond of him; she was. Why was she so hesitant to sleep? She already knew. Another dream was waiting for her to turn out the light, rest her head on the pillow and close her eyes to the world of the awake; and in Edinburgh right now, the world of the awake was probably rather limited.

It was a weekday night; most normal fatigued working people would have already closed the curtains and said nighty-nite to Aunty Sue. She was in an exclusive club. She kind of liked that thought; she'd never really fitted into anywhere before. The Insomniacs and Seriously Deluded Club. IASDC, for short. She still remembered the image of his hair; normally shoulder length and silky, now matted with blood beneath her fingertips. She'd pretended not to notice, as he looked into her eyes from the roadside. Instead, she'd smiled at him. He smiled back, said he felt cold; didn't have the energy to smile for long. She had been there until the life faded from his eyes, and finally he'd let go, welcomed to another world, or into darkness. She sighed, and as she'd predicted, the room began to grow cold. Shivering, she closed the window, and as she did, her candle blew out.

"Goodnight," she whispered, to the empty room.

26

"A woman who looks like a girl and thinks like a man is the best sort, the most enjoyable to be and the most pleasurable to have and to hold." – Julie Burchill

Stanley Hobbes

"You're absolutely fascinating." Stanley sat on the couch opposite, so as to keep an appropriate amount of space between them; he didn't want to get too close, no matter how drawn to her he felt. It was odd, having her there in his small flatted dwelling. Almost surreal, even down to the way she held her mug. Even though he'd never heard of her by name before, she had a certain something about her that he could not simply ignore. Jasper was now sprawled out on her lap, and had begun to purr as she gently stroked the soft fur between his ears. She'd obviously made another fan.

"What's so 'fascinating' about me, the fact that my lipstick stays on even after drinking hot chocolate? It's amazing what they can do with make-up these days, trust me, it's nothing spectacular – I find the modern women of today even expect it."

"No, not that. It's just... you, I guess."

"Of all the stars in all the world..." she started.

"... None could shine so brightly, as you," Stanley finished.

"Awww... and that's right, it *is* just me! You should never put me on a pedestal, or else how are we supposed to conduct this interview with any hint of professionalism?" She raised an eyebrow at 'professionalism'.

"You realise I'm not recording any of this, right?"

"Uh-huh... but you are up here," she pointed to her head,

"and that's all that counts."

"If you say so," he replied, lacing his hands together and finding a more 'professional' pose. It was difficult, but he kept a straight face.

"Now don't do that... that – pose! Far too sexy, how am I supposed to take that seriously?"

"Sexy? Me? I'm sorry. How do you want me to sit?" he asked, unsurely.

"Like this," she said, ridding her lap of a disgruntled Jasper; in one swift movement she was next to him, her eyes briefly meeting with his before she gently picked up one hand and place it on his thigh. The other, she placed on the arm of the chair. "There, very relaxed," she smiled. "Now you just have to tell your face!"

They laughed, but then her expression took on a more serious tone. "You're not used to this, are you?" She asked.

"Well no, I've got a star in my living room, not really sure how to act," he replied, only half-jokingly this time. It was true; it wasn't a situation he was familiar with.

"Oh, pass me a bucket! You know, it's funny - I looked into the abyss, and the abyss looked back at me. But then I realised I was really the one who was staring back. It put me off dinner parties for a long time."

He looked at her for a moment, but before he could speak, his phone began to vibrate in his pocket. Taking a look, he realised it was Gill, probably worried about what'd happened to him earlier. Regrettably, he pressed the 'busy' button.

"Who was that?"

"Just a colleague, from work," he replied, which was kind of true. She met his gaze, and something in her eyes told him she knew that wasn't quite the right answer. He looked at her fingernails. They were long and painted black. He could imagine her painting them in long, smooth strokes, as if she'd been doing it her whole life.

"I want to... get used to you," he said. It seemed

153

appropriate.

"Well, you'd better get used to me, because we're meant to be," she said, and something in her tone told him she meant it.

"Really?" He got closer.

"Yes, really," so did she.

He paused. "How do you know that?"

"I just do. This moment, right here, is meant to be."

"So if I did this..." he leant in to kiss her. Their lips found each other with minimal effort; as if they weren't even supposed to be apart... it just felt right. Their kiss was soft; her lips warm. She tasted of sweet hot chocolate.

"Mmm... and how about if I did this..." she said, loosening his tie.

"You can do whatever you want..." he replied. That was it. Suddenly they were all over each other, kissing passionately on the sofa, her hands in his hair, then down his back, pulling him on top of her. It felt good.

"Where's the bedroom?" she whispered, taking his hand and standing up.

"Marcella... I'm not used to one night stands."

"Good, because this isn't one," she replied.

"Phew," he said, allowing her to lead him into the bedroom.

"Wow, so is this how you imagined your room to look like, when you were all grown up?"

"Not exactly. Are you saying there's something wrong with my room?"

"No... oh my God, look at your ties! Why do you have so many?"

"That's my collection. You haven't seen the half of it," he said, opening his wardrobe out fully. Marcella gasped, hand to her throat in a dramatic gesture of pure awe.

"Look at these things! You're obsessed!" Before he could stop her, she was pulling the ties out in an almost curious

154

fascination that would otherwise have been adorable – like a cat, playing with twine – but the mess on the floor would nevertheless have to be tidied and the ties put back into their order according to colour and texture.

"No, I wouldn't call it that," he said, refusing the urge to pick up the ties and at the same time attempting to brush off how close to the truth she actually was.

"You know, we could have some fun with these..." she said, her voice taking on a slightly naughtier tone.

"Oh really," he said, a question that really wasn't a question at all.

"Mm-hmm," she murmured as she pushed him back on the bed, armed with a particularly expensive purple silk tie. Then she was on his lap, kissing him and pressing her firm body up against him in a way he couldn't quite refuse. He couldn't even refuse when she stealthily began to tie his hands behind his back. "Again... I'm not used to this," he said, trying to stay calm at the prospect. She had a look in her eye that he didn't recognise. She'd removed her jacket, and now the blackness of her hair contrasted dramatically to her pale exposed shoulders, and down to her cleavage. He wanted to touch her. Instead she started to unbutton his shirt, which again was a little weird considering he had no control over the situation. He could feel her nails running lightly over his chest, her leather-clad thighs wrapped tightly around him.

"Are you teasing me now?"

"Maybe," she said.

"You think I'm really going to be held against my will by a bit of flimsy material? You'd better think again, I could break out of this if I wanted to."

"Just try it, I dare you," she taunted.

"Those are expensive ties," he reminded her.

"Knew it, weakling," she muttered.

"Your lipstick's come off," he said.

"Oh, shut up," she kissed him again, harder this time, as

her hand reached for another tie. The jade frog dropped onto the floor, with a barely audible 'clink'.

27

"Despite crime's omnipresence, things work in society, because biology compels it. Order eventually restores itself, by psychic equilibrium." - Camille Paglia

Duke Edmund Ford

The Duke fumbled for the leather gloves inside his brocade jacket and carefully watched the corner of the alleyway as the heavy footsteps got gradually louder, before finally materialising into the familiar figure of Kane McAvoy. He was a large clout of a man, bigger than the Duke by far. A bruiser. He was, pretty much, the Duke's dog. Not that he'd ever tell him that, of course. After all, dogs could turn on their owners, and he rather needed this particular dog for a rather particular and dastardly deed.

"Mr McAvoy," Duke Ford hissed, "I didn't think you'd be taking the liberty of joining me this fine evening. Where on earth have you been?"

"Apologies. Couldn't really get away; I think we've got a wee problem," McAvoy panted, with utmost sincerity. His voice was deep and growled in a pissed-off Glaswegian manner that Ford could never really decipher. The Duke cringed. Not because of the voice, but because a 'wee problem' was the last thing he wanted to hear of.

"Oh?"

"That's right. Oh. Your pal the reporter, he's becoming a bit of a nuisance," McAvoy continued.

"Don't I bloody well know it! Did you find him?" The Duke asked, bracing himself for the worst.

"Did more than that," McAvoy made fists.

"Oh, for God's sake... what did I tell you? What mess have you gotten us into now? Damn that Garlic Tony for ever suggesting..."

"Not a lot... the sod got away. The marbles thing didn't really help matters either. Didn't want to leave them on the ground, scooped to pick them up, was sent reeling backwards and hit myself on the head. Might have a concussion. Look, it's still bleeding," McAvoy reached up to his head, and winced.

"Do you think I really give a flying squat about your concussion? What happened with Mr Hobbes? Tell me, man!"

"I thought he'd got away, thought he'd probably gone straight to the police. So I got the most pleasant surprise later, when I was waiting for Foxy and that brother of hers."

"Go on," said the Duke, mildly interested now.

"It was your reporter. Stood there talking with her, bold as brass. I tried to be inconspicuous, like, but I think they saw me. Anyway, they both left together."

"Oh buggery-bludgery-bollocky-shit!" The Duke paced, his hand reached to his brow as his headache now hit him full-on. McAvoy stood watching silently. Ford allowed himself a deep intake of breath, before continuing.

"This is getting far more complicated than I would have liked. I mean, this is really rather serious now," the Duke muttered, almost to himself.

"What do you want to do about it? You're the boss, after all."

"Going to have to take care of it..."

"A third party?" McAvoy enquired.

"Something of the sort, yes," the Duke sighed. "I didn't really want to have to do this..."

It was all getting well out of hand for the Duke. They were pulling him in, making him out to be something he wasn't... and those damn knives, taunting him. Well, they had asked for it. Will was such a child, didn't know what he was doing, an embarrassment. The whole sorry state of affairs was an embarrassment. And then there was the wench... never trust a wench to do what you should have done yourself in the first place.

"She wouldn't tell him anything anyway, would she?" McAvoy asked, "I mean, nothing that can be traced back to you. She didn't even know it was you that indirectly gave her the Bogleur tip-off."

"So what the buggering hell are they doing together then? Maybe he was in it all along!" the Duke said.

McAvoy shrugged.

"And maybe he knows nothing. Maybe after tomorrow we won't have to worry about either of them," he said. "Am I still all clear?"

"What? Oh, yes, come by around tea-time and I'll make sure that you're all sorted. But call first. Going to cause quite a stir, is it not? How exciting," the Duke rubbed his hands together in a way reminiscent of an old-school villain. McAvoy supposed that was true, in a way.

"Yeah, you could say that, but... sure this is necessary?"

"Everything's necessary. Everything in its place, and all that. Eh? And we all stand at the fence together, eh?"

McAvoy screwed up his eyes. It was becoming clearer and clearer to him that the Duke was not really 'all there'. Probably too much time dunking rich tea biscuits and talking about fox hunting. Or lack of it. He'd pretty much made up his mind to go ahead with tomorrow and then high-tail it with the money. But now it was looking rather bad for his bank account, and yet more things needed to be 'taken care of'.

"Eh?" the Duke goaded.

"What fence?"

"Oh, never you mind that! Just come by tomorrow, and remember to get out of that Theatre before... well, you know what. Or don't, save me the expense that way."

"Sure you're ready for the fall-out?"

The Duke sneered. "As long as you do your job

correctly, there won't be any fall-out for me to worry about."

"You think we can still pull this off?"

"I think you can."

"What about the file?"

"I told you, I'll take care of it," the Duke replied.

"Right, get you; and then the bank transfer?" The Duke forgot that McAvoy liked to ensure he'd get his Scooby Snacks at the end of all this.

"Here," said the Duke, reaching into his pocket, "take this for now, you'll get the rest via BACS later."

"How later?"

"When we get ourselves out of this mess... and don't even think about dropping me in it, I have friends in lower places than you, don't you know."

"As if."

"So, are we back to being 'bosom buddies' then?"

"Oh, always." At least, that's what he thought.

28

"Hike up your skirt a little more, and show the world to me." –
Dave Matthews, 'Crash'

Stanley Hobbes

It wasn't something he'd expected. Not again, so soon. The elevator doors swished open to reveal the familiar scene, and this time he knew all too well what was coming. It was always his worst nightmare to return to the dream exactly where it last left off, instead of back at the start where at least he stood the slightest slither of a chance with Lorraine. He was thankful for that slither. But something had happened, hadn't it? Something she might not be too happy about. He imagined Marcella, lying next to him in the real world, curled in the warmth of fuzzy sleep. He wished he could wake up. Instead he felt cold, lost.

He stepped forward, hoping that she'd be at least clothed this time. Why was he doing this, again? Would it always be his fate? He imagined this was like hell, forced to repeat the same actions, the same fears, over and over again without ever conquering them. Never coming to terms with Lorraine's death, never facing his cruel fate in her hands – hands so cold like ice. Perhaps he should just let himself be caught by her, her dead eyes, scratching nails, scraping of bone... perhaps then it would end.

He closed his eyes, and felt something in his gut that was close to stabbing fear. He felt the cold marble under his bare feet. It was too real. Why wasn't he dressed? He checked himself; the only thing he was wearing was his tie; a checked burgundy colour this time. It bared a horrifying resemblance to the one she had used when she... he didn't want to think about that. Instead, he hesitated. An unusual sound stopped him from moving any further forward. It was unusual for such a sound, but it registered.

The corridor stretched out before him, and suddenly he felt like he wasn't completely alone. Still, it wasn't a bad feeling. It lifted the fear, and the memory of her touch came flooding over him once again. Her kiss, oh it'd been sweet... so sweet. *Marcella.* Her pert breasts; the line of her waist; her hips... and then lower... So sweet.

"Stanley."

It was his name. This time the sound seemed to be coming from somewhere else. Still far out of reach, but closer than before. Nevertheless, it was a familiar voice. He felt the dream fading. This time it would go away. This time he was saved.

"Stanley?"

He opened his eyes. She was standing naked in the middle of his bedroom, surrounded by a mess of ties. They covered the floor, but he was too transfixed by her beauty to care. He blinked, then, lazily rolled over.

"Funny... I dreamt that you were naked, too," he said.

"It's amazing how perceptive the human mind can really be, even in dream state." she replied. His eyes had adjusted fully now; most definitely naked, all right.

"Nah. You look a lot better in the flesh."

"Oh really."

"Yeah," he said, getting up. He was not so naked; he often slept in his boxers.

"Don't get up, I was going to make you breakfast in bed!" Marcella said, indignantly. She turned for a second, as Jasper entered the room.

"Morning, kitty," she purred, "I bet you're hungry too, huh?" She turned back to him.

"Wait, turn around, I want to see your tattoo," he said. She obediently obliged. On her lower back, sat an intricately decorated snake, almost definitely the sexiest tattoo he'd ever seen. He was behind her now, and ran his fingers over it, making her shiver.

"You know, I'm not usually the submissive type..."

"Oh no?" she feigned surprise. It was sexy, like in a '40s movie; only this particular heroine was completely exposed, unsuited to the false modesty her pose projected.

"No. So why don't you bend over, and have a good look at the mess you've made of my room." Again, without a word, she obliged. Ties scattered the floor and hung off just about every surface visible to the naked eye. He was far more interested in other matters. He ran a hand down her back, lightly tracing the outline of the snake with his finger.

"Mmm, lower," she said as she shivered visibly.

"Stand up," he replied. He spun her around and lifted her, pushing her up against the wall. She ran her nails down his back as they kissed deeply, and she gently bit his lower lip. Her eyes said it all. Her legs were wrapped around him and she could feel how hard he was through the light fabric of his boxers. Eager to touch him, she moved her hand down but he brushed it away, instead lifting her slightly higher before licking and sucking her hard nipples, teasing her with his mouth.

"Touch me," she whispered, "feel how wet I am."

"No, not yet," he said. Instead he set her down on the floor and she turned to face the wall, once again giving him a delicious view. The tattoo was still prominent as he kissed down her back, stopping briefly to lick the snake before his lips found her smooth firm buttocks, perfectly round. He held her wrists as he kissed her there, and she arched her back, showing him her need to be taken. Her exposure was just begging for his tongue, his cock, even a finger, but instead he slapped her smooth roundness and murmured for her to wait.

"No, fuck me now, please," she pleaded in a low moan. He let go of her wrists, standing fully and running his hands up her body, before firmly grabbing her breasts. It felt good. She gasped as she felt his weight on her, and she let out a single solitary moan as he finally penetrated her. His erection filled her up in one deep thrust, causing her to shudder and give in to her orgasm. She leant forward as much as the cold wall allowed while he held her firmly and fucked her, enjoying the feel of her tight warm sex around him. It felt like heaven, sweet and so very carnal, so natural. He almost felt like a different person, as if joining with her gave him a power he had never quite felt before and it grew with every sweet thrust. He caressed her breasts before pushing a finger into her mouth. She sucked eagerly, while his other hand played with her firm buttocks. Then, when he withdrew his wet finger he slid it into her asshole, moving his other hand around to play with her clitoris while he fucked her slowly. Her pleasure started to build again until she couldn't quite take it anymore, and she came so hard she cried out in pleasure as he felt every little muscle tighten and contract around his swollen penis. His breath grew shorter and he thrust into her harder, and he gasped as she whispered what she wanted.

"I want to feel you come inside me, Stanley. Oh God, fuck me till you come."

He moved his hands tightly around her hips, and thrust into her deeply. He could see the snake in even better detail now than the night before; its markings were odd, but he was sure they meant something. The pleasure was just starting to take over his body, building in the base of his spine, when he heard a familiar calling.

"Stanley."

"What..."

"Stanley?"

"What?"

He opened his eyes, to find himself back in bed. Slowly his vision came into focus, and saw she was standing there, this time with coffee. The room was still littered with ties.

"Ugh... I had the strangest dream, and in it you were

164

standing exactly like that, only minus the coffee," he told her, his voice slightly croaky.

"Oh really, and what did you do?"

"Do you really want to know?"

"I do."

"Put down the mug, and turn around," he said.

"But it sounds like you need the coffee," she replied, playfully but obediently putting the coffee on top of the dresser. He knew it'd leave a ring but the thought was automatic; it didn't matter. He stood up.

"Now," he said, running his hand over the snake tattoo that looked ridiculously similar to how he'd remembered it in his dream. "Bend over..."

29

"*To deal with violence in this country we need more Jane Austen's 'Persuasion' and less Quentin Tarantino's 'Kill Bill'*"
– Clive Woldfendale, Deputy Chief Constable

The D.I

Detective Inspector Thompson stared disdainfully at her morning coffee as Boris drove towards London Road. It was a dark thick brown, and strong; she imagined the sugar sludge gathering in the bottom of the Styrofoam cup. It was 8:30am and the sun shone brightly through the car window. She squinted, wishing she'd brought her sunglasses. She didn't want to answer the door with one half of her face looking like a salted slug.

"Are you sure he'll want to come in?" Boris asked, breaking her trance.

"Don't see why not, he doesn't seem like he has anything to hide," Thompson replied, a hint of annoyance seeping into her voice. She was always snappy in the mornings.

"I suppose," said Boris, lips smacking as he chewed his gum. That was another thing that annoyed her. It'd been five months since she'd been lumbered with her new partner, and she was still in the adjustment period. Boris didn't seem to mind – in fact, he seemed consistently unperturbed by most things. She couldn't make up her mind whether that was good or bad.

"I just don't understand what is going on here; first the Bogleur incident, then McBeard – I mean, Dennis Fotheringham... oh, whatever his name is! And then last night... that poor boy didn't stand a chance. Of all the stupid stunts they could have pulled. They said someone switched the knife!"

"Do you think there's a curse on this year's festival?" Boris asked, without looking away from the road. She shot him a serious glance.

"No, and that kind of talk is not going to get us anywhere - but there's definitely something not right. And without closing down the entire festival, I don't see how we're going to find out what before anything else happens," she said, her brow furrowing. There were so many people; it was going to be difficult to distinguish any real possible leads. That's where Mr Hobbes came in. Just then, Boris's mobile ringtone in the form of the Black Eyed Peas blared out from his pocket, interrupting her train of thought. Boris pressed a button on his Bluetooth headset, and answered it.

"Hello? Alright, mate!"

Boris grinned in a stupidly happy manner. Too happy, in the D.I's opinion, for that time in the morning.

"Hahahah – he was totally out of it last night!"

"No, but I drew a magic wand on his face. What? No, what? What did you say?"

The D.I sighed in the background. Boris did not seem to notice.

"No, mate. Have you got any?"

"Boris!" D.I. Thompson interrupted. Boris shot her a quick look.

"Nah, nah... yeah, I know, really got to go now. Chicken ciao for now." He pressed another button on the headset, and then turned to the D.I.

"That was just my mate, Bytey."

"Bytey? What kind of friends do you have exactly, Boris? I mean, what kind of a name is Bytey?"

"Nah, he's really cool. He's a proper geek; he's getting an RFID chip implanted into his hand; doing it himself with some mates."

"An RFID chip? That sounds... dangerous," Thompson stated, mildly interested now.

"Yeah, it is," Boris replied. "They could hit a nerve or it could get infected or he could bleed to death..."

"Okay, that's enough. I'm going to pretend I didn't just hear that."

"But, but but... he'll be able to do all sorts of cool things with it!" Boris exclaimed, turning back to the D.I. and dangerously gesticulating with both hands, which should really be on the wheel of the car. The D.I. allowed herself a sharp intake of breath.

"Just focus on the road, Boris."

As they pulled up to London Road, Thompson checked the address one last time. "Right, this should be it," she said, keeping her cool.

"Aye, Captain," Boris said. Thompson shot him another look; she didn't have to say a word. When Boris was by her side, she reached out and rang the buzzer. After a pause, they were let in. The stairs were quite dark, and Stanley's door was on the second floor. After a minute, she was about to knock, when the door opened to reveal Stanley. He looked slightly sleepy, and was in the middle of fastening his tie.

"Hello again Stanley, do you remember me? I'm D.I Thompson and this is..."

"Boris," Stanley interrupted, with a look of mild amusement on his face, "Yes, I remember."

"Sorry to bother you," Thompson continued, "I just hoped we'd be able to catch you before you left for work. Would you mind accompanying us down to the station for some questions?"

"Ummm... no, I suppose not. I'm not under arrest or anything, am I?"

"No, - no, not at all, it's just, we need everything we can get and you're perhaps one of the best eye witnesses we have at the moment. We've been trying to get in touch with you at your work, actually."

"Oh, right, yes. I've been out reporting on the Fringe,

168

I've just been writing the reviews and sending them straight through," Stanley lied, as he was yet to send anything through at all.

"So, are you free to come with us now?"

"Yes, just hold on a sec and I'll be right out," he said.

Thompson waited. Boris smacked his lips together, and she held back from saying a word. She had a feeling it might rain. She heard Stanley talking to someone; it sounded like 'will you wait here?' - a female voice answered; girlfriend, most likely. Then he was back in view, tie nicely done, throwing on his jacket and not bothering to lock the door behind him. Definitely a girlfriend, the D.I. thought.

"Ready?"

"Yes, let's go."

30

"The world is a great book; he who never stirs from home reads only a page." – Saint Augustine

Winnie Hobbes and Magdalena

"Are those angels in the sky?"

Winnie Hobbes smiled. "No, Magdalena, those are just clouds. Doesn't it look beautiful?"

"It's scary... so high up. Why don't we fall?"

"Oh dear, you'll get used to it. It's nothing more magical than anything humanity has achieved over the years."

Magdalena sat back, and nodded. It was curious, the way she seemed to take in knowledge like a sponge, but at the same time calmly accept all she was told. She was a logical girl, and Winnie liked that. Still, she wasn't sure if she'd done the right thing; she hoped it was the right thing, considering they were now around 30,000 feet in the sky and were was no easy way of turning back. The flight to Edinburgh had been delayed by two hours, and soon Magdalena's excitement had turned to sleepiness. Now, fully awake again, she was staring wide-eyed out of the window.

Of course, the only way to take the girl with her had been to adopt – but she didn't plan to remove the girl from her homeland completely, at least not at first. No, they would return to Ghana together until Magdalena decided what she really wanted. But Winnie already felt so much love for her. It seemed together, they could conquer the world. She wanted to show her so much, teach her all about the wider world, while she still could. Magdalena looked into Winnie Hobbes's eyes with a special kind of attentiveness. They were old eyes; the wrinkles around them proved that, but they were also kind eyes. And deep down, they weren't old at all. Magdalena didn't need a great deal explained to her; she could feel it more than she could speak it, the gentle bond between the two of them. It wasn't something that was easily translated into words, especially as she still had a limited vocabulary of her own. Only one thing troubled Winnie; she *was* old. Fit, but there was no denying her age. And of all the love, wisdom and support Winnie could offer Magdalena, she knew that one day she would have to leave her behind for another journey entirely. Then again, she reasoned, the love that one old lady could offer was perhaps better than no love at all. Her heart had not withered over time, bound by the aging body that seemed to remind her every day that she would never be immortal. She hadn't said a word of this to Magdalena; somehow she felt she didn't have to. It was as if there was a quiet understanding between the two of them – although perhaps spurred on by the day the girl had first spoken. That was indeed why they were on the plane now. Her words still echoed in Winnie's mind, and if she let it, sent a faraway chill down the back of her spine. Winnie only hoped they were not too late.

"Don't worry, it will all be okay, you'll see," Magdalena said. Winnie turned to face the magazines that'd been piled up in the pocket of the seat in front. She sighed, unsure of what to reply with. "Trust me, we can help," she said.

But help with what?

Winnie played with the ring on her finger. It seemed strange; she was fascinated by the girl and the words she used, the possible meanings behind them, but at the same time, and despite knowing better, it still made her slightly uncomfortable.

"How do you know that?" She found herself asking the question.

"I just feel it."

Winnie was silent; Magdalena was looking at her, with expectant eyes.

171

"Well, I hope you're right," Winnie said, affording a small smile.

31

"I would like to see a return to the good old-fashioned policemen: 16 stone and 6 feet 4 inches tall." – James Horsfall.

Stanley Hobbes

It was a room just like they showed on TV; all in all, pretty bland. Beige walls, a small table, digital recorder and a chair that seemed to be an enhanced version of what he'd had back in primary school. If he let it, it was going to make him feel very small indeed. He fidgeted with his hands, the way he always did when he was slightly uncomfortable.

"So Stanley, how did you know Dennis Fotheringham Ford?"

Stanley blinked. "You mean, Captain McBeard?"

"Yes, of course... that was the name of his act."

"I didn't – know him, I mean. I only met him at the bar after his show," Stanley said.

"And you were there for your job, as a reporter?" Thompson almost fired the question. Either she'd been doing this a long time or she was just bored.

"Yes, that's right."

"Were you by yourself?"

"No, I was with Lionel. He's a photographer who works for the paper, the main Fringe photographer, actually," Stanley replied.

"I see. And was he with you the whole night?" The D.I looked up from her notes. Stanley didn't know why she was taking notes. He didn't see any point as they seemed to be recording the whole thing, anyway. "No, he had to go off to another show, but we did share a taxi at the end of the night... is that a problem?" D.I. Thompson looked up from her notes, eyebrows raised.

"No, don't worry, we're just trying to establish the facts, that's all," she said, managing a friendly smile at the end. Stanley returned it, but that didn't stop him from fidgeting.

"So, you said you usually work on the obituaries? What brought you out reporting on the Fringe?"

Stanley shrugged. "Editor's decision. I guess they were a man short this year, or something."

"Ah, I see. And have you been enjoying it?"

"Not particularly. I mean, I wouldn't say that... it's been interesting."

"But you got into the habit of drinking on the job?"

"No, I wouldn't say that."

"But you went to the bar with McBeard after the show was over?"

"No, not with him. I think we must have met up with him around an hour or so after that, at the Belly Bar."

"What was he like?" The D.I. pushed.

"Pretty pissed, to be perfectly honest; talked a lot. Seemed an interesting guy though, from what his show was like."

"Do you remember if he said anything of significance?"

"I'm still trying to remember... I did have a few, myself," Stanley replied, unsurely.

"And you had that hook? You said he gave that to you on the night?"

"Yes, that's right. He went off to the men's room, but before he did he said he wanted me to look after it for him, so I just assumed he'd be back for it. But before he left..."

"Yes?"

The D.I's eyes widened; he'd caught her attention now. But something made him hesitate.

"... I can't quite remember what he said, it's probably nothing, anyway."

"Stanley, it's important you tell us everything you can remember, it might just be that –

The D.I. was interrupted by a knock at the door, before a serious-looking man in a suit entered.

"Thompson, we need to speak to you, now,"

The D.I. sighed. "Can't this wait?"

"No, it's urgent."

"All right, give me a minute," she said, looking agitated once more.

"Stanley, we'll continue this at a later time, okay? Until then, please try to remember any other bits of information you can about that night, I can't stress to you enough how important it just might be," the D.I said as she started to stand up.

"Will do," Stanley nodded.

"Okay, you're free to go."

"Wasn't I always free?"

"Of course you were. Don't let the door hit you on your way out," the D.I. smiled, before making her way out of the room. Boris smiled, nodded, and then followed. Stanley stood up, and picked his jacket up from the seat. It'd been an unusual experience, being interviewed by the police. In a way, it was just like being on 'The Bill'. All wasn't silent in the corridor. Two doors down, he could see the D.I. and another officer arguing through the glass. Their voices were muffled and he couldn't make out the words. He stopped, and still staring (spying) he started to put his jacket on, when Boris exited the room and turned the other way.

"... But why the Festival Theatre of all places, do they think we're fucking stupid?"

"Do I look like I know what the hell they are thinking, I just think we should get down there before..."

"I know, we should tell the staff to keep their eyes open, just in case..."

The D.I had been holding the door, and as she exited the room with the unnamed officer, she saw Stanley looking

175

sheepish, half wearing his jacket. In that moment, she looked almost like a deer caught in the headlights, at least her eyes narrowed and her posture changed to that of a defensive nature.

"Stanley... were you listening just then?"

He avoided, and then gave in to her gaze. It was difficult to lie.

"I might have been, but don't worry, I don't care about a story, it's just..."

The D.I. shook her head, and started to walk away, followed by her colleague, who shot him an annoyed look. Stanley gave chase.

"See, I have a friend at the Festival Theatre – she performs there. If something's going to happen, I'd prefer to know about it," he called from behind her shoulder.

"It's just a precaution, okay? I'm sure your friend will be fine," the D.I sounded agitated, and Stanley knew not to push it.

"Okay, but I'm allowed to be worried, aren't I?"

"Look, we have to go now but give me a call if you remember anything else. I'll be in touch."

He nodded, and he watched her leave. Boris was waiting in the foyer. They seemed to be in a rush, and he felt a wave of something he couldn't quite place in his gut. He had to think, hard. He'd been battling in the beige room, whether or not he should mention the Duke. There was no hard evidence, and then there was the incident last night with the marbles. Surely he'd sound completely stark raving bonkers. Surely she'd question why he didn't go straight to the police then. In fact, he didn't even know himself, apart from the whole thing had seemed so surreal. There was no proof that it'd been anything to do with Duke Ford - at all. However, he was up to something without a doubt and Stanley had a bad feeling about just what. It was then in the car park, that he made a decision. He took out his phone, and with a slight cringe, found the number in his phonebook.

"Hello, Rory? It's Stanley," he said.

"Stanley? Where the fuck have you been, I – I mean,

we've all been worried," Rory said. He wasn't sure if it was his imagination, but something about the editor sounded different; something in his voice gave it away.

"I've just been questioned by the police," he told Rory.

"What about - the murder at the Underbelly? What did you tell them?" He shot the questions quickly, as if he was firing at gun.

"Just what I know... but Rory, there's something else going on. I think Duke Ford's involved, or at least up to something. I almost got beaten up last night-

"Beaten up? Who by?" A hint of concern.

"Yeah... I don't know, some guy I'd seen before, think he might be connected to Duke Ford somehow," Stanley said. There was a pause on the other end of the line.

"Wait – you didn't tell the police anything about this, did you?" It was an unexpected question. In fact, if he wasn't so caught off-guard he might have found the time to be offended.

"No, not yet. I can't make sense of it myself, but... maybe I should," Stanley said, quietly. The thought had occurred to him before, but he hadn't really had a chance to think.

Rory sighed. "If you find out anything else, tell me before you go to the police, okay?"

"Okay, sir, but... is there a reason for this?"

"A very good one. I want to know what the fuck is going on!"

"I see."

"And Stanley?"

"Yes sir?"

"Try and stay away from Duke Ford for now... not sure he'd appreciate being linked to this."

"... Will try, sir."

The phone went dead. Stanley managed a small smile to himself; it was the same Rory, all right. Still, something seemed a bit off. It was mid-morning and the sun was out in full. He

177

guessed he'd be walking, wherever he was headed. Stanley supposed, since he was suitably dressed, it might be a wise idea to show his face in his office at least once this week. He wondered if Marcella would still be waiting when he got back; he hoped so. He didn't actually miss being in the obits office, which surprised him. Feeling a slight twinge of guilt for Clive, Stanley crossed the road and made his way to the nearest bus stop – he was fit but not that fit. Besides, he was in no mood to walk. Just then, his phone rang. It was Gill.

"Hello, and for what do I owe the pleasure?" He asked, playfully. He knew she wouldn't be too happy about him hanging up the other night, but it hadn't occurred to him she'd actually be worried.

"You know full well - what the hell happened last night? Do you know they took that poor boy to hospital? Are you okay?" The concern was there in her voice, and suddenly he felt bad about not picking up the phone when she'd called.

"Yes, I'm sorry about that. I'm fine, just been interviewed by the police about McBeard." He heard a muffled laugh on the other end of the phone.

"Sorry, I shouldn't laugh but that name... anyway; you know what you were saying about the Duke?"

"Oh God, not you as well. I know there's no proof and this sounds completely nuts, but..."

"No wait, I was going to say I think you might be onto something."

"Really?" The thought surprised him. "Even if I am, I wouldn't know how to go about finding out – Rory just warned me off Duke Ford."

"But he didn't say anything about me, did he?" Gill asked, conspicuously.

"Well, no..."

"You know I used to be a mystery shopper, and I'm exceptionally good at sneaking backstage when I can't get myself a press pass. I can do it, I'll go and interview Ford – he won't have a clue."

"Interview him, about what?"

"Oh, I'll just spin some crap about his presence at the festival, rah-de-rah-de-rah, you know, same old bullshit."

"And what, have a poke around his kitchen cabinets when he's not looking? I'm not sure if this is a good idea..."

"Well, I don't know! It's better than nothing."

"You're right, but Gill, if he's dangerous..."

"Don't worry, I'll be fine. I've got some write-ups to do though, are you coming into the office at all?"

"I'm on my way in now," he said, checking his watch. "I should be about half an hour."

"Okay, when you get here, I'll make myself scarce and you can finish my write-ups! Deal?"

"Okay... deal. You just want a skive don't you?"

"Not saying a thing. Bye!"

"Bye."

32

"It's only if a man's a gentleman that he won't hesitate to do an ungentlemanly thing." – W Somerset Maugham.

Gill Gallagher

An hour and a half later, while Stanley was sitting at Gill's desk surrounded by pieces of ripped-out notepad and attempting to make sense of the chaos tornado that was his friend, Gill was standing in the doorway of Duke Ford's townhouse. She had diligently rang the doorbell three times, and was just about to give up, when a muffled voice came through the intercom.

"Hello, I'm here to see Duke Ford?"

"Reason?"

"He knows why," Gill said.

"Who is this?" The voice sounded almost agitated, and definitely not that of the Duke's.

"This is Gill Gallagher for the Edinburgh Times... look, I did call beforehand so he should be expecting me," Gill said, sounding slightly narked now. She was in no mood to put up with housekeepers (she assumed that was what he was) with a God complex.

"I see... wait, please."

Gill sighed, and cast an admiring look at her new silver Guess bag. It had been worth the money; it glistened in the sun, and she squinted up at the large colonial style building with the impressive engraving above the door. It looked a bit like Latin, but she'd never really paid attention in school; everyone knew you only took Latin because it was a skive.

Her attention was distracted by the sound of disengaging locks followed by the opening of the outer door. It swung open to reveal an elderly gentleman with a rather sour face, pale brown hair and cheeks of a ruddy complexion. His nose was droopy and fairly red, as if he'd had a bit too much of a 'wee drop o' the creature' in his middle-aged years. His eyes were pale and shrewd, and peered beneath bottle-thick spectacles with silver rims.

Despite the hot weather, he was wearing cords and a plaid jacket, unbuttoned with a heavy beige jumper underneath.

"You'd better come this way," he said.

"And you are?" Gill asked.

"Humphries. Mr Humphries, to you. I'm Duke Ford's personal assistant and... friend." He said the last word as if it were almost an insult.

"I see," Gill replied, following Humphries into the reception hall.

"The Duke is in his office, please follow me," Humphries continued. The man walked with a deceivingly fast gait, and she imagined him in his rightful domain, high on a hill with a shotgun in one arm and a deer corpse on the other. She smiled, amused by the thought.

"And what, pray tell, is so funny?"

"Oh, just something someone said to me earlier. I have a habit of doing that; laughing at the most inappropriate moments."

"May I suggest you get that seen to, Miss Gallagher, or at least keep it in check while you are within the hospitality of this residence?" He shot Gill as sharp look, and continued on down the corridor, which incidentally, seemed to go on forever. Old portraits were hung and displayed almost in order of darkness and sourness of face, or at least Gill thought so. Then again, perhaps Humphries had hung them himself. His shoes, a deep burgundy leather, barely made a sound on the oak wooden flooring, whereas Gill's heels clickety-clacked almost uncouthly, making her feel even more out of place than she already did. She was glad when they stopped at one of the final doors, and Humphries made a gesture which seemed to say 'wait' in some long-forgotten sign language of the immensely-more-sophisticated-and-you-know-it variety, before knocking in a rat-ta-ta-ta-tat manner on the rather sturdy office door. She half expected to hear a cry of 'Come!' from behind the door, taking her once again back to her schoolgirl days. She checked her notepad was still in her pocket, and as the door began to open, she was greeted with the familiar regal features of Duke Ford. His skin was a deep bronze, as if he spent half a year cruising around the Caribbean in his own private yacht – at least that's what Gill imagined he did. His shoulder-length hair was brushed back from his aged face, and his wrinkles seemed to almost wink at her as he first pursed his lips and then smiled. The smile did not, however, extend to his steely blue eyes.

"Ah, Miss Gallagher, I presume?"

"Yes, that's right," Gill said as pleasantly as she could manage, "I hope I'm not disturbing you, Sir."

"Oh no, no, no, don't worry about that, come in! Can I offer you anything, coffee, maybe?"

"Oh, go on then," Gill said.

"Humphries, can you manage that?" The old man nodded.

"Milk and two sugars, please," Gill said to Humphries, who looked sourer than ever.

"Certainly, Miss," he said as he left the room with stealthy silence. She imagined she wouldn't like to have him in charge of her housekeeping... the thought of him prowling around in the night, quite frankly, gave her the creeps. In fact, the only one who kept her flat was herself, and she didn't do a very good job at the best of times.

"So, Miss Gallagher," Ford continued, casting a glance at his fingernails in a manner that looked oddly camp.

"Please, call me Gill," Gill interrupted, noticing his distraction. "Those are very... clean hands sir," she remarked, "very small cuticles."

"Oh, I was actually in the middle of giving myself a manicure. Would you care for one yourself?" The words were out of his mouth before he'd properly had a chance to look at her bitten nails, which she hastily (sheepishly) covered up.

"Oh no, I couldn't... I'm not very good at keeping them nice. Within 10 minutes of putting nail varnish on I always balls it up."

"How interesting," remarked the Duke.

"Not at all, it's just the way I am." There was an uncomfortable silence, which was gratefully filled by a brief knock, following by the opening of the door.

"Ah, that was quick, Humphries. Scones too! Excellent, on the game today, I see!" Gill reserved the urge to burst into laughter at that last remark, and watched politely as Humphries set the tea set down upon Ford's rather large desk, while Ford made room by shifting his manicure set to the far right. His slight fingers were elegant, if slightly wrinkled with the natural age spots that befell most people of his particular age group; old.

"So Gill, I had guessed you actually came here for a reason, am I right?"

"Yes, like we discussed, I'm here to talk about the Fringe and the role you are playing in it this year."

"Scone?"

"No, thanks, I'm on a diet."

The Duke frowned, but took one for himself and began to spread cream and then jam onto it with an almost elementary precision that Gill imagined could only have been learnt in the public school manner of the late 1950s. After a fashion, with scone safely prepared and delicately put onto the china, ready to eat, the Duke looked up.

"We were saying? Ah, yes... as we discussed." Gill raised an eyebrow. "Why do I find that so hard to believe, young lady?" He asked the question as if he was asking about her horse riding technique, or how much those premium leather shoes cost.

"I-I don't know what you mean, sir."

"Oh, pull the other one! Why on earth would you choose *me* to interview about the Fringe? I've nothing to do with it!"

"Well... you've become quite the familiar figure, and we're choosing people... might I say, close to our hearts, to give their little snippets of insight into the..."

"In that case, why wasn't I informed of this prior to this morning?"

"It was... spur of the moment. We press have to think fast on our feet, sir, as I'm quite sure you understand," Gill replied quickly, certain she'd tackled the question rather well, considering.

"Well quite," the Duke said, encouragingly, "I can see that. Indeed, I see right through it, what with all that's going on at the moment."

"I can assure you," Gill tried to continue, her brain now whirring at the speed of light as alarm bells had started to go off in her head. She needn't have worried.

"You want me to give you the inside track on my nephew, don't you? Stupid accident, never before has this family been so embarrassed, never mind the type of... establishment he'd chosen in the first place - this is purely off the record, by the way?"

"Of course, but really, I didn't mean to – I mean, it hadn't really occurred to me..." The Duke laced his (well manicured) hands together, reminding Gill of an evil genius plotting to take over the world. His mannerisms, however, were more abstract. "Oh like hell it hadn't. But I want to make no comment on that matter, aside from a passing reference which shall only be customary and beneficial to my nephew."

"Yes, well that goes without saying."

"May I point out right now, that I do not take very kindly to any intrusion on my private life, or that of my family's. In actual fact, I find it, and take it as a personal insult –

I no more want you here than I'd invite a vermin to my dinner table and feed it my prize stilton. I don't even see how you can call yourselves 'press' with such a low brow publication, and I will be watching very carefully – while you are under my roof, and otherwise. Understand?"

Gill gulped.

"Never mind; now, let's get on with this little pleasantry and let you be on your merry way. I'm sure you have men of much greater interest to interview, most probably with tighter jeans and 'manscara'. Jolly good."

Fifteen minutes later, Gill had shook the Duke's hand and was on her way to being shown out the door by Humphries.

"Oh, you don't mind if I just nip to your loo, do you?"

"No, of course, go ahead... let me show you the way," replied Humphries, who by this time only looked slightly aggravated. Gill noticed his cuticles were not quite so neat, but were instead the hardened, weathered hands of a gardener; her father was much the same.

"Oh, don't bother yourself really; I'm sure I can find it myself."

33

"Women must learn how to be complete nutcases and crazily committed to ideas, ideologies, interests, anything! We must be positively bonkers about something other than men." – Elizabeth Wurzel

Stanley Hobbes

All was quiet when Stanley returned to the flat on London Road. He'd managed to get away from work early – hardly employee of the month material, but for once he didn't really care. The hall was dark, and at first he thought Marcella had left after all; that he was alone, except for Jasper of course, who would be curled up asleep on the windowsill, revelling in the sun as per usual. He was surprised when he saw a glow coming from the living room. Small tea lights scattered around the floor, the coffee table, the fireplace, the window sill. Jasper was keeping well away, and looked rather annoyed that his rightful place had been filled with smelly burny bright things. The flat also looked unusually sensual, but he couldn't quite place what she'd done to it.

"Marcella?"

"You're home!" She came from the bedroom, dressed in a long black t-shirt she'd borrowed from his wardrobe, and nothing whatsoever on her smooth pale legs. Although the t-shirt was baggy, there was something sexy about her wearing it. It actually looked better on her than him, Stanley thought to himself.

"Yes, I wanted to get here early, to see that you were all right," he said, confused at the amount of ties she was holding in her hands. She put her arms around him, and he gathered her up and kissed her softly on the lips.

"Why the candles, and what were you planning to do with those?" He indicated to the ties.

"Oh, never mind the candles now," she said, skipping from place to place and blowing out each tea light with an enthusiasm Stanley didn't quite understand.

"I have something to show you, upstairs."

"Upstairs? You mean, the roof?" he asked, incredulous as she pulled him by the arm, ties still firmly grasped in her left hand.

"Come on!"

"Alright, I'm coming... this better be good."

They ascended the stairs and before he could stop her, she'd opened the (unusually small) door to the roof with ease, and gestured for him to go through first.

"Wait, how did you get the key?" He scratched his head. He'd never been on the roof before, had always assumed it was off-limits.

"The supervisor gave it to me," she replied, matter-of-factly.

"Just like that? He just gave it to you?"

"I explained it was for a good cause," she stated, impatiently.

"Oh, well that makes it all right then," he smiled, bowing his head under the low door frame in order not to render himself unconscious-by-concrete.

On the roof, he was met with an unusual sight; a blanket, a massive pile of ties, a homemade bonfire contained in a large metal bin, what looked like a picnic basket and a bottle of red wine with two glasses.

"What the hell?"

"You need to get rid of all... all this," she gestured to the large pile of ties.

"But why? Do you realise just how long it's taken me to collect all these?"

"Yes, and it smothers you. You need to take control of your life and stop being so obsessive about goddamn ties! It's symbolic, trust me. Claim back your life. Just think, what would Data do?"

"Data?"

"Yes, Data. He never wore ties, apart from fancy dress on the Holodeck."

"But... he was on the star ship Enterprise. They didn't need ties," Stanley sighed. He knew that underneath it all, she was right, but the Data reference was the most ridiculous idea he'd ever heard of.

"Okay, let's do this. Is that all of them?"

"Yep, these were the last," she replied, excitedly. "Quick! It's almost time!"

"Time for what?" He asked, perplexed.

"Look at the time! It's almost 3:16pm and that means it's Stone Cold Steve Austin time!" Marcella exclaimed, excitedly.

"Stone Cold Steve... who? And what significance does that bear on the complete annihilation of my tie collection?" Stanley just looked confused.

"I always notice when it's 3:16pm, it's the time to do or say something crazy!" Without any further warning, Marcella stepped towards the bin, and held the ties over the fire.

"Do you want to go first? I think you should start."

"Okay... are you sure this is safe? What about the environment?"

"Fuck the environment for one day!"

"Now you just sound like Jeremy Clarkson – of course, you look nothing like him. Thank God." Stanley took the ties from her hands, gave them a quick look over, and then nodded to himself. He turned to her, as she checked her watch.

"Okay, go!"

He dropped them into the fire, which seemed to burn brightly for a few seconds, before returning to usual. Stanley

188

imagined he could smell the materials burning; a mix of expensive silk and cheap nylon affairs going up in smoke. Marcella had already grabbed the next load.

"Wait! Not that one – that's my favourite," he pleaded.

"Okay, you are allowed to keep this one, but only that one. Come on, let's get this done!"

It took them under 10 minutes to rid the world of the collection Stanley had spent years accumulating. It felt strangely invigorating to Stanley as they danced round the fire in an almost primal ritual.

Marcella poured the wine, and together they collapsed on the blanket, kissing passionately.

"You were right, you know."

"Of course I was. I'd had all day to look at the ridiculous order you had that flat – I can spot OCD a mile away. My brother has it."

"Your brother? You never mentioned one before," Stanley said.

"I have more than one brother. There are many things you don't know about me," she replied, hands clasped over her chest. She looked relaxed and free of the make-up from the previous night. She was naturally beautiful, in every way.

"I'm going to enjoy finding them out," he said. She cast a worried glance at him, which made him laugh.

"You can try," she replied, cryptically. "So, do you feel good now?"

"I feel amazing. You're amazing."

In a moment he was kissing her, and she was responding with her tongue. She tasted of wine. He pressed his body against hers, and their hands were suddenly all over each other. They made love on the roof, with the very real possibility that Mr Jones the supervisor would walk in on them at any moment to check exactly what they were getting up to. It was somehow better, sweeter, and each little moan she made set him on fire. When they were done, and the sandwiches were all gone, they

189

lay together looking up at the clear blue sky. A single solitary tie – the one survivor from his collection – lay next to them.

"So, when are you taking me to Easter Island?" Marcella asked, breaking the peaceful moment between the two of them.

"Easter Island? You mean with all those massive stone heads?"

"Yeah, that Easter Island," she replied, matter-of-factly.

"Why would you want to go there?" he asked, confused.

"I don't know. I've just always wanted to go there. The history of the place just kind of fascinates me," Marcella explained.

"Oh?"

"It's like the whole struggle of humanity, survival thing. The story goes that some people one day got on a boat and found this plentiful island, almost like a paradise. They use up all the resources building the stone heads, and eventually fight over everything that's left until of course, there's absolutely nothing left to fight for. They all leave, or die, and now all that's left are the stone heads, just staring out into the sea with an expression on their faces as if to say, 'what just happened?' It's like the story of life. It's exactly what we're doing to our planet but on a much smaller scale... depressing, isn't it?"

"Yeah... now that you mention it," he replied, thoughtfully, "maybe those heads aren't as dumb as they look."

They lapsed into silence, and she reached out for his hand. He took it in his, and squeezed.

"You know, I wasn't expecting to find this here," Marcella spoke, interrupting the calm silence that had washed over them after the pleasure.

"Find what?"

"Love."

He was too shocked to speak. Instead, he squeezed her hand, and another silence fell over them. But it wasn't an awkward one. Nothing was awkward with her. A bird squawked overhead, bringing them out of the reverie, Marcella blinked.

"I have to go; otherwise I'll be late for rehearsal."

"Do you really have to?"

"Yes, I said I have to. I didn't make it this afternoon and they'll be worried about me." She started to get up, but he held onto her hand. She turned and looked him in the eyes.

"Marcella... just be careful, okay?"

She nodded, and something unmistakeable passed between them that didn't have to be spoken, or addressed, or broken down to give it meaning, bit like the stone heads really.

"Now give me back my hand."

He watched her leave, not tall enough to duck under the doorway. He was alone, but instead of tidying up the mess, he just lay there for a while, and thought about nothing, then everything. Then it started to rain.

34

"Bollo just landed in Big Apple, where is Big Banana?" – Bollo of the Mighty Boosh (via Twitter)

Granny Hobbes and Magdalena

Magdalena looked up at the sky in almost childlike wonder. It was as if she'd never seen rain before. Of course, Winnie knew that to be untrue.

"Does it rain a lot here?" She asked, reaching her hand out to gather the tiny droplets.

"Oh yes, that's a bit of an understatement," replied Winnie Hobbies.

"Understatement?"

"Never mind for now," Winnie smiled. "My, my, it's been such a long while since I've been here, I have no idea where anything is."

"Winnie, look at that, and her clothes!"

Winnie looked. A young woman wearing orange baggy trousers, a white and green checked shirt and scarecrow make-up passed on some stilts. Magdalena had, of course, never seen anything like it. "Yes, I should have remembered about the festival. I have a feeling you're going to see some very unusual things over the next few days," Winnie replied, amused at Magdalena's reaction.

"Look, that statue just moved!"

"I think you'll find that is in fact a man dressed as a statue. Watch him; he is very good at his art."

Magdalena ran up to the man, who was perched atop a mock-concrete block where a small crowd had gathered. For a minute or so, the man stayed completely still, before he saluted to Magdalena, and she jumped back in surprise.

"It is a man!"

"Yes, now come with me while I become accustomed to the city again... strange, being here. And to think Stanley's here somewhere. We could run into him in the street."

It was a nice thought; one that Winnie had not allowed herself to contemplate until she had firmly found her footing in the great city of Edinburgh.

"Where are we going?" Magdalena asked.

"This way, I think," replied Winnie, gently taking Magdalena's hand in hers. The child was happy enough to trust her, but that trust had been built over the period of a few months. She was curious to see how the young girl would react to the presence of strangers. She, of course, still had to think of Magdalena as a child in the strictest sense; whatever gifts she had shown were merely speculation and not something to be addressed... at least, not yet.

"There's somewhere I used to like to go... a place of a friend of mine. A small bistro called Scaly Tivets', I do recall. If only I could find it..." muttered Winnie. She would, after all, enjoy dropping in on Nigel after such a long time. She wondered if Stanley still visited there.

"Maybe ask someone for the way?" Magdalena asked.

"Good idea."

"What about her? She's pretty."

Winnie turned to where Magdalena was pointing, and was about to remark that it was indeed rude to point, when she was distracted by the sight of a beautiful young woman dressed all in black making her way along The Royal Mile. Her flowing hair was long and she had a dark but exquisite look; she almost seemed to glow. In fact, if it wasn't for the rain that made her draw her leather jacket close in an almost troubled manner, Winnie would have said she was ethereal.

"Excuse me, Miss?" The young woman stopped and for a second she looked serious, before she smiled. "Yes?"

"Do you know the way to Scaly Tivets'? I seem to have forgotten how to get there," Winnie explained, relieved that she had smiled after all.

"I'm sorry... I don't really know the way around myself," the young woman replied. Her voice was surprising, smooth and almost undoubtedly Russian.

"Oh, not at all – you're not from around here, are you? No, neither am I," Winnie said. The young woman seemed to hesitate, and looked almost uncomfortable before she spoke again. "Sorry I couldn't be of help. I'm already late."

"Well, thank you anyway!"

Marcella waved a regrettable response. Magdalena watched her walk away, but to Winnie the moment seemed again to hold little or no significance to their predicament.

"Magdalena, it's rude to stare... Wait! Yes, I know where I am now! This way, dear child, hurry up, hurry!"

35

"If in doubt, stick your left out." – Henry Cooper.

Marcella Dimitrieva

When she eventually arrived late for rehearsal, Marcella glanced briefly at the others as she left her bag on a nearby chair and began to limber up. She avoided her brother Dante altogether, yet she could feel his eyes burning into her even though she had her back turned. She massaged her ankle as she felt a slight twinge, and waited for the coming onslaught. But no-one said anything, each in their own little world – the way it had to be if they were to keep up their routine and perform together as one living, breathing unit. They worked as one, each part a vital cog in the living machinery; to be a work of art took a lot of time and patience. Although the show had just opened, they'd already devised some small improvements to the overall performance, meaning little insignificant changes here and there, only adding to the complexity of the routine. She supposed it added to the danger, too, but she never really thought of what she did as dangerous. After all, she was infallible, a goddess in the dance between time and space. Not that she really thought of herself that way; well, maybe only when she was in character. She was stretching each leg with experienced precision when Sergio came over to her, a towel hung neatly over his shoulder.

"Hello, Poppet," he said – it was a nickname she'd always hated, but she could never hate her older brother. His hair had been dyed a bright blonde, almost to the point of white, and styled in exaggerated spikes that came down almost to eye level. He wore the routine black, although not as understated as the other men in the group. Marcella didn't think that was because he was gay, but merely because he liked to be different.

"Hi, Serge, what have I missed?"

"Oh, father's angry at you. Where have you been all this time?" His face had a hint of mock concern, but mostly she could tell he was just happy to see her. She could see it in his eyes, green like a pure forest.

"None of your business," replied Marcella with a smile.

"Oh, so it's like that then, is it?"

"Uh-huh, until I say any different," she said, playfully.

"Is he at least good-looking?"

"Unbelievably so," she said, stopping her stretches and picking at her black cropped leggings. Because of her curves, she'd always been rather aware of tight clothing, but they were the most comfortable thing to train in. Her legs were muscular, but never fat.

"Another thing," he said, "the police have been sniffing round." She shot him a look, and a small sliver of dread crept into her gut before she could stop it.

"The police? Why?"

Sergio shrugged, and an almost undetectable detail passed through their eyes – at least, undetectable to anyone else.

"Who knows," he replied, "but we should perhaps keep a discreet eye out."

"They're probably just making checks of all the venues, you know, after..."

"Yeah, that's probably it. Still, be careful," he warned her. Not that she needed it, but she nodded, and arched her back in a graceful stretch that he was undeniably envious of. It released some of the tension; her muscles felt taught and ready for anything; which was always good before a show.

"Uh-oh," Serge whispered, but she'd already looked up to see Dante on his way over. His hair was dark, like hers, and he had dark brown eyes that seemed to hold a fire in them, always burning.

"Marcella, this is the third time you've been late for

rehearsal, you really need to take this more seriously," Dante's voice was much sterner than her other brother's. He was extremely serious about his work, but it could easily be mistaken for a bad temper. She wished he'd lighten up every once in a while.

"Like you, you mean?"

"Yes, why not? And you do know the police have been around? What is in your head lately, apart from that ridiculous CD you listen to every chance you get? You are in your own Dreamland, never mind his."

"Oh, shut up, Dante, I'm here now, aren't I?"

"Yeah but your head's still somewhere else! Always somewhere else!"

"Even if that were true, you can leave my music tastes out of it. And that's not why I'm late," Marcella stated, shooting him a look as she removed her wrap cardigan and placed it over her bag. She walked toward the trapeze on centre stage. As she did so, she began to hum the notes to 'There May Be Trouble Ahead'... not only a classic, but one of the songs from Brent Spiner's CD. It was the part right before Maude Maggart got shot, if he recalled correctly.

"Ooh, touchy, touchy," replied Serge, but he knew when to let it drop. After all, he remembered the days when the two of them used to watch Star Trek: The Next Generation on those cold, windy nights. If anything, he'd had more of a crush on Data than Marcella had. It was the ethereal look that had captivated his attention; it was around that time he really discovered he was gay.

"Well... Look at her, still just a girl in a woman's body..." Dante muttered as he left the stage. Sergio shook his head, and then laughed as his sister did an extravagant take-off from the trapeze ladder. Her hair was tied back in a simple pony tail and her skin was pale and free of make-up; she reminded him now of the same 12-year-old girl who drank hot chocolate and huddled under a blanket on those cold nights. But he knew

Dante wasn't giving her enough credit. Marcella was a woman; a very capable one, who showed promise, feminine power and infinite possibilities, if only she would realise it. Unbeknownst to her, he had made a copy of that CD. He rather liked it.

36

"The only control we have is the power of control over ourselves, no regrets, look under every stone, and never look back thinking, 'what if'." - @Slipfinger (via Twitter)

Fair Summer

Fair lay awake in bed, knowing that she could force herself to sleep no longer. She looked sceptically at the stones by her bedside; unfortunately they had not worked this time. It was time to be honest with herself; they had never really worked. It wasn't that she hadn't slept well – but the dreams had come in terrible floods that swept in and out like white flashes of terror, while she was left stranded in the darkness. Throughout the day she had been drifting in and out of consciousness in an attempt to avoid the visions that swept over her; the raging storm in her mind. At first it would be calm, cloudy, and the clouds would serve as a protection from the worst of it. It was more like a vague sensation of foreboding, a sign of things to come.

Sometimes, after a while, the clouds would pass and the sky would be clear after all; it was those days she felt lucky – of course, she considered herself even luckier when there was no dreams at all, sometimes not for months. But mostly, after one of her dreams and when the clouds had cleared, the images would come flashing down like lightning, striking her when she least expected it. The fear would lash down like heavy rain, all the while stranded in that dark place, the one from her dream. The place she could never quite remember – it was more of a feeling than a location. She wasn't really there at all – it was light, and she was awake; in her room, at work, surrounded by friends, or all alone. The dominant feeling would be there, waiting, weakening her reserve.

In the dream she had reached out for Jack as if he would appear just in the distance, but of course, he hadn't been there. She couldn't even remember his face; perhaps that was what made it so annoying, or the knowledge that the one thing she wanted, the one thing to make it all better, was somehow unattainable in this endless nightmare. As the scene unfolded around her, she had been helpless, forced even deeper into the darkness as she watched it take place. It was out of her control, almost like a graphic movie without an eject button. It was only later, when she awoke, that the images began to take on their full effects. At first, they made no sense, but throughout the day they'd start to get worse until she felt like her mind would implode. Her head would throb, she wouldn't make much sense and she'd lose concentration at entirely the wrong moments. What good was a sub that missed typos? So she'd called in sick. Her logic was to sleep, to hide, until hopefully they'd wash over her like a calm sea; another harmless dream, nothing left but the dregs. Even if it was not, there was no way to recognise the place in her mind. She recognised none of the streets, the people, the dark alleyway where the fire and smoke exploded onto the innocents. Then there was the terrible smell of burning flesh, skin, the screams, the panic that tore over the building... but which building? She didn't want to think about it – couldn't think about it. *Why is this happening again? Why now?* Yet the sun had crept in through the curtains and she had hidden from the day, crippled, unable to come out from beneath the covers. It was no way to live.

She felt guilty about work. They would no doubt wonder whether she was okay. She imagined them talking about her; imagined Gill had heard her fakery on the phone. Fair hated liars. Luckily when she forced herself to sleep a second time and even a third, the dreams did not follow her. Funny, how the sleep that had been the source of so much torment in the night had become a place of refuge in the day. A hiding place where she could wait for the passage of the dream in which she had weaved. It was often the way; the images had found their way out of her slumber and now haunted her waking hours. She would not let them. No, instead she'd be a coward. But what if it was not just a dream? *What if it's real?* Again, she could not think about that, for fear of it becoming true. She never wished death on anyone, but she would be powerless to stop it. What was the point in knowing beforehand, if there was absolutely nothing she could do? There was a chance it had already happened.

She sighed. She needed to get out of bed. Tried to get out of bed, but froze as new wave of false memories hit her. It was blurry, far off, yet an unusual feeling crept in to the back of her mind. Whatever it was, she knew it hadn't happened yet. *What if it's real?* She would get up, eat some cereal (completely wrong time of the day, but her stomach was empty and it was food) and switch on the television. She'd see nothing more interesting than the latest swine flu updates. Maybe a school protest. Okay, she wasn't that accurate but nevertheless, there would be nothing more interesting than any other day.

Her train of thought made her very uneasy. It was as if she almost expected it would happen – and if she really thought that, surely she had to do something about it? She winced; a glimmer of pain shot up her forehead, and she leaned back on the bed. She reached out for her water, and took a sip from the strong glass. It tasted old and lukewarm. As she put the glass down and stood up, she instantly felt the weakness in her legs. Nevertheless, her stomach growled and that was a good sign to make it to the kitchen. In an attempt to blank out her mind, somehow block it from any future onslaught, she ignored the ringing phone. Funny, she hadn't even become aware when the ringing had started. Instead, she moved towards the kitchen and switched on the kettle. Step one, sorted. Next, instead of cereal, some toast, and then a little bit of catch-up with the news. Most of the day had passed her by, and in a way that saddened her; a waste. She felt groggy, unable to remember the base elements of the dream; unwilling to remember. The phone had ceased its ringing, and the flat was silent. Sunlight flooded in through the kitchen window, and the world began to feel more real. The objects had substance, the kettle had boiled and she had assembled a mug of tea. She liked sweet tea, with milk, when it was available. She began to relax, as she moved away from the dark place and towards the small table to wait on her toast. She could hear children playing outside. A car went by. The faint aroma of the toast seemed to spark something off in the back of her mind, and she a vague look glazed over her eyes. It had found her.

37

"I am scared of my own hands." – Noel Fielding.

Stanley Hobbes

When the rain eventually drove Stanley to find shelter in the flat, he found his phone was ringing. Dropping the wet blanket on the floor and awkwardly placing the picnic basket (also containing the empty wine bottle and glasses) atop the table, he reached for the receiver.

"Hello?"

"Stanley, I've been trying to ring you!" It was Gill, her voice was unusually strained. He could tell she was outside from all the traffic noise.

"Sorry, just got in. Was ermmm... on the roof," he said, awkwardly.

"The roof! In this rain? Oh, never mind, I'm about 20 minutes away, I'm coming over," Gill said.

"What?"

"See you soon!" The phone went dead before he had a chance to protest. More or less 20 minutes later, a rather wet and disgruntled-looking Gill sat on his sofa. Her hair was stuck to her face, and her new Guess bag was looking slightly soggy; he hoped for her sake it was waterproof.

"What's with all the tea lights everywhere?" Gill asked.

"What do you mean?" Stanley looked around, confused for a second. "Oh, you mean the candles? I don't know why people call them 'tea lights', to me they're just little candles – actually until today, I didn't even know I had them." Gill raised an eyebrow, and cast a long look over the rest of the living room. Jasper opened one eye sleepily from his place at the window sill.

"This place looks like it's had the woman's touch," Gill remarked, her expression difficult to read.

"Oh, does it? So anyway," Stanley said, moving swiftly on, "What were you so desperate to tell me? What happened with Ford?"

"Oh, that man is an old crab cake," Gill replied. Stanley laughed, and sat on the opposite sofa.

"Did you get any dirt on him when you checked his medicine cabinet out?"

"No, nothing. Bugger all. In fact, it was far too... neat. I made sure I went to the biggest bathroom I could find too, his en suite."

"You did what?"

"Well, he's hardly likely to have anything interesting in the toilet he keeps clear for his guests, is he?"

"No but – how did you manage that?"

"I happened to have a couple of press tickets to Thursday night's Opera le Voltaire. Humphries was only more than happy to oblige."

"You bribed the housekeeper?"

"Yes, actually. Strange that, when he claimed to be Ford's friend," Gill replied.

"Suppose that's what happens when you treat your housekeepers like shit."

"Oh, it was nothing, not like the time I had to infiltrate Garlic Tony's lair. You know, the faux Italian pizza mafia boss who ran the fast food protection racket from his allotment shed? I had to get past his hound, Donough, I think it was. And every time I tried to ask him a question, his reply was always 'dunno'. Do you remember?"

"Yeah, that was pretty funny. I remember you called me up because you were tearing your hair out over the stench of the garlic," Stanley smiled.

"Anyway," said Gill, "it stank big time at the Duke's

house. Not literally, but there's something far wrong with being that neat, having no trace of... personality."

"Well, he doesn't actually live there all the time, though. Spends a lot of time up in Glendevon, doesn't he?"

"That's beside the point, he's here now and if that was me I'd have that bathroom in a right state by now."

"Of course *you* would but you have to remember, in this world there are people like you, and then there are people like me," Stanley explained.

"Wait, that's it! Do you think the Duke has OCD?"

Stanley shook his head. "That's not what I was getting at..."

"But he could have, right? When I went to interview him today, he was giving himself a manicure and everything!"

"A manicure? I never do that," Stanley replied, almost insulted. He was almost proud of his no-nonsense nails. They were almost as bad as Gill's when he forgot to trim them right down. Gill shrugged, and looked at her own, bitten nails. She wasn't quite so proud, but most of the time she never even thought about them until someone pointed them out – and mostly when she was in the salon and they wanted to get more money out of her. It was embarrassing.

"But what did he actually say?" Stanley said, interrupting her train of thought.

"Apart from all the usual nonsense? He described the press as vermin, made a reference that could insinuate killing me, and was generally a grumpy old sod. I made a mental note never to go back there again."

"The bastard. I bet he said it in a way that could be contrived as old gentlemanly sod talk and nothing incredibly serious?"

"Oh yes, but his eyes Stanley... they're so cold." Gill shivered, and Stanley only just realised how cold she must be. He stood up.

"Let me get you a fresh towel," Stanley replied, leaving

to find one in the utility cupboard. He took out a medium-sized towel and almost reached for a large one to protect his sofa, but resisted.

"There was something else," Gill mentioned, gratefully receiving the towel and shaking her hair through it. Jasper stared unpleasantly as he was hit by a droplet of water.

"What was that?"

"Do you know why the Duke would have tickets for some show at the Festival Theatre tonight? They were just lying there, on the table... but they didn't have his name on them." A chill went through Stanley, and he turned a whiter shade of pale. With the towel over her head, Gill failed to notice, and was now murmuring names to herself.

"McTavish... no. McArnott? No... McAvoy! Yes, that was it, like the actor!"

Stanley could only utter a single word. "Shit!"

"What?" Gill looked up, taken aback.

"Did you say tonight? Are you sure?"

"Yes, absolutely sure, the date was today. Some weird named show, Kaska..."

"Kaskadiori," Stanley muttered, going paler than usual.

"How did you..."

"Wait here, I just have to check something," Stanley interrupted a confused Gill, before leaving the room in a hurry and entering again with his work bag. Without saying another word he brought out the plastic folder Rory had given him.

"Bogleur was monitoring some of these acts... the list's right here. If I'm right... oh God," he muttered. The now-familiar Russian word for 'risk takers' was written down before him in black ink: Kaskadiori. But what could it mean? His head was spinning.

"But how...? Stanley, I'm confused."

"You're not the only one. We have to get down there," Stanley interrupted, "I have a very bad feeling about this." Gill's eyes widened.

"What, now?"

"Yes, right fucking now!"

"But it's raining... I've only just got dry!" Gill moaned, looking only slightly less worse-for-wear than when she came in. Stanley ignored her, and was throwing on his jacket before she had any further chance to complain. Gill swore under her breath, and realising there was no way of getting out of this, clutched her bag and looked out the window, doubtfully. Jasper did likewise, although he had no bag to clutch.

"I mean it, Gill! You can take my umbrella," Stanley told her, "It's a big one."

She turned back to him, a look of sarcasm on her face.

"Gee, thanks."

38

"Despise not any man, and do not spurn anything; for there is no man who has not his hour, nor is there anything that has not its place." – Ben Azai, Mishna

If it was any other day, it would have still been light and full of festival promise. But instead it was dull and foreboding; dark clouds hung in the sky, menacingly, as the rain poured down harder than ever. Gill had clung to the umbrella for dear life until they managed to thumb down a taxi, and now they stood outside the queue for the Festival Theatre, with plenty of time to spare before Kaskadiori's performance. People were huddled under umbrellas and the Theatre looked very different to how Stanley remembered it from the night before. Thinking of it, it was hard to believe he'd only met Marcella less than 24 hours ago; it was corny but he felt like he'd known her a lifetime. And he didn't do one-night stands, either. Something had definitely gotten into him lately, but he couldn't quite place his finger on what. The colleagues stood close together to avoid the rain; Gill looked longingly at the Theatre entrance while Stanley figured out what to do.

"Okay," Gill said. "So we're here. What are we supposed to be looking for?"

"Let me think," Stanley replied. "Shit... what would Data do?"

"Who! What?"

"Oh, nothing."

"Are you going to tell me why the hell we're here? Who *is* McAvoy?" She was looking at him, confused, as he pressed his fingers to his lips.

"Just... let me think." It wasn't the answer she'd been hoping for.

"Stanley!" Gill looked at him, exasperated. He gave her a sideways glance, but it was clear he was preoccupied.

"Can we at least go inside?" she asked at last, shivering.

"Yes, let's."

She took his arm as they tried not to poke anyone in the eye with their umbrella, artfully avoiding the slowly dissipating crowd until they could keep their cover no longer. Then Gill rushed for shelter as Stanley took down the large umbrella; she waited for him in the doorway, hair plastered to her face in an almost childlike manner. It would have been cute at any other moment; she looked like a wildcat caught in the storm. Stanley scanned the crowd; secretly he was hoping to see Marcella, but he knew she would be backstage preparing for the show. He supposed it was so busy now because of the weather outside – the show had turned out to be quite a hit at this year's Fringe. No sign of McAvoy, either. Gill had gotten a sense of his concern by now, and was looking at him in suspense. He ignored her questioning eyes as they inconspicuously (Stanley hoped) circulated the room. "If he's not here yet, he will be," he muttered, more to himself than anything.

"Who is he?"

"This isn't right... it's just not right."

"Stanley," Gill spoke softly now. "You're starting to scare me."

"Sorry." He looked around the room once more and then his eyes focused on Gill, who gave a small sigh of relief. He was still Stanley. She just wished she knew what was going on.

"Have you seen any police? I need to find D.I Thompson, or Boris, or... anybody."

"Boris?"

"Never mind... I should have told them while I had the chance. Maybe they're outside, I'll go myself."

"What, in that? You'll catch your death, look, just about everyone's inside now. People are starting to take their seats."

"Exactly, which is why I'm just a little bit tense," Stanley muttered.

"Are you going to tell me what you're tense about?"

"No time," he replied absently as he started to head out the door. Gill grabbed him arm.

"Wait," she said, knowing she would regret it. "I'm coming with you."

The pair braced themselves as they stepped out into the rain. Few lingered outside now as it poured down even heavier than before. Gill grimaced as the heavy droplets of water made it hard to see. Apart from the odd group huddled under a rare shelter, it was mostly quiet on the street now.

"I don't see them here," Gill said.

"No, I know," Stanley muttered, wracking his brains.

"Maybe they decided there was no call for alarm after all?"

"Maybe."

He started walking, searching for some sort of clue. Not that he really expected to find one. When he came to the alleyway, she stopped him.

"Stanley, this is madness. If you're really concerned, shouldn't we go inside and ask to speak to someone? Or call the police?"

"Wait – who is that?"

A small, almost recognisable figure was walking towards them, but because of the rain he couldn't make it out in any detail. The rain seemed to be almost overpowering it, holding it back.

"Who's there?" Gill called. There came no response, but the figure started to get closer.

"Are you all right?" Gill called, louder this time. Still no response, but the figure seemed to hesitate in the distance.

"Wait a minute..." Gill said. "Is that..."

Stanley narrowed his eyes, but it didn't help. The rain was coming down thick and hard, making it almost impossible to distinguish any recognisable features. But there was something... "Fair?"

No response. Gill looked at Stanley, concerned, she moved forward. He put a hand out to stop her. She was just about to speak, when a flash of lightning nearby make both of them jump, and illuminated the face of the stranger. It was Fair, but she didn't look anything like her normal self. She was wearing a large dark rain slicker, most of her wispy blonde hair covered up by its overwhelming hood. Small bits of hair clung to her forehead, and her face was distorted in an almost agonising wail. She was almost unrecognisable. They both ran to her, and caught her just as she was about to fall back.

"Fair! What's wrong, talk to me?" Gill cried out over the loud hammer of the rain.

"No... don't stop me."

"Stop you from what? What's wrong?"

"Don't worry about me," Fair seemed to stutter, and then hesitate, almost as if it pained her to even say the words. Gill turned to Stanley, who looked just as concerned.

"We need to get her inside, Stan," she said.

"No! NO!" Fair almost screamed.

"Why? Tell us, what's the matter?"

Gill was holding her now, rubbing her back in a way she perceived to be calming and helpful, but Fair was struggling against her now.

"We need to get everyone out of there... Just go, please, tell them to get out!"

"What? Why, what's going on?"

"JUST DO IT!"

"What should I say?"

"Tell them... tell them there's a bomb... or an explosion, just get them OUT!"

Stanley's heart seemed to stop for a second. Gill went

pale and loosened her grip on Fair's rain slicker. The rain continued, and a loud grumble of thunder erupted.

"You go," she said to Stanley, barely audible. "I'll stay here with her." The next few seconds seemed to happen in slow motion, and as he turned to run, she called back to him with wide eyes.

"Stanley?"

"What?"

"Be careful."

He didn't care about the rain anymore as he ran through the street wildly missing anyone in his path. His mind was blank of all thoughts except thoughts of her. *Marcella.* There were few people left in the foyer now; most of them had gone to take their seats. A line of people had formed on the stairs and were waiting to enter the main hall. Without thinking any further for fear of hesitation, a soaked Stanley took a deep breath, and shouted for them to stop.

"Everybody, listen up, you have to get out!" Only a few people turned to look at him, with curious expressions. The rest continued up the stairs. He took another deep breath.

"Everybody, you need to evacuate the building, please!"

By now he'd gotten the attention of the stewards, one of whom was running over to him with a worried look on her face. She had long blonde hair held back with a glittery head band, and big wide eyes heavily lined with thick black eyeliner. She was only about 5'2.

"Excuse me, sir, but what do you think you're..."

Stanley turned and, (probably looking more than a little deranged) followed by the steward, made his way to the emergency glass. The steward, realising what he was doing, continued to reason with him with gradually a increasing screech quality to her voice.

"Sir, please wait, you can't..."

"What am I doing..." he muttered, before bringing his fist down hard against the wall. He smashed the glass, and as the alarm sounded he turned to her and shouted louder than he'd ever shouted before.

"Look, there's a bomb in this place and we need to get everyone out, RIGHT NOW. Did you hear me, there's a BOMB, there's going to be an explosion. Now, are you going to help me?" As the foyer filled with people, the steward bit her glossed lip and nodded.

"Everybody, make your way to the exits right now, please! This is not a drill, I repeat, this is not a drill!"

There were murmurs of 'I don't see any fire' and 'what about our tickets, I hope we'll be offered a refund...' and even 'that guy, never seen anything like it... like something out of Die Hard'.

"Sir? SIR?" He turned around to see the little steward and what appeared to be her manager alongside her.

"Yes, look, I need to get backstage, I... there's someone..."

"You NEED to evacuate the building, sir, just like everyone else!"

"But..."

"Whoever it is will no doubt have the good common sense to do the same."

"But," he sighed, "I suppose you're right." The steward's boss was looking at him suspiciously.

"How did you know about this? The emergency services are on their way, you're going to have to explain all this to them!"

"Yeah... of course," Stanley muttered as he was lead through the front door. A large crowd had now gathered outside in the rain, most of them looking puzzled and more than a few complaining.

"Are you going to tell us what's going on?" One man called as the manager walked past.

"I wish I knew myself," the manager snarled, as he held onto Stanley's arm uncomfortably.

213

"It's okay, I'm not going anywhere," Stanley said, before the man grudgingly let go of his arm.

"But, where's the acts? Shouldn't they be out by now?"

"That's none of your business," the man almost growled this time.

"It is, you see I have a friend..."

"Oh God..." Stanley looked up just as the blast began to erupt throughout the building. The noise was deafening, and things seemed to happen very s-l-o-w-l-y.

39

"The insurance man told me that the accident policy covered falling off the roof, but not hitting the ground." – Tommy Cooper.

Bang. BANG. But then a curious silence. Noise, then no noise. No sound whatsoever. Faces in the crowd, people running scared, everything moving s-l-o-w-l-y. There were people still in the door when it happened. He watched as gravity seemed to vanish and they were picked off the ground, still in that slow motion, like something out of a movie. The glass shattered. Then thick smoke and deep burning flames from the inside of the building; it felt like his ears had just popped. Still no sound, only a high-pitched tone; where was she? *Marcella.* He was in a sound bubble. There were people all around him, but it was as if none of them existed; only she existed. Was she safe? All he could think about was her. *Marcella.* People, so many people. Some of them were on the ground. Others were running to help the ones on the ground. Some of them were screaming. A man; a girl; the same couple from earlier. *Die Hard.* A hand on his shoulder. He turned to see a man, his face almost bright red – no, not his whole face, just underneath his left eye. *Lisa Left-Eye Lopez* he thought, and repressed a giggle. She had been the one that had worn the condoms under her eye - TLC. She was dead now. The man was saying something, but he couldn't figure out what. *No sound. Turn the volume up.* Then something popped in his head, and he was back in reality, the sounds of the chaos flooding back into his system. "What?" he heard himself ask. His voice sounded strange, alien somehow... not quite right.

"Are you all right?" The man asked; a faraway quality to the concern in his voice. He was wearing a blue anorak, and his hair had a certain comb-over appeal to it that strangely suited his face.

"Yes, I'm fine... I need to... I need to find someone. Sorry," he said, although later he wasn't sure why he said the last part. What did he have to be sorry for? He started to walk over the devastation around him; it was surreal. The smoke made him cough slightly, and the rain didn't seem to bother him anymore. It was hot. The building was now on fire, and he could hear the sound of approaching sirens. He stumbled slightly, and rested his hand against a nearby wall to steady himself. There was another exit; he knew there had to be. Where was she? He had to find her. *Marcella.* He moved around the building in a daze, avoiding the stares of the people around him. Their eyes were all around him and he could feel them. *Why are they looking at me? It's not me. I didn't do this.*

"Stanley?" It was out of the blur, a moment of focus, his name. *Marcella. But no, that's not my name. My name's...*

"Stanley!"

"What?" It was Gill. She was staring at him, wild-eyed. Fair had almost disappeared into the wall, as if she wanted to just melt away. Gone.

"Are you okay? Where are you going?"

"I've got to find... got to find..." *Marcella.*

"I'll come with you..."

"No! Stay here." With that he was walking again, only this time he'd found his feet and the reality of the situation was really beginning to sink in. More people up ahead. His heart leapt when he saw the small gathering. *Costumes.* It was the performers, Kaskadiori – it had to be them. He saw them through the haze, as if he'd been running for miles and everything was faded. His eyes scanned the faces, searching for hers, but there was no sign of her. His heart was pounding in his chest, and he almost stumbled again. He could hear their voices, but there was another sound now; a strange, dog-like panting. He realised it was him. He tried to slow down his breathing, but coughed instead. They were talking in raised voices, but he couldn't make out the words. He frowned, confused. Why couldn't he make out the words? *Russian, remember? Oh yeah.* They seemed to be gesturing inside the building; towards the door. And although he didn't want it to be true, Stanley knew at once what they meant. *She's still in there, isn't she? Tell me she's not still in there. Shit. She's still in there.*

*

Gill felt swamped by the people who had gathered in the alley. It was almost claustrophobic, but she stayed beside Fair, protective and strong. But Fair wasn't really there; she'd clammed up; refused to talk, her eyes in a faraway place - off to a distant land. The location of said distant land remained a mystery to Gill – almost as much of a mystery as how Fair knew about the explosion before it happened. She watched as Fair shivered, huddled against the wall. Gill used the umbrella to shield her, almost like a mother would do for her child. Around her people were hurt, shocked, confused. Her ears were throbbing and she was shaking herself. She'd watched Stanley leave towards the back exit. Her mouth was dry as she waited. For what? What was the outcome of all this?

"Fair... I need to go after Stanley." Fair said nothing.

"Will you be okay here? I won't be long, I promise." A slight nod. That was okay. A nod was good. It meant there was still someone in there, somewhere; a living, breathing person. Gill managed a smile. She gently patted Fair's shoulder, and then stood, unsure of her heels. One of them was unsteady, and she almost stumbled. Vaguely, almost unaware of the action, she removed her shoes and went after Stanley.

*

Fair, now alone, stared into the abyss in which she'd hidden so easily in the past. But they were all around her now, just like in the dream, only with the added extra of Gill's shoes. They sat looking injured and abandoned beside her, awaiting a pair of dainty ladies' feet to fill them. They were pretty shoes, but Fair's feet were too small to fit them. Although it wasn't quite the same as the dream - the smell, for one, was not there – the scene was all very familiar. But the people around her (thankfully) seemed more dazed and confused than actually hurt. That was something, at least. She wished they'd all melt away and she could wake up in bed. *Wake up, wake up.* But she was really here. Somehow it was really happening; or maybe she'd stopped it from happening. Or had she made it happen? No, surely she wasn't capable of that. She thought she was alone, when a hand gently brushed her cheek. A child's hand, soft yet electric to the touch, she looked up. A young girl with black raven hair and dark skin looked into her soul with big brown eyes. The same girl found the energy to smile, her dress a deep purple that hung off her thin child-like body.

"W-who are you?" Fair asked, her voice sounding alien to her own ears.

"It's okay. It's all love here, now," the girl spoke with a beautifully exotic tongue. She seemed to be African in origin.

"You did it. You helped," the girl whispered in an almost unintelligible tone.

"What do you mean?"

The girl only smiled, and looked up. Fair also looked, and noticed the rain had stopped. Something had passed between them. Then, Fair smiled too.

*

The smoke was thick and black now, billowing out from the door. Stanley stood, unsure of what to do, unnoticed by the gathering crowd; just a little person. A misfit. He wanted to go in, to find her. The sirens were getting closer now. *Marcella.* There seemed to be a sudden rush of excitement from the crowd. An older man was being held back by two younger men,

218

and a woman. He was shouting. Someone pointed towards the door. Two figures were emerging from the smoke. One tall; slender but well-defined, the second shorter; more feminine and was being supported by the former. There were shouts as people rushed over to them. Stanley gave a sigh of relief as he saw she was safe. *Marcella.* It was her. She was okay. She was being held by the older man, who first rushed to hug and kiss her, and then to the younger man – maybe her brother. He had bright blonde hair, which was dirtied greatly by the smoke; it looked almost skunk-ish. He was gesturing back towards the door.

Marcella was shouting, looking around. *Turn to me, please, look at me. Let me see your face, I need to see...* And then she did, and it was really her. Her eyes caught his and in a moment they lit up. At the same time, the man she was with broke away and began to fight his way back through the door. The older man tried to follow him in, but was again held back by the others. Marcella turned to the door, then back to Stanley. Then she ran into his arms. It was another surreal moment, almost dreamlike, but as soon as their bodies touched, the earth seemed to centre once more on the two of them. It hit him like a brick, like falling, hard. Then she was in his arms and she was crying, and his heart was still pounding, and his hands were in her hair and then they were kissing. *God, I missed you. You smell like fire. You feel so warm. Your heart is beating; beating hard. That's good. So is mine. You're beautiful.* Her lips still tasted sweet. Then she broke away, her gaze caught on something in the distance, directly behind him.

"Who's that?" she asked.

He turned, to see Gill standing stock still in front of them. Her eyes were still wide like a wildcat's, her expression unreadable. She was shaking, and Stanley noticed, also barefoot. She just stared. It was then he noticed the rain had stopped. Before he could say anything, the door smashed hard against the wall, and two more figures appeared from inside, the striking dirty blonde and this time another man, slumped and coughing.

"Dante!" Marcella shouted. She broke free from his arms and ran to her brothers. "Get help, please, somebody help them!" He could hear an ambulance in the distance. He did not follow her, not this time; he was still the outsider. He felt Gill's presence as she stood next to his shoulder, they said nothing.

*

It was later when D.I. Thompson was surveying the damage that the explanation started to get a little messy.

"Are you going to tell me what the hell happened here?"

"I don't really know. I was worried after what you said earlier and then... I got a call and..." Stanley replied, still clutching Marcella close to him, next to an uncomfortable-looking Gill. "This is the friend I was telling you about, Marcella."

"You perform here?" The D.I. directed the question at Dark-haired beauty. Marcella nodded, speechless. Stanley turned to her.

"Are you all right? Look, we should really get you checked over," Stanley said, the concern showing in his voice.

"Really," said Marcella, "I'm fine."

"Thought you were supposed to be keeping an eye on this place?" Stanley asked the D.I.

"That's none of your concern," replied D.I. Thompson, "but I'm going to need to get eye witness accounts from all of you down at the station. And you realise, Stanley, that because of that little scene, you're going to make yourself a suspect in this case?"

"I can explain myself," Stanley said, "It's really not what it looks like. I got a tip-off. You know me, I'm just the obits guy."

"That doesn't matter, I'm going to need answers," the D.I. stated. She looked worn out, bags under her eyes. He didn't assume he looked any better.

Gill sighed. "For fuck's sake, Fair..." she muttered under

her breath. Stanley looked at Gill. Gill looked at Stanley.

"Where is she?" he asked.

"Who?" the D.I. asked, confused. Gill shrugged, and gestured behind her.

"You mean you just left her? Alone?" Stanley demanded.

"I-I was worried about you!" Gill exclaimed, the anger coming through all of a sudden in her eyes and the tension in her voice. But it was obviously not Fair she was angry about.

"We'd better go and find her, maybe she can..." Gill faltered as Stanley shot her a glance, "We should check that's she's all right."

"Right, well I'm coming with you," replied D.I. Thompson, who had (thankfully) been too busy with her notes to witness Stanley and Gill's brief exchange.

It wasn't hard to find Fair; she was in exactly the same place, albeit not alone. Gill narrowed her eyes at the small girl who seemed to be trying on her shoes. Her dress blew in the wind and looked out of place on her narrow body. The shoes looked about five sizes too big for her.

"Fair?"

To Stanley's relief, she turned to him and smiled; a lacklustre smile but a smile nevertheless. If she was exhausted, it didn't show on her features and in the orange street glow she looked like a pixie. The hood had come down from around her hair and it looked mussed but somehow appropriate.

"Stanley," Fair said, the relief showing in her voice, "Is everything okay now? Did everyone get out?"

"Yes, don't worry, it's fine," he replied, and looked to D.I. Thompson. "This is Detective Inspector Thompson; she wants to get all our statements down at the station." The D.I. nodded.

"And who is this? I'll take my shoes back, thanks very much," said Gill, directing the last part to the young girl who looked up, startled and wide-eyed as if she'd been lost in her own little world. Fair gave her a reassuring smile.

"I'm not sure who this is, but she likes your shoes," said Fair.

"I like my shoes, too, funnily enough," replied Gill.

"Are you... Stanley?" the girl spoke in a hushed voice, her expression now completely taken in by Stanley.

"Yes, that's right. What's your name? Are you lost?"

The girl seemed to hesitate, not sure whether to speak, almost as if she had said something bad.

"Her name is Magdalena," a familiar voice from behind made him jump, "And she doesn't usually talk to strangers."

Stanley couldn't quite believe his ears - surely not. It couldn't be... but he was too afraid to turn around just in case it wasn't. But the others appeared to be staring at direction of the voice that had spoken with such pleasant and warm tones, the same voice he'd grown up with as a child being read bedtime stories at night; of mythical creatures and Irish legends. He turned around slowly.

"Granny?" he spoke, unsurely.

"Stanley!"

40

"To wisdom belongs the intellectual apprehension of things eternal; to knowledge, the rational apprehension of things temporal." – Saint Augustine

Stanley Hobbes

3a.m. It had been a long night when Stanley finally drew the curtains in his second-storey flat. With six of them in such close proximity, it was anything but spacious. The world outside seemed a delicate, fragile place, that was capable of caving in at any moment; this was their protection. He was the protector; the only man. It seemed a bit caveman-ish, when he thought about it like that. Still, he somehow felt a responsibility to keep them safe as they all sleep under the one roof. Or ceiling, at least; his ceiling. He'd invited them into his odd little world, and it was almost nice, in a way. At least, it would have been if the circumstances had been any different and not quite so traumatic.

Magdalena lay asleep on Winnie Hobbes' lap, a blanket draped over them both – Stanley had insisted they spend the night there, as they were both exhausted when they'd reached the London Road flat. Winnie sat drinking tea – perfectly usual behaviour, in a perfectly unusual situation. He found it an incredibly odd experience, to see his long lost (well, almost!) grandmother sitting on his sofa. It looked like she hadn't aged a bit since the last time he'd seen her wave goodbye in her mock-safari suit and straw hat that they'd bought her as a joke. Her hair had grown longer, and looked no less elegant than it always had. In the village where he grew up, it was often thought best to tackle their issues with humour, so the hat had been a way of coping with the loss. Looking at her now, he felt

223

overwhelmingly glad she was back. He had taken out the sleeping bags he always kept in the cupboard for emergencies, and now Gill lay curled quietly in the corner, snugly wrapped in warm blue padding. Stanley wasn't sure if she was asleep, but he hoped she was okay. He needed to talk to her, but it could wait until morning.   Marcella had wanted to go to the hospital with her brothers, but Serge had reassured her. At the police station, she'd gotten a call to say that Dante had broken a bone in his leg. That was quite serious, for the physical activity the act required. But, with the venue closed down, that was really a moot point. He crept quietly over the floorboards, so as not to wake anyone. Jasper the cat was awake, and purring next to Marcella, who grasped his hand as he walked by.

"Are you okay?" she whispered.

"Yes, fine," he smiled. "Just glad you're here."

"Me too," she said. She looked beautiful and radiant even in the darkness of the room, her pale features no longer highlighted by the light of the moon. She was her own light, and he smiled. She smiled back, but she seemed distant as she brushed her hair back from her face. It had been more traumatic for her than anyone.

"Need anything from the kitchen?" He asked quietly, as he gently stroked her bare shoulder. She looked up at him with her dark eyes, and shook her head, smiling a sad smile. He managed to pull himself away from her with great difficulty, eventually kissing her on the forehead before retreating to the hall, careful not to squeak the floorboards too much on his way past. Fair was in the kitchen making toast when he walked in. She looked so small under the harsh lights, her expression a surprised one.

"Hey, it's okay," Stanley told her.

"Stanley, I... just wanted to say. Thanks, for... you know. Keeping my secret, like this."

He'd told the D.I. he'd received an anonymous tip-off. The story might not hold, but it was going to have to do for the moment.

"I don't really know what to say. How did you know what was going to happen?" he asked her.

"I find it hard to explain even to myself. It happens sometimes. I just... know," she replied, unsurely, as if the words were trying to escape her. He could tell it hadn't been easy for her; none of this had. She looked uncomfortable in the small flat, but she was there, and he was glad.

"How long have you had this... this thing for?"

"A long time. Too long," she said, very matter-of-factly. She brushed some hair away from her eyes as she said it. She looked wide awake, unlike the others. He wondered if she ever looked tired.

"But how...?"

Fair just shook her head, and he knew she didn't have the answer. Just then, her toast popped up from the toaster, making her jump slightly.

The evening had been surreal. He felt a pang of guilt when he pictured the D.I's face at the station, and how he'd assured her he knew only what he'd already said about the bomb... If it had been a bomb at all. *McAvoy.* Maybe she knew something was up, and it was only a matter of time before he'd be back in the same room, devoid of colour. That's why he needed to speak to Gill. Jasper had joined them in the kitchen, and meowed as Fair lightly buttered her toast; when she did it, it looked more like a fine art than a menial chore – which to Stanley, it was. If he could choose have his toast pre-buttered in the mornings, he would.

"You ever get the impression you're just sort of... clearing space?" Stanley asked.

There was a silence, before Fair replied. "I think I know what you mean."

"When you were younger, did you ever used to play the old Megadrive games? Sonic? Those were kind of tougher than they have these days; no save games."

"Yeeess...?"

"I used to play those for hours, not because I was really absorbed in the game play, not that I didn't enjoy it... but whenever there was trouble at home, I would kind of just blot it out. And I'd play. You know? The start of the first level was sort of like embarking on a journey, and it didn't matter how well the game went or how many lives I lost or picked up along the way, I'd know that by the time I was finished – the end of the game – everything would be better, in here," he pointed to his head. Fair sat down at the table, and offered him a slice of her toast. He shook his head, and she took a small bite from the corner. She nodded. "Yes, I know that feeling. It feels the same when I start sketching. Just mainly doodles now, but still."

"It feels like that's what I've been doing, all along. Maybe I'm waiting for the calm. Even through all this."

Fair replied, "That's good, Stanley."

"You know, I used to think the secret lay in doing something familiar. My games, your drawings. But in this case, I just don't know."

What had it been? Did it even matter? *The man's mad.* He pushed the echo away with a slight pull in his stomach.

"All I know for sure is that I don't want to go back to the way it was before. Like floating. Only half there."

"I know. But right now, there's nothing much we can do. It's just fallout, Stanley," Fair said, as she gingerly moved crumbs around the empty plate with her finger. It was almost hypnotic. There pair sat in silence, until it was interrupted again by Stanley.

"So, now what?" he asked, uncertain. Fair shrugged, and frowned at the floor.

"Your cat seems to be playing with something," she said. Stanley looked, and grimaced at the floor.

"Oh, it's another caterpillar. I've got them all round the place," he replied. Fair frowned again, and seemed to hesitate. Meanwhile, the 'caterpillar' crawled along the floor at an alarmed rate.

"I think you'll find those aren't caterpillars, Stanley. Those are Dermestes Peruvianus larvae... you've been seeing the beetles as well, I presume?"

"Sorry, what? Beetles... well, yeah, but not so much," he replied, slightly stunned.

"Probably because your cat takes care of them before they can develop to that stage," Fair smiled. Jasper, now scratching his claws against the wood of the doorpost with almost savage ease, meowed as if in agreement.

"Great, I have an infestation of... I can't even pronounce it."

"You can buy formula to take care of them. It's no biggie," said Fair, polishing off her slice of toast with another dainty bite. She seemed much more relaxed now, but then her eyes narrowed on the floor.

"Thanks, I'll look out for it," he murmured.

"What's that?"

"What? I don't see anything," he replied, looking by the door.

"I see a bit of fluff in the corner... should really dust more."

"No, not that – that, over there," Fair said, pointing, before bending down to pick up the object. Stanley recognised it almost instantly. It was the same jade frog he'd picked up from the Underbelly.

"Oh, that. It's nothing, just something I ermmm... picked up. Maybe Jasper was playing with it."

"It's a funny little thing," Fair said, looking in great detail at the small frog. The way it was carved caught the eye under the light.

"Evil, you mean."

"Evil?" Fair looked up at him, taken off guard.

"Yeah, evil. At least, that's what the shop assistant told me when I asked her. She said it summoned up 'bad juju', or some sort of yoke."

"Weird, you found it?" Fair replied, before very carefully placing the frog down on the table. Stanley nodded, not really sure of what to say next.

"So, Marcella seems nice," Fair seemingly nonplussed.

"Yeah, she is, isn't she?"

"Very pretty, in a dark and exotic sort of way," Fair replied, continued.

"I know what you mean," he replied, thinking that he knew exactly what she meant. And more so. Marcella was beautiful, like an exotic creature he could never really keep to himself. She demanded attention the way a light bulb demanded energy. And in a way, she shone.

"Am I interrupting?" It was Gill. Her hair was dry now, but she looked like she'd been dragged through a hedge backwards. Frizz central. She still looked paler than usual, and almost sweet as she squinted at the two of them.

"No... I think we'd better talk. Bedroom?"

"Ooh-err, Mr Hobbes," Gill started, but one look at his face made her rethink the joke. "Okay, bedroom. Wait... isn't that the frog you found at the Underbelly?"

"It's an evil frog, apparently." Fair said, without looking up from the frog's evil eyes. Now that she thought about it, it seemed to stare back with almost malevolent intent.

"I just... found it," Stanley replied to Gill. "Why do you ask?"

"No, it's just weird, that's all. I just remembered, I saw a whole stash of them in Duke Ford's dresser, before."

Stanley's eyes widened, "Bedroom, now."

Stanley closed the door behind them, as Gill sat down cross-legged in the middle of his bed. He'd never pictured her on his bed before; it was odd to say the least. Especially after the other night, before the whole Marcella business; but it was far more meaningful than that. He knew it, but did Gill? Could she read it in his eyes? No, that was silly.

"So, I feel like I've been hit by a sledgehammer or something. Do you have a hairbrush? Actually, silly question, considering it's you, you probably have about 25."

"Hey, that's not fair. I'm not THAT much of a neat freak," Stanley replied, feigned insult. "Here," he said, handing her the nearest hairbrush to hand – it just happened to be his favourite.

"Ooh, nice. Can I keep this?"

"No."

"Fair enough. So are we going to talk?"

"Definitely."

She looked at him in quiet expectation.

"Look... I'm sorry I didn't tell you about Marcella."

"Stanley, it's really not an issue. We're friends, that's all," Gill smiled, reassuringly.

"I know... I know."

But he still felt awkward to look at her. It was an awkward pause. It wasn't something he'd ever expected with his friend. *I'm sorry*, he wanted to say. But before he could say any more, Gill broke the silence.

"So, what do we need to talk about?"

"The frog. We need to work out how it's linked... what it means."

"So that frog there could be evidence of some kind? Good job, Stanley," Gill said, sarcastically.

"Thanks. And now you've told me the Duke has... how many of these things?" He asked, curious.

"Loads, I didn't count."

"There's no doubt in my mind now that he's behind all this," Stanley said, stroking the stubble on his chin. It was one thing about being a man that he could really live without. He narrowed his tired eyes. Gill sighed.

"So, what do we do about it?" she said, brushing the knots out of her hair. "I mean, do we even have a motive for why he could be behind this? It's a pretty serious allegation to make. People could have been seriously hurt, or worse. Why would he do something like that? Do you think it has something to do with Bogleur? Maybe he failed to do things the back-handed sleazy way, and that somehow makes Ford think he can get away with... well, with this?"

"I don't know, maybe he's senile, but we have to go back to the police station. I think we should go first thing in the morning, and spill everything," he replied.

"Everything? You think that they'll take us seriously?" Gill raised her eyebrows.

Stanley raised his own eyebrows. "As we can keep Fair's secret... But, then again, I might have a better idea..." he said, intentionally ignoring the last question.

"Going to share?" Gill nodded, placing the hairbrush down firmly on the bed as she said it. He still couldn't read her bambi eyes, or look into them for long. It was like looking into the sun; too long and you'll burn your retinas.

"Nope, just follow my lead. And get some rest."

41

"Enough is enough! I have had it with these motherfucking snakes on this motherfucking plane!" – Samuel L Jackson, 'Snakes on a Plane'.

At first, the cool blue of the walls hurt his eyes as the elevator swished closed behind him. He was back in the dream again, a far cry from the warm bed he was sharing with Marcella. He hadn't wanted to fall asleep; he'd wanted to watch her, her soft skin, her soft sweet breaths in and out as she slumbered. To feel her firm, supple naked body against his as they entwined in post-coital bliss. Instead, he was here, and it was happening... Again. There was only silence, pregnant with intent as he faced the empty corridor. And although he knew what was coming, it was the anticipation that made it ten times worse. He wanted to wake up, but instead he was helpless, a slave to the dream. *Oh no, God no, not again, please not again... If I have to look at anything, just one, terrible image, for the rest of my life, then let it be anything – anything – but not those eyes. Not again.* Yes, he knew it was coming. This time, he was dressed in his usual attire. The same blue tie, blending nicely with the walls; *blues, always blues.* But he frowned as he noticed an added extra. He was holding something in his right hand; a small, hard object. He didn't even have to look to know it was the jade frog. *It's bad juju, put it down, why are you holding it, don't you know it's bad juju? But... she's bad juju, too. Maybe it takes one to defeat another?* He moved the frog around thoughtfully in his hand, as if it were simply a toy he'd picked up, maybe from the Jenner's' toy department. But he doubted they'd sell anything that looked quite so ugly and so... *evil.* Not to children, not to anybody. He felt himself moving forward; one foot in front of the other. Exactly the same way he always moved towards certain doom in this dream. Still, he wanted to force his eyes shut, to stop himself from seeing her figure as it ran across his vision. Or at least, the thing that wasn't quite her. The thing that had been her, but had been so hideously morphed over time by his warped memories, the deluge of emotion that had slowly developed into... well, this thing. This scraping, needing, soulless being that craved a warmth that it could no longer know. He was sure it'd eat him alive one day, if he let it, for it was no longer Lorraine at all. Still, the corridors beckoned. The air felt fuzzy and thick. *Lost in the maze, I'm looking around, and I'm trying to find my way out but each and every time I'm here I'm unable to follow any other route than the one she wants me to take. It won't let me go. Bad juju. Protect me, help me, save me from her.*

It would play out the same way as it always did, and he was unable to stop it. He remembered Gill's advice; *lucid dreaming. You can do it.* But could he? Did he really want to try after last time? The frog felt almost hot in his hand now. He felt himself jump slightly, still in the bed yet standing before her as she ran across the distance in front of him. The same white dress... Just a glimpse. He moved forward, to that same point. It was impossible to sift through the confusion, to overcome the dreamlike veil that dropped over him like – well, like a dream. Except he knew by now, it was a nightmare. He could feel his heart in his chest, beating faster. It was the game, always back to the same game. *The chase.* It was always his turn to chase her, before it would be reversed into some horrible dependency that he had no way of stopping. *Dependent on what? I don't want this. I don't want you. Leave me alone.* He could hear the words in a faraway sense, almost as if he was hearing them underwater, and he took him a while before he realised he was the one saying them. His lips were moving, but the sound was muffled. He laughed. *I'm talking into my pillow, aren't I? Marcella, wake me up. I love you, now wake me the hell up.*

Did he love her? Yes, he thought he did. It was a wonderful thought. But the warmth of the feeling soon turned to icy cold shivers, as he heard her laugh from behind his back. It was razor sharp, and pierced through the air like broken glass. *Voice of broken glass, damaged vocal chords. You did this to yourself.* He was thankful she was behind him, sparing him from the sight of her dead eyes. Her hands reached out for his back, and he felt her fingers icy cold against him, nails scraping through his clothes, against the skin. Dead nails, blackened nails, veins standing out on the hands. He didn't have the strength to move, to resist, to push her away. He was paralysed to the horror of her touch. Then her hand reached out to the front, and he saw he'd been right, exactly as he'd pictured it. He could imagine the rest of her, as she leaned up tight against him now. He could feel such a terrible coldness, like icy pins and needles. *So cold.* He imagined the coldness would consume him, if he let it; like she would consume him. But even the warmth of his blood could not bring nourishment to the shrivelled blackened pit of her heart. *Nothing can help you now, so don't even try.* But she didn't want to consume him. It soon became obvious that she wanted something else entirely. *What are you doing?* Her hand was now unfastening his trousers, the button and then the fly. Now she was reaching... *No, don't do this. Please.* But she did, and then she was. He shut his eyes and squeezed the frog, as she squeezed him. It was a sort of excruciating pleasure, one that he really didn't want to bear. He groaned, wanting to tell her to stop. Unable to tell her to stop. *Please, make this go away. Stop it, now, please. Lorraine... no. Oh God, what are you doing to me...* It was slow, and all the time he could feel her eyes bearing into the back of his head, could imagine them in his mind. *Dead eyes... wide eyes.* He squeezed the frog again in his hand, turning it over with his fingers, the only bit of reality he could control. He bit his lower lip and pleaded in his mind for it to stop. She seemed to relinquish her hold, instead drawing her attention to the thing he held in his hand. It seemed to be getting hotter the longer he held it.

"What's that?" the voice asked, but it wasn't quite what he was expecting her to sound like. The broken glass texture was gone, and that seemed to spark a distinct change in the dream. Suddenly things seemed to be breaking apart, moving very slowly as if the walls would fall around them. But the only movement he could feel was her hand around his...Momentarily confused, he asked, *"What?" Am I talking out loud? Did I... say that... out loud. L-o-r-r-a-i-n-e. S-t-o-p.* "Your hand, what's that in your...

"What?"

"Stanley? What's that in your hand?"

It didn't make any sense, and suddenly he was falling away from the coldness, away from the blue walls and (*thank God*) away from her. *Lorraine.* Falling through a bed of broken eggshells, into the darkness, gradually becoming brighter until...

He woke up with a start. Marcella was looking at him, her eyes wide and concerned, the spell of the nightmare broken; the shame gone. He groaned, and rubbed the sleep from his eyes. "Are you okay? You were sweating, looked like you were having a nightmare. What's that you're holding in your hand?" Marcella asked, her hand resting gently now on his shoulder. It was warm, a nice hand. Smooth skin. Perfect. He tried to vanquish the image of the nightmare hand from his mind. He looked down. He was holding something. He opened his palm, to see the small jade frog greet him a good morning. Its evil eyes stared ferociously up at him. He laughed.

"That's weird... I swear I dreamt about this frog," he said. The delicate fabric of the dream had been torn, and it no longer seemed like bad juju at all. In fact, the frog almost seemed like his protector. *Thanks,* he thought.

"Why would you want to dream about a frog?" she smiled now, the concern in her eyes, for now, banished. He shrugged, unable to answer the question.

"Why would I want to bring it to bed with me? I don't

recall doing so, yet I'm holding the ugly beast in my hand."

"Not ugly. Just... aesthetically challenged, maybe," she replied, before kissing him sweetly on the nose. He smiled back at her. There was one pleasant thing he remembered from the dream, and that was the feeling he'd had when he thought of her. The sun shone through the window, illuminating her pale skin and the messy dark mane of hair that so perfectly framed her features. A long curl crept over her small nose, and she brushed it back. Even better, when she moved her arm across the bed, the sheet pulled back to reveal that she was naked. He saw just enough of her pert breasts to want more. All thoughts of the dream were now entirely forgotten.

"You look so good in the mornings," he told her.

"Well, you don't," she teased back.

"Ha ha ha, come here, I'm going to get you for that..."

42

"I want to have a threesome with Rupert Murdoch and George Bush Jr." – Maynard James Keenan

It was a hot August day outside, with no sign of yesterday's rain; the kind of day the Fringe was invented for, yet the atmosphere was a rather sombre one. As the pair approached Duke Ford's residence, Gill clutched Stanley's arm tightly, nervously. He didn't stop her.

"I said I never wanted to come back to this place," she grumbled, keeping her head low to avoid any unwelcome gaze from the windows above.

"Never say never," Stanley said, coolly.

"Are you sure we can pull this off?"

Stanley nodded, calmly. He wasn't as calm on the inside as he was on the outside, but the cool demeanour he projected to Gill was one that he'd like to believe he was capable of feeling on the inside, too. James Bond, eat your heart out. Humphries let them in, and immediately Gill made her way through the hall with her clickety clack heels that weren't quite comfortable ever since the heel had become loose.

"I'm sorry, is he expecting you?" Humphries called after her, expressing a worried glance at Stanley. Well, as worried as his face could allow, which, really was not very much.

"He can bloody well expect all he likes! In the office?" Gill called behind her.

Humphries nodded. Stanley followed Gill's lead, and nervously fumbled with the frog in his pocket. *Bad juju.* She was way ahead of him, past all the horrible paintings that adorned the wall, and already stopping outside a thick wooden door. She looked like she was going to pound on it with her fist.

He felt butterflies in his stomach, and not the good kind. He motioned for her to stop for a moment. Humphries was still behind them, looking bewildered. Gill mouthed, '*what?*' as he caught up with her, annoyed at the implication that she had to wait for his permission. She looked at him, questioningly, as if to say '*can we just get this over with?*'. He nodded. She knocked on the door, three polite raps. There was a silence on the other end. Stanley fidgeted. Humphries looked like he was about to speak. Gill reached for the door. But before she could grip the handle, it swung open to reveal the Duke in his elaborate dressing gown. He stared at them with piercing eyes. They stared back at him. He raised an eyebrow. He looked haggard, old and almost frail as he stood in the doorway, his hair mussed and a far cry from his usually very presentable – if slightly eccentric – self. Eventually Gill broke the silence.

"Just got up, have we? Did we not get much sleep?" she asked, accusingly.

"Actually, it's a smoking jacket," the Duke sneered, "not that you would know."

"You look like an old pimp," she replied, "All dried up and washed-out."

"What, pray tell, are you doing here? Humphries, get my gun, would you..."

"Unfortunately, shooting them is not an option, 'Sir'," he almost spat out the last word.

"Hmm, you're probably right. Well, can you at least poison their tea?" The Duke asked dryly, as he motioned for the pair to enter his office.

"Will see what I can do," Humphries replied detachedly, as he sauntered off down the hall. He was unusually light on his toes, Stanley thought - it was a most definite saunter, as compared say, an amble, or a mince. For Humphries was most definitely not gay. But he did seem secretly happy about the whole scenario. Gill and Stanley stood in front of Duke Ford, Gill with her arms crossed, and Stanley looking ever-so-slightly

237

awkward. They were hardly the deadly duo, or even good cop, bad cop. The Duke motioned for them to sit, as he took out another cigar from the box on his table. It really was his smoking jacket.

"So," the Duke said, offering first Stanley then Gill a cigar from the both. Both declined. "What can I do for both of you?"

"For starters, you can tell us why you almost killed a theatre full of people last night," Gill said. Even through her reluctance to return here, she seemed to be taking the lead, almost as in some sort of defence mechanism. The Duke was silent. "Well?" Gill goaded. Stanley bit his lip. Duke Ford put down the cigar, and seemed to grit his teeth.

"I beg your pardon?" he growled, almost like an angry dog that was well and truly on the chain. Only the Duke was not on any sort of chain, he was most definitely off the chain, and Stanley was very aware of that fact indeed.

"I said..."

"I know what you said, young lady, but why on earth you are saying it to me is another matter. Do you have any idea what you are implying? Or indeed, who I am?"

"We know exactly who you are," Stanley said, finally speaking up, "and what you're doing. Why would you do it? Wish I knew."

"Then why are you accusing me of... of this?"

Stanley took out the jade frog from his pocket, and placed it down on the table. Duke Ford twitched, but apart from that, did not react.

"What did McBeard ever do to you? Was it intentional, or did he just get in the way?"

"I don't... I don't know what you are talking about," The Duke muttered. He didn't look either of them in the eye, either. It was then Stanley saw the initials embossed on the Duke's robe, and it struck him.

"Wait a minute... Ford. Duke Edmund Ford..." said

238

Stanley, almost inaudibly, Gill ignored him.

"Don't tell me you're innocent. He was nervous about this frog before he... well, before he was murdered! And I found a whole stash of them upstairs in your drawer, how can you explain that?"

"If you must know, Argos delivered a whole box load of them by mistake," the Duke replied, indignantly. Stanley's mind was busy whirring away. *What had been McBeard's name? Dennis... Fotheringham... Ford! He knew there'd been something similarly eccentric about the two men. Of course – they had to be!*

"He was your brother! You killed your own brother!" Stanley exclaimed, catching Gill (and Ford) completely off-guard.

"I did nothing of the sort!"

"But you're not denying you're related?"

The Duke seemed to consider this, before slowly shaking his head from side-to-side, almost as if in disappointment with Stanley. "Dennis? That man was no more a brother to me than a sewer rat. And now... now you're accusing me of murder? Is that it?" the Duke asked, incredulously.

"But you wouldn't do that yourself, would you? You'd get someone else to do your dirty work... by the name of McAvoy, is it?" Stanley asked. The Duke was staring at the frog on the table. It stared back at him with its evil eyes. Gill picked up the pace where Stanley left off.

"Why the hell would you want to ruin your own nephew's show? Was the other boy getting all the attention, or was it all just another embarrassment for you? Did Uncle Ford just have to make it all better, huh?" She paused for effect, the Duke remained silent.

"You knew Stanley saw you with the knives, saw what you did. And you tried to have him beaten up! How could you be so stupid? Who do you think you are, I mean, you're hardly Garlic Tony!" It was hard to tell what the Edmund Ford's reaction was. He was staring at the frog, eyes averted and completely still, although it was hard to tell if he was shaking from the force he was exceeding on the table, or from something else. Either way, he looked like he was about to explode, and not in a good way.

"What else have you done? Why are you doing this to good people? Do you know what happened to Bogleur? What really happened to him?" Gill demanded. Even Stanley thought she'd taken it a bit too far; there was no evidence, at least that *he* knew of, that suggested any foul play in Bogleur's death. Aside from the phone call... The Duke's head shot up, almost as if something had snapped inside his mind. His eyes looked madly around, first at Gill, then focusing on Stanley, who was beginning to wonder what was taking Humphries so long with the tea. The Duke's hand bashed down on the table, causing the manicure set to fall to the floor. Something smashed.

"I'll tell you what you need to know about Bogleur! You know that little bitch, the little hole you've been using? Not quite so innocent, there!" This time it was Stanley's turn to be taken off-guard. "W-what... do you mean?"

"Why don't you ask *her!*" the Duke cried, a look of either evil or pure insanity in his eyes.

"So are you admitting it, then?" Gill asked.

"Admitting no such thing, now why don't you just fuck off the pair of you, before you find yourselves up to your necks in it. I know you're all in it, together! But you're not taking me; you're not taking me back to that bloody..."

"What?" Gill asked, confused. "He's lost the plot..."

"You've been caught, Ford, you can't get out of this one," Stanley said.

"Also, you broke your nail varnish," Gill smirked. The Duke appeared to be nonplussed at the latter remark.

"You know, those are some pretty fucking serious accusations you're tossing around without a care or a thought. So disrespectful. I hope you know what you are doing, and the consequences of your actions. And by the way, it's not me you need to worry about now. You should tell your little whore to watch her back," the Duke sneered snarkily. His right eyelid seemed to be twitching and his voice was becoming increasingly shrill, "and don't worry about me. I'm quite mad," he continued, reaching into his desk drawer.

"Well, at least he knows it," Gill muttered. Stanley ignored his friend, suddenly feeling quite nervous of Ford. He was indeed quite mad. It was quite obvious. Stanley was surprised he hadn't noticed before now. The Duke seemed to be reaching for something unseen, and then suddenly it came into view. It was a shotgun. He raised it to eye-level, his hands shaking in the process at the weight of the massive weapon.

"Do you have a licence for that?"

"Shut up. Of course I do," the Duke replied. Not that it really mattered, to a mad man. Gill gave Stanley a worried glance. Stanley gave the shotgun – which was now staring him right in the eye – a worried glance, before a loud knock at the door made everyone jump.

"Sir!" It was Humphries.

"What? I'm rather in the middle of something here, Humphries!"

"I tried to stop them, but..." The Duke's housekeeper was interrupted by a familiar (to Stanley) female voice.

"Duke Ford? It's the police; we're here to arrest you on the suspicion of murder. Open the door, please," D.I. Thompson said, and not a moment too soon.

43

"The hardest part is knowing I'll survive." - Emmylou Harris, 'Boulder to Birmingham'

The flat was much quieter by the time Stanley arrived back home. Gill had gone back to her flat to get changed for work, after clearing it with a raging Rory (*are you actually saying that you two still work here?*)

Fair was already in the office, having left for her own place before Stanley and the others had even woken up. As he stepped into the hallway, a floral note lay on the table, scribbled in very familiar handwriting. It read:

Dearest Stanley,

I have taken Magdalena back to the hotel, but look forward to catching up with you later in the day. It would seem you have much to sort out. Lovely to see you again.

Yours,

Granny Hobbes.

x

Stanley smiled vaguely, and left the note where it was. He heard a noise from the bedroom, before Marcella called out, "Stanley? Is that you?"

"Yeah, I just got back," he replied, not even finished the sentence as she appeared in the hallway and put her arms around him on tippie-toes. She smelled nice, and he sighed into her hair, losing himself momentarily in her presence. Eventually she released him, and took a step back.

"I've just been having a clear-up around here, you know, after last night..." she continued, stepping through to the living room. "I was hoping it would have been all done by the time you got back, but it's not quite there yet."

"You don't have to do that," Stanley replied, as he stood in the doorway.

"I know, but I want to."

"But still, you don't live here, it's none of your concern," he said.

"Don't be silly, it's..." she faltered, turning to him now with blankets in hand. She'd picked up on something in his voice, something not quite right. Her eyes met his, questioning.

"Is there something wrong?" she asked him, straight out.

"Marcella..."

"Yes?"

"There's umm... something I need to ask you."

"Please, sit down," she said, motioning to the empty sofa, now free from the blankets she held in her hand. He shook his head. She let the blankets drop to the floor.

"Go ahead then, ask it," she said, her eyes showing no emotion now, her voice straightforward cold. In his head, he wondered if... but that was silly. He took a deep breath.

"What did you have to do with Bogleur?"

"What? What did I have to do with – what?"

"You know the recent news about Jeremy Bogleur, the MSP?"

"Oh... yes. Of course. He died of heart failure," Marcella replied. Her expression was hard to read.

"You didn't have anything to do with it?"

"Why would I... why are you asking me this?"

"Because of something Duke Ford said, right before he was arrested for suspected murder. He knows about you. He pointed the finger," Stanley looked her in the eye. "At you."

"But how... Oh God," she said, slumping down on the couch. She was trembling. Part of him wanted to help her, the other part just wanted to listen. He waited in the doorway, silently.

"Okay, I'll tell you," she said after a long minute. "I went there, that night. I had a file with me. I wanted to tell him to stop doing what he was doing... how he was going to stop my family performing our act."

"Why would he do that?"

"Just listen. I don't know why, maybe because certain people don't like variety at the Fringe, they think it's getting out of control," she shrugged. "We had done nothing wrong – I promise you! I just wanted to catch him in the act. He was a dirty, perverted old man."

"What happened when you got there, did you catch him?"

"Oh yes. I even took a photo; was kind of enjoying it, in a sadistic way. I just wanted to warn him... to make him stop. But it kind of went wrong... it was right, the reports of heart failure."

"How so?"

"He had a heart attack, alright, right in front of me! *Because* of me. I lost it, I didn't know what to do so I left the file and I... I just left! Called downstairs, said 'call an ambulance' and then... I left."

"Is that really what happened? Why should I believe you?"

"Stanley! Because I'm telling you, that's why!"

"How did the Duke know?" he asked, in full interrogation mode now. Funny how he should get a handle on being a journalist at the most inappropriate time. She shook her head, silently, unable to find an answer in her head. She looked up at him, her lips shaking as if she was holding back tears. Eventually she spoke.

"I don't know... I swear! Maybe *he* was the tip-off... Oh God, what's going to happen to me now..."

"I can't believe this. Wait, that day... that voice on the

phone – that was you, wasn't it? You called the paper?" It had only just struck him. Of course, the voice had been her. It had always been her, all along.

"Yes, I'm sorry, I didn't know what else to do!"

"I need to think," he said, backing away slowly into the hall. He felt a strange feeling in his stomach and in his chest, almost like anxiety, a knotting that he couldn't control. He swallowed, and felt for his keys; still in his pocket.

"Ask the police about the file! If they didn't take it then... McAvoy! That's why he was following me... Of course, that's probably how Ford knows about all of this!" Stanley felt slightly dizzy. He reached for the door.

"What should I do? Do you want me to stay here and wait for you to come back like some little lost dog?" She was shouting now. In her eyes was hurt and indignation and somehow shame, too. Standing before him was a lost, scared and guilty little girl that he wasn't entirely sure he recognised.

"Do what you like," he said, as he slammed the door shut.

"I threw the camera in the Forth!" she screamed after him. He pretended not to hear. His head was racing, and he realised he didn't really know her that well at all. *It's only been a couple of days, for God's sake.* But something on his heart snagged on her words as he played them back in his head. He didn't want to think about it, it was all too confusing. What could have been in the file? He wished he'd had the foresight to ask. As he walked down London Road, the day grew dull and he knew not where he was headed.

44

"We have forty million reasons for failure, but not a single excuse." – Rudyard Kipling

The drapes in the hotel room hung down like giant fabric doilies. Tartan ones. Stanley sat on the chair opposite Winnie Hobbes, while Magdalena sat on a small stool by the dresser. She was staring at him, wide-eyed. She wore jeans and a stripey top which resembled something he'd expect to see in a catalogue, or in the window of Marks & Spencer. At the same time, it looked kind of sweet. The bed was also tartan and contrasted to Winnie's pale beige trousers and demure oversized white shirt as she sat in what could have been the lotus position. She looked really rather good for her age.

"Nice decor," said Stanley, "very... Scottish."

Winnie smiled, but there was an undertone of seriousness in the air of the room. There was also something else, something he couldn't quite place.

"So, are things... okay now?" Winnie eventually spoke up. The creases around her eyes gave her the concerned look he was so unused to seeing these days. His granny, undoubtedly older and yet somehow still exactly the same, was questioning a situation which was already weird enough without having her sat across from him on an overly-tartan bed. All the time he had the same horrible feeling in his chest, in the pit of his stomach, every time he thought about her. *Marcella.* So no, things were most definitely not all right.

"Well, not really," Stanley replied, looking sheepish and unable to say any of what was really on his mind. It was as if a deep crevasse expanded between them, much wider than the simple distance from the sofa to the bed.

"Oh, not really, is it? So now, tell me about the girl. Where is she?"

"I don't really want to talk about it right now..." he said.

"And why not?"

Stanley fidgeted. He felt like he was 12 again.

"Stanley, have you two had a falling out?"

"We might have, but really let's just leave it. We've got plenty more to talk about..."

"Maybe so, but you know I just want you to be happy, don't you?"

"Of course I do."

"If you've had a falling out, you should really go and sort it. She's special, that girl is, just ask Magdalena."

"Magdalena? Why?" He turned to the small girl, confused. She smiled; an almost unsettling smile.

"I like her," Magdalena said. Her voice had an interesting quality, and combined with the accent it made him almost forget where he was. The curtains brought him back down to earth. "Oh? Did you speak to her much?"

Magdalena nodded.

"Granny... why did you come back? And Magdalena... is she...?"

"Is she what?"

"Why is she here, with you?"

"I adopted her, legally, and I came back, well, to be honest, because of you."

"Me?"

"Yes, you've been on my mind lately. I wanted to come and see you."

"I'm glad you're here," he said, the awkwardness fading all at once. She was, after all, his granny. It was still surreal to be in the same room with her again.

"I'm glad too. But, the girl," Winnie said, turning once again to the girl with the wide eyes, sitting quietly in the corner.

"Magdalena?"

The wide eyes turned to Stanley. It was difficult to decipher her stance, or why she seemed a lot older than she was. *How old can she be, about eight?* She seemed to have something to say, something that quietly commanded his attention in a way that was rare for one so young.

"What is it, Magdalena?"

"You and her. You are joined, tied, destined. Go after her," again the enchanting voice carried him off to somewhere else, but this time he was acutely aware of the words and their meaning. He laughed, unsure of what to say. Winnie was looking at him, a serious but almost quietly amused expression on her face.

"Is she for real?"

"She is," Winnie replied.

Magdalena nodded. "For real," she said.

"She tells me things sometimes. When I first met her, she didn't really speak at all. In all honesty, my being here is down to her."

Winnie had poured some tea, and he clutched the mug now in his hands; it tasted sweet; too sweet. He sloshed the liquid around in the plain white mug, the way he normally did when he was nervous. It was somehow calming, either that or just another symptom of OCD – which he still wasn't convinced he actually had.

"I don't know what to say to that," he said, after a considerable pause. When he looked up, Winnie was still looking at him. Magdalena was playing with a doll.

"Well, say nothing. But you should go to her, go to Marcella," Winnie said, calmly.

"She probably won't even be there when I get back," Stanley replied, suddenly feeling the wave of guilt hitting him again. The way he'd left her there, slammed the door behind him as if it had been nothing. *What should I do? What would Data do? Wish I watched Star Trek more often.*

"Maybe not, but you should find her," Winnie said,

adjusted her foot with practised ease. "Look, I might not know what's going on, Stanley, but I think it might be a dangerous time here in the city. Maybe you should go after her, you know?"

"Don't you think we should... catch up first? I've barely got to talk to you."

"I've been around this long, Stanley," Winnie said, assuredly, "I will probably be around a little bit longer, touch wood." She knocked on the table to prove her point.

"Maybe you're right... I just don't really know what to think at the moment," Stanley replied. Winnie reached out for his hand.

"Stanley?"

"What?"

"Just be careful," she said.

"Why does everyone keep telling me that?" Just then, his phone started to ring, it was Rory.

45

"I like work; it fascinates me. I could sit and look at it for hours." – Jerome K. Jerome.

Clive Quigley

The dull light of the small, boxy office provided a perfect backdrop to the perfect beige day. Clive's beige day, to be precise, and he rather liked it that way. Fortunately for him, his keyboard was beginning to turn nicely beige too; although he'd heard talk recently that he was to receive an upgrade to those fancy black computers with the flat screens. This didn't really bother Clive as much as he would like. After all, he didn't really have time to ponder it at all, for he was up to his neck in obituaries. He had been offered some outside help from Jenny, the bright little junior, but she was far too happy and explaining all the ins and outs was far beyond his energy level, and took precious time away from doing other things. Like solitaire. He couldn't get through a whole day without at least three games of solitaire. It calmed his nerves. Besides, Jenny wore an awful lot of pink for his liking. Too fresh-faced; a life in the newsroom would soon see to that, of course.

In the meantime, he'd just have to get on with things himself. Everything in Clive's life was just about 'getting on' with things. Whether it was his job, the vacuuming, the weekly shop at Tesco. He always had something to 'get on' with, and each task would be completed with the neat and timely precision it deserved.

The Bogleur obituary was turning into a bit of a farce. He had no idea who had written it in the end, but he knew it hadn't been him or Stanley. Something was most definitely a bit fishy about the whole sorry affair. It was even worse than when Gill Gallagher went undercover to get the dirt on Garlic Tony and came back stinking of pizza and grease. As for Stanley... well, he missed his friend. And he couldn't help but feel he was being kept out of the loop about something. Unbeknownst to Clive, he was about to find out what...

Clive was eating an easy peel Satsuma orange when the phone started to ring. He sadly put down the tiny, half-peeled orange upon a piece of pre-ripped kitchen roll, daintily wiped his fingers, and picked up the phone.

"Hello, obituaries?" Clive asked in his usual calm, relaxed and well-pronounced manner.

"Clive, it's Stanley," said Stanley. Clive frowned.

"Stanley? Where are you? Is everything...?"

"Look, I don't have time to explain so please, just listen. I need your help," Stanley said, the stress in his voice not quite alerting Clive to the problem-at-hand.

"*My* help? You need *my* help now?" he asked, utterly astounded at the revelation.

"Yes, is that so hard to believe?" Stanley asked, impatiently.

"Well, it is a bit... I'm quite happy in the world of obituaries – very happy in fact – so do not tell me you are going to drag me from my warm cocoon and into the cold harsh world of current affairs, because that's not for everybody, you know. I know I trained as a journalist but... I'm too far gone, Stanley, I'm just too far gone for..."

"Calm down, Clive. No-one is going to take your obits away, okay?"

"Okay. So, what is it?" Clive asked, uncertainly now.

"I need you to do me a favour... this is very important."

Clive sighed; he played with his Satsuma, rocking it back and forth upon the piece of kitchen roll (he had a stash under his desk for such Satsuma occasions).

"I'm listening..."

46

"The spy who came in for a cardie..." – Mike Coleman

Gill Gallagher

The day had almost come to a standstill; dead on its feet. Although she was anxious about Stanley and the Ford incident, Gill was also on Twitter. Her screen read:

BertieBarkingmad @GillGoGo So generous, sweet. Need to go and affix my heart labels now before the glue stops sticking. Take care xx

GillGoGo @BertieBaker Thanks! Look out for next week's, there's some really SWEET Prada peep toes in there!

BertieBarkingmad @GillGoGo Those are the sexiest ballet pumps EVER! Do you have a style guide out for those yet? Love your column, BTW.

GillGoGo @ShooFaery: Teeheeheeee!!! LOL

ShooFaery @GillGoGo Don't know but I'm saving up, got just about enough in the piggy-bank, until I see my next love affair!

GillGoGo @ShooFairy Oooh those are the cutest! But do they have the pink version that Schuh have? Irregular Choice all the way, baby

ShooFaery @GillGoGo Look at these bad boys!

GillGoGo OMG has anyone seen the new DM boots? I'm usually a stiletto girl, but those are sweeeeet!

Just then, her concentration was interrupted and she quickly tabbed away from her bright pink screen.

"Donuts!"

Just the mention of the word, never mind its strange context in the office environment caused Gill to look up from her screen in interest.

"Come and get your fresh donuts, people, they won't stay around for long!" Kev called. He was standing next to his desk, gesturing to a rather large bag of donuts. Yep, it was definitely Kev, all right. Just not the one she knew. His blue check shirt, for one, was properly ironed and wrinkle-free. His hair looked almost... nice, but she couldn't quite place what he'd done to it. Gill frowned as, even more out of character, Kev sidled through the office, whistling 'Lovecats' under his breath, before starting to... sing! He had intercepted a awkward-looking Jenny, who swiftly backed away in disgust, before Gill shook her head. It was all a bit, well... baffling, really. Fair was smiling from her desk, and Gill mouthed, "What's up with him?" Fair just shrugged, but her overall demeanour made Gill suspicious. As soon as Kev had gone into Rory's office, she got up and slinked over to Fair's desk, grabbing a donut on the way, for good measure, of course. "Does he know something I don't? I mean, seriously, the last couple of days there's been a definite change in that man!"

"You're right; he does seem to be in better spirits these days, doesn't he?"

"But you're telling me you don't know why?" Gill asked, the question slightly muffled by a mouthful of donut. "Mmm, jam," she said.

"Nope. Couldn't possibly make an assumption, it could be that he's just started getting out of the right side of bed in the mornings," Fair replied. *Or it could be the dusky healing stone I left on his desk the other day,* she thought. Gill nodded, but it was clear she was not satisfied. Her journalist's nose was most definitely sniffing for clues.

"Have you heard from Stanley since this morning?" Fair asked.

"Only briefly. I think he had a fight with Marcella, apparently she had something to do with Bogleur. Anyway, he asked me what Data would do..." Fair just kept on smiling, that is, until she saw what, or rather who, was en route. Gill swallowed. Fair looked with surprised eyes, trained on the sight ahead of her. A silent hush shifted around the office dynamics, almost unnoticeable but ominous in its presence. It was as if an imaginary darkness or grey cloud was swooping down from beyond the office corridor, a great cool breeze from beyond the grave; like a whisper of sweet darkness, *my old friend*. Or a great mass of silken black ties all taken off and thrown over the coffin at a funeral – apparently that's what happened at Noirio Twiddle's funeral, at any rate. But it was none of those things; it was Clive. Not even dressed in black, but instead his trademark beige, vampire-like Clive was a sight mostly unseen in the office. It was rumoured he liked to start the day earlier than most, and leave when it got as dark as darkly possible, even in summer. Of course, that part was not true, but he still stayed later than most.

"C-Clive?"

"Hello, Gill. Got the email," Clive said, standing awkwardly between Gill and Kev's desk.

"Which email was that?"

"The one about the donuts."

"Oh, *that* email. Yeah, right," Gill replied, holding up her own donut, "Mine's jam, very tasty."

"I like jam, I hope I get jam," Clive replied, taking a donut of his own.

"So, Clive... how is life in obits?"

"Ach, it's not quite the same without Stanley. I'm going to have to attend a... *board meeting*, later," Clive made a face, although the way he'd said board meeting meant it wasn't entirely necessary.

254

"Oh, I'm going to that! Excellent, I'll have someone to sit beside who won't bore me to death," Fair said, before realising what she'd said.

"Ahahah, death! Obits! Get it?" Gill laughed. Fair looked at her, witheringly. So did Clive.

"Oh, well sorry! I'd better get back to work anyway. I've got to phone a woman about that dog who saved the ferret... or something." Gill returned to her desk, which left Fair and Clive together. Fair didn't seem to mind. She found Clive interesting and mysterious. His glasses sat well on his face, and she noticed underneath he had thick eyelashes; he was looking down at his feet.

"So," Fair said, trying to maintain communication, now that this enchanting being had made his presence known. "How long have you worked here, I barely ever see you around the office?"

"Far too long," Clive muttered. "But yes, sometimes it's nice to get out of the box I work in. I like your... outfit." Fair looked down. She was wearing pale grey coloured skinny trousers, a pale orange long-sleeved top and a faded turquoise waistcoat, teamed with a skinny scarf, multi-coloured.

"Oh, thank you. Ebay," she said.

"Nice."

"I like yours, too, very cute, very beige, though."

"Indeed. I suppose you'd expect me to wear black, but I don't think it does my complexion any good."

"No, you working in obits and wearing nothing but black would make you such a stereotype. Far too obvious," Fair replied, intelligently. Clive smiled.

"That's what I thought," he said.

"I'm glad we think alike," Fair replied.

"I'd better be getting back. I have to go and phone a man about another man who... had a ferret. Or something."

"See you at the board meeting?"

"Look forward to it."

255

47

"Diet soda is poison." – Brent Spiner

Stanley Hobbes

The Gothic Aquarium was a show that Rory wanted a feature on, and he wanted an interview ASAP with its main star, Milla Twilight. Stanley didn't have to be reminded that he *was* on Fringe duty, after all. Before he entered, he'd reluctantly tried calling Marcella at the flat. No answer.

From the posters, Milla Twilight looked like a wicked witch of the goth rock legion, if one existed. Long, black hair and deep purple eye shadow drew the attention to her pale sharp cheekbones, upon which a single star was tattooed on the left. Her lips were thick, dark berry colour and she was dressed provocatively in a corset and black velvet choker. Her fingernails were a sight to behold, also black with white spider web designs covering them.

The show was, most aptly, taking place in the Edinburgh Dungeons, in a small room that had not been in use for fear of its being haunted. The owners had agreed to open it for the Fringe show, in support of all things dark and gothic. This knowledge made Stanley feel slightly on edge, as he stepped through the main doors and onto a floor that was not quite balanced; he looked down and saw why. It was covered in black lacy material, which reminded him of how his dad used to cover the floor on paint days when he was decorating the house. When a hand tapped him on the back of the shoulder, he jumped most visibly, before turning to see a very small, vertically-challenged and shapely gothic bell with bright red hair and bosoms bigger than her head. "Hello there," she said, her voice ringing with a definite Cockney twang. She was wearing a PVC zip-up top and a long skirt that looked to be designed for someone much taller than herself. She was completely dressed in black.

"Oh, hello," Stanley said, forcing an uneasy smile. "I'm here to interview Milla Twilight before the show?"

"Ah, yes, this way! I think she's just getting the finishing touches on – I believe they are stitching up her corset as we speak. A most dangerous task, I do say."

"Oh really? Why is that?"

"Well, for one thing she's hung over, and another, she refuses to eat anything over than Nutella-covered digestive biscuits. I heard you should always eat healthy-like, bananas or somefink, at regular intervals while wearing a corset, otherwise your intestines will stick together."

"Oh God... I think I feel sick."

The gothic maiden giggled, and led him up a spiral staircase before gesturing to a room beyond with a small black door.

"This is it, luvvey; enter first, think later, eh!"

"All... right." Stanley said, as he watched the girl descend the stairs, her long lace skirts trailing behind in her a manner that could be considered dangerous. He knocked at the door.

"Come!"

Turning the knob, he let the door swing open to reveal a very black room with bright lights and mirrors. It looked a bit like the lap-dancing booth his brother had forced him into when he was 17, for a 'laugh'. From within, a very large woman dressed in black velvet had her back to him, and was pulling very heavily on some strings. It took him a moment for his eyes to adjust, and to see the very small creature that was pressed up against the wall, bent forward in an almost sexual way.

"Hello?"

"Hell-o... I take it you must be Stanley? Come in, please, take a seat. I'm... Ah! Sorry, I'm just getting some help with my cor-SET! Ahhh... there, just a bit more, Helena."

"I see. Is it always this difficult? I never knew corsets were quite so... fiddly," Stanley replied, a little embarrassed and not quite sure where to look. Luckily the large woman's behind was blocking most of the view.

"As with most good girly things, Stanley, they are a bit 'fiddly' but the rewards are very great," Milla sighed. Stanley said nothing, and fidgeted in his chair. He felt for the frog in his jacket pocket, but realised too late that he'd left it at Duke Ford's.

"Almost done," Milla called.

"Okay, no need to rush on my account." Stanley looked around the room. It seemed to be decorated with silver ink scrawlings and pentagrams. Posters for the show were on the wall, along with lipstick markings over the mirror. On the table, some digestive biscuits and a tub of Nutella stood out.

"There we go, mistress! Now, can we stand upright?"

"Just about. Thanks, Helena, now leave us."

The large woman turned on her heel, and smiled at Stanley, patting him on the shoulder as she walked past.

"Look at it, Miss, better be careful with this one. Delicate little flower."

"Oh, I can be nice. Gentle," said Milla, as she turned to look him in the eye. The door creaked closed and the two of them were left alone.

"Ermm... so, let's get started with the interview then, shall we?"

"We shall," Milla purred. The corset she wore was breathtaking, in a deep gold colour that was most unexpected. Black lace adorned it, and her skirt dripped with it, almost like a biblical creature. She was even paler in the flesh, and her eyes were violet. Contact lenses, of course, but still they shone under the light of the dresser and danced into his.

"So, ummm, let's see... Firstly, why don't you tell me about the show! It's a new concept, isn't it?"

"Everything's a new concept, darling. But then, there are no new concepts, only the same regurgitated ideas in one wild variation or another."

"Variations on a theme?"

"Indeed."

"So... is this new, or old?"

"This is both new, and old... older than the passage of time."

"You're talking in riddles."

"It's what I do, dear. Just go with it, it'll sound cool enough on paper." *Really? Are you sure about that?* he thought, but didn't say, instead raising his eyebrows and taking down the words in shorthand, making a few notes of his own while he was at it. "That's a cool name you have, where was it inspired from?"

"Twilight Eyes, one of my very favourite books by Dean Koontz, actually. In it, one of the characters had purple eyes. It was beautiful, hence," Milla answered, pointing to her contact lenses.

"Those are startling."

"Why, thank you," Milla said, getting closer to him on the couch. Her purple eyes were staring directly into his and it was making him uncomfortable to say the least. Her hand touched his arm; it felt cold, vampire-like. Unlike the photo, her lips were pale nude colour, which was just as well as anything red would remind him of blood. He was half expecting her teeth to look like small milky sharp daggers. He could feel her breath now... it smelt of Nutella and Diet Coke.

"So, what goes into each show?"

"Well, I don't want to give too much away, darling, we can't be having that! But I will say, a hint of darkness, a touch of magic and a slither of sex..."

"Right, I see," Stanley said, standing up. "I think that's all I have time for right now, but that's been great."

"Going already?"

"Yes, but don't worry, we'll team the interview with a review of the show. Better be going, really have to... be somewhere... else. Bye!"

"Ta ta," Milla pouted. Before she could stand up and give him a goodbye bite, he was out of the door and down the staircase, desperately packing his notepad and pen back into his pocket. He could almost feel the sunlight on his face, when he saw a familiar sight ahead of him. *No, surely it can't be...?* But it was. McAvoy. Waiting. Stanley backed up before he could be seen. What was he doing here? Was he being followed? He watched as McAvoy checked his phone, managing to look calm and menacing at the same time. Just then, a voice boomed from behind him; it was the red haired Goth.

"Stanley! You forgot your... posters." The girl finished as McAvoy shot a glance up at Stanley, and Stanley dashed back up the staircase, not one level, but two. He could hear the woman below saying, *"And who do you think you are?"* He knocked at the door, then opened it dived in, before slamming it shut as quietly as humanly possible behind him. He was not alone. A single tall female figure with long white hair and a very slim frame dressed in black rubber stood up at his entrance. He recognised her.

"Edw- I mean, Alice!"

"It's you! Stanley, isn't it?"

"Yes, yes, that's right," he looked nervously behind him.

"Who are you hiding from?" she asked, perceptively.

"A man..."

"Quick, hide in here!" She opened the coffin lid, the very same one he'd helped her transport down Fleshmarket Close. It looked very black and foreboding inside.

"Come on, no time, just get in!"

"Oh God... okay," he gulped. Coffins were really not his strong suit, especially not ones that looked completely black and airtight. Cautiously he got in the coffin, before she closed the lid shut above him. Placing a few boxes on top before sitting down demurely, she had began to brush her hair again when the door burst open. Stanley lay in the dark, listening. His heart was pounding in his chest, and he had a strange compulsion to laugh.

"Excuse me? Who do you think you are, busting in on a girl like this! Could have been naked, or anything!"

"Wouldn't want to see that," a man with a gruff Glaswegian accent grumbled, "are you the only one in here?"

"Yes, and I prefer it that way."

Stanley resisted the urge to sneeze, as he imagined the man silently looking around the room, checking she was in fact alone. After a moment of awkward silence, he heard Alice's heels clacking on the floor.

"Now, if you don't mind, this is private – that means not open to members of the public. The show doesn't start until later!" Stanley heard the door shut behind them, before their footsteps faded down the stairs. He was beginning to feel claustrophobic, but he knew the coast probably wasn't clear yet. He tried to still his pounding heart, but for a while all he seemed to hear was his own heartbeat.

Time seemed to pass slowly in the close blackness of the coffin. He could smell a curious scent of lavender, and the silk lining felt smooth as he rubbed it beneath his fingertips. It seemed like an hour had gone by in the space of a minute, when he heard the sound of Alice's heels on the staircase once more. When the door creaked open, there was a pause, and another creak, and he strained to hear before a loud knock on the coffin almost made him jump out of his skin.

"Oi, still in there? It's only me, Alice," Alice said, as she lifted the lid on the coffin. He'd never been so glad to see a Goth in all his life. "It's okay, he's gone now."

"Thanks for doing this," Stanley replied, climbing out of the coffin as quickly as he possibly could without falling over. The smell of lavender seemed even stronger in the air now, and he realised it was coming from Alice; her perfume.

"Why was he after you, anyway?" she asked, the intrigue

showing on her snow-white face. Her hair looked almost like a fairytale in the dimly lit room, and large black material roses adorned her clothing.

"Long story, but I think he's been following me," he said, unsurely. His legs felt a bit like jelly.

"Seemed like a charming bloke," Alice said, as she watched him make his way across the room, before sitting on a bean bag to steady his nerves. It was a black leather bean bag, of course.

"Oh, he certainly is. So, I never knew you were part of this show."

"Oh, I'm only helping out a friend," Alice replied, moving her long white hair away from her face, "what brings you here, anyway?"

"I was interviewing your star for an article in the Edinburgh Times," Stanley said, finally feeling like a proper journalist and liking it.

"Oh?"

"At least, I was before..."

"Well, you're safe for now. I escorted him downstairs... might have followed him outside a bit, too. Was on his mobile, said something about going to London Road."

"What did you say?"

"London Road, he said... right before he got in the car."

"Oh shit," Stanley muttered, his gut sank. "Oh shit, shit buggering shit bollocks."

"What?" She looked at him, questioningly, her long slim hand wandering up to nervously her hair once more. "What's wrong?" The Duke's words echoed in his head: *And by the way, it's not me you need to worry about now.*

"It's nothing – can't explain. I really need to go though. Now... right now."

"Something I said?"

48

"Never bolt your door with a boiled carrot" – Irish Proverb

The day was already starting to dull and fade when Stanley arrived back at the flat on London Road. On the way there, he'd told himself there was nothing to worry about; that his flat would have been empty, or had she been there she would have ignored the buzzer. It was as if his mind had taken him somewhere else as he fought to get back to her, fought and struggled in the losing battle to utter panic. It was almost like a dance in his head, the place he retreated to when things weren't quite going right but there was nothing he could do about them. When that happened, he mostly saw colours; shades of pink and grey and green and blue, instead of pictures and words and people and memories and fears and loathing and panic. Those things would surface to, of course, like a loop or a broken record spinning around his mind. It was a weakness. *Why did I have to leave like that. Marcella. It wasn't you, I know that now.* But did he know it? His heart told him 'yes' but perhaps that was only what he wanted to believe. *It's my fault, all my fault. Please God be safe, be there waiting for me when I get back.*

All he could think about was Marcella; Marcella and the way she'd talked that night on Arthur's Seat, Marcella and the way she looked in bed, the way she'd burned the ties, the night when he thought he'd lost her and had held her tight in his arms. He hadn't lost her then and he didn't want to lose her now...couldn't lose her now. He turned the key in the door and ran up the stairs, unable to think straight, pausing only at the top of the stairs. The door to the flat looked perfectly normal, silently ominous. He listened, but could hear no sound. Carefully, silently as so not to alarm an intruder, he turned the key in the door before slowly pushing it open and stepping inside. All was dark in the hallway. Nothing looked disturbed, yet he felt unable to call out. Instead, he stepped forward with the same trepidation he felt in his reoccurring nightmare. Only this time he didn't know what to expect.

As he stepped towards the living room, the floorboards creaked underneath him. He remembered again the hurt look on Marcella's face as he'd left the flat. He remembered all too well as he felt the panic slowly creep up into his heart again. *Panic heart.* It was the same feeling of horror he'd felt when he knew he'd made a terrible mistake, first in a school exam, then at the paper. But this felt at least ten times worse. He bit his lip, and walked into the living room, only to discover it empty. Nothing, no trace of Marcella lingered in the room. She'd obviously cleared up. That was good. Maybe she had left before McAvoy had a chance to get to her.

Quickly checking the kitchen, study and bathroom just in case, and finding them empty, he paused just ahead of the bedroom. He heard a faint noise from inside. His hand reached for the door, and he realised it was shaking. *Breathe. Just calm down.* Before he could consider any further options, he opened the door quickly, sharply, and stepped back, almost sure of the onslaught. But nothing happened. No shouts or lunges forward, no attack from McAvoy with a loaded gun. No Marcella, either. He looked around the room, and for a second he was so sure that McAvoy was standing in wait, he actually saw him there, in the corner. Alas, it was but a shadow, and his heart started beating erratically in his chest.

Jasper the cat meowed as he stepped over the bed to greet his owner. It was almost as if he had his own little language, and seemed to be talking to Stanley in an angry and animated rant that only he could understand. Stanley smiled. It was only when Jasper pounced from the bed to the floor and two 'somethings' fell with him, that Stanley stopped smiling. It was the jade frog. Beside it, now also on the floor, was a brochure for the show, 'Kaskadiori' at the Edinburgh Festival Theatre. Scrawled in black ink across the back, was simply: *"Danger, danger, risk taker. Will you save her?"* His heart sank, and he dropped the card. Jasper nestled against his legs, wondering what the matter was. Stanley picked him up, and stroked him gently. "Did they hurt her?" he asked the cat.

"What did they do?" Jasper stared up at him with his confused and cat-like eyes, and licked his lips the way cats do from time-to-time. He purred.

"I know what you're thinking. You're thinking I need to get a grip." Stanley sighed. But it was too late for that. It was too late for just about anything remotely involving sanity. *W.W.D.D.*

"Wait, what am *I* doing? I need to go and I need to go now," he said, putting the cat, which seemed to meow in agreement, back on the floor.

49

"What Darwin was too polite to say, my friends, is that we came to rule the Earth not because we were the smartest, or even the meanest, but because we have always been the craziest, most murderous motherfuckers in the jungle." – Stephen King.

It was close to dark when he made it to the theatre, which loomed ahead of him like a broken-mirror version of the truth. It wasn't in the best shape, and had been cordoned off for a full-scale police investigation. However, it looked deserted of all life. There was a sadness that seemed to hang like a black cloud in the air and seeping through the fabric of his clothes in an almost undetectable mist. He stood, unsure of his next move. It was almost a certainty that Marcella was in there. Most probably, McAvoy was too. He suspected the building had been cordoned off for more reasons than one; it was probably dangerous, the foundations unstable. The inside looked dark and foreboding, calling to him from deep inside. Unable to take his eyes from the sight in front of him, he pulled out his phone and dialled Gill's number. She picked up on the second ring.

"Stanley? Where are you, what's wrong?" she asked.

"I'm at the Festival Theatre."

"The what? Why?"

"It's McAvoy. I think... I think he's got Marcella. Will you call the police? I'm going in."

"What? Stanley, no! Can't you just wait until they arrive? Why haven't you called them?"

"Because I think he wants me... I can't let him hurt her, Gill. Just call them."

"But – wait! Stanley, did you ever think she might be in on this? You don't know her, Stanley!"

"So?"

"You know me! Listen to me!"

"Is that what this is about?"

"No! But for God's sake, be careful!"

"I... I'm going in. W.W.D.D," he replied, his mind already somewhere else.

"What?"

He ignored it. Instead, he pressed the 'call end' button, and on second thoughts, switched the phone off before slipping it back in his pocket. He knew he couldn't hesitate any longer as he approached the building and ducked under the tape that was supposed to keep him out. It looked even worse the closer he got; broken glass crunched under his shoes, making him grimace weakly. He was on edge as he stepped into the darkness, the smoky smell of burnt carpet consuming him. It was almost overwhelming, and he could imagine the fire starting all over again, sweeping over him like a ghost. He shut his eyes. *Get a grip, need to get a...*

He opened his eyes again, before stepping delicately over the debris that lay in his path. It was getting darker, and his eyes were failing to adjust; he wished he'd brought a torch. At least it could not only provide light, but also an adequate weapon. He realised he had nothing bar his bare hands to protect himself with; to protect Marcella with. He scanned the parts of the floor still illuminated by the light outside, and found the closest thing that resembled a weapon; a crude wooden bar from the stairs. He grasped it firmly in his hands, squeezed it tight, willing it to steady himself. It seemed to work. It wasn't a gun, or a sharp blade, but it would have to do in the event of violence.

"God help me..." Stanley muttered to himself. He climbed the stairs, keeping as close to the wall as possible. Looking ahead, he could see nothing more than a few vague shapes in front of him. How was he supposed to find his way, to find her, when he couldn't even see where he was going? He felt around with his hands out in front of him, just like in a Scooby Doo cartoon. He imagined he looked quite silly. Eventually he found the left door to the main theatre hall, and hoped to God he was in the right place.

A noise in the distance stopped him in his tracks and his heart leapt in his chest. It sounded as if he was going in the right direction. He stood pressed against the door, listening intently for any further clue; there was none. Eventually, he found the courage to silently push the door open, and creep stealthily into the blackness. He felt his way forward, wondering if he was alone. It felt like a million eyes were watching him from the seats. Apart from the lingering smell, it was impossible to tell there had been an explosion in the darkness that enveloped him so completely. In the back of his mind, he half expected his nightmare to become reality in that darkness. First a hand from behind, the nails down his back, the awful eyes staring into the back of his head, the smell of decaying flesh... *Lorraine.* But that was ridiculous; it was but a nightmare. This was real, and it was happening right now. The stage was up ahead, and he felt the rough velvet of the chairs on his way past, counting. It was still hard to see in front of him, and he almost fell over a chair that had somehow been detached and lay on the floor. Eventually he reached his destination, and pulled himself up in search of any clues. That was when he realised something lay crumpled in the middle of the stage. He felt fabric, then skin and the silkiness of human hair. It dawned on him that the lifeless body was Marcella.

"Oh my God... Marcella?" He held her in his arms, but her skin felt cool to the touch. She was unconscious, her body limp. Then he felt the wetness, and realised she was bleeding, broken. She was bleeding onto the stage, and as he felt around he touched something cold and sharp; a knife.

"No... no Marcella... wake up," he whispered, pleaded. No response. She was gone. He felt an overwhelming sadness take over him, and all he could find in his heart was... was...

"I love you."

He placed her down gently on the hard wood of the stage, as up ahead he heard laughter. It was a deep, growling laughter, cold and humourless; McAvoy. Stanley looked up to see a figure in the dark. He stood beside the curtain, mocking. Suddenly the love was replaced with a rage so blind and pure it took him over completely. The wooden bar and knife forgotten about, he stood up, careful to avoid the blood, and ran towards McAvoy.

"Noooo!" he shouted as, filled with an anger he never knew existed, he launched himself at the figure, who retreated behind the curtain. Before he knew it, he was grasping at empty material and trying to keep his balance while tumbling to the floor. He scrambled to his feet to see only shadows.

"Come on, you fucking coward! I'm here! Come get it!" But there was no reply. He didn't hesitate as searched backstage, almost tripping over a box filled with props. A very clumsy hero or perhaps a failure was more accurate, he thought to himself. Something fell from above, just barely missing him as it skimmed his shoulder. It was a spotlight; useless now. He looked up, to see the figure of McAvoy disguised in the shadows.

"What do you want? Why don't you face me?"

"I want to talk," McAvoy said; his accent thick and deep.

"Well I'm not really in the mood for talking," said Stanley, ascending the slim spiral staircase, his shoes clacking on the metal. It wasn't long before he was at the top.

"You know, you press disgust me... Garlic Tony was a friend of mine," McAvoy growled.

"Where are you?"

"Look," McAvoy started. His tone seemed to soften as he continued, "She knew my name... my face. It was too much. Couldnae let her just..."

With that, Stanley lost all rational thought, the full

weight of his loss finally hitting him hard in the gut. It was so much worse than any physical pain.

"You fucking killed her, you sick fuck!" Stanley threw himself at McAvoy, who stumbled back, taken by surprise. He bared his teeth, his expression drawn back in a grimace as he moved towards Stanley, his fist clenched tightly. Things seemed to move in slow motion after that. McAvoy's fist was coming closer to connect with Stanley's face, and Stanley was directing his whole being towards McAvoy to stop him, do something, anything, because all that mattered was Marcella and Marcella was gone. He couldn't bring himself to use the word 'dead'. Not yet. Things seemed to be suspended in the air, all kinetic energy drawn up and brought together in a spark of mass power and they were entangled for better or for worse. McAvoy's large, thick frame and Stanley's slim boyish one. There was no match and it seemed to Stanley like he was losing his balance against the full force of McAvoy's weight. He stumbled, and righted himself, holding on tightly to the enemy's jacket; the only thing stopping him from falling from, perhaps not a great height, but an uncomfortable one, especially for an acrophobe. Then, seemingly from out of nowhere, a separate fist connected with the side of Stanley's head, and hit hard. Then Stanley was falling. He didn't have time to register the source of his downfall, or where he was headed, only that he was no longer on solid footing. It was a curious sensation. Falling. Falling through the air. F-a-l-l-i-n-g and then everything went black...

50

"*The doctor said I was a paranoid schizophrenic. Well he didn't actually say it, but we knew he was thinking it.*" – Robert Rankin, The Curse of the Voodoo Handbag.

Where are you? Why can't I see you? Blue... why is it always blue? It's all so vagu... what am I doing here again? I was falling, I... if only I could hold onto something, something solid. Call to me, use your voice, call my name and I'll find you... I'll find you. I promise. I won't let you down again. Marcella. I'm falling. Did it feel like falling for you, too? Did you fall the way I did? I fell for you. It was all for you. I didn't know it at the time, but I do now. Oh God... I need you. I'm here now. Where are you? Let me see you. I just want to see you, to touch you... I won't let anyone hurt you ever again, never. I love...

He was back in the blue corridors, searching for something. Searching but alone. His hands were empty, his feet bare and cold on the floor. A feeling of confusion made his head thick and fuzzy. He had no idea how long he'd been there for, but it felt like a long time. Suddenly the old feeling of the dream came back to him, and he knew he wasn't alone. It was all too familiar, all too uncomfortable. She would be there soon. It was all the same, but somehow different. *Here there be monsters, kid.* Marcella's voice echoed in his mind, as one of the first things she'd said to him in that ridiculous 'interview'. The same blue walls, the same cold floor, only this time he could feet it under his bare feet. No shoes. *Why?*

The corridors seemed to stretch out forever, and he was again like a rat caught in a maze. Time seemed to stop and he was lost for thoughts; what had happened? Why was he here, was it a dream? Of course it was a dream. Unless of course, he was... dead. But what utter hell would it be to relive this nightmare over and over again, what had he done to deserve such a punishment? Of course, he knew. *Lorraine.* He could have saved her, could have found some way to stop it from happening; to stop her from doing that... to herself. To save her from death, take her in his arms and tell her it didn't have to be like this. Surely that was the real crux of the matter? Surely that was why he was here now? His head hurt; a lot. He couldn't be sure, what he didn't think he'd experienced pain in any of the dreams before. The thought terrified him. It meant she could do whatever she wanted to him, and he could feel it, actually *feel* it. Suddenly it didn't feel like a dream anymore. Suddenly he was sure he was not waking up. *What the hell happened? Why can't I remember anything?* Then he could remember. There was darkness, falling somehow. He could remember the falling. He'd been hit, and then flailing, and then falling...the energy. The fight with... *McAvoy... Marcella. Oh shit, Marcella.* It took him a few seconds before he realised he could hear sounds. They were fuzzy, distant, a faraway beeping in the distance. Where were they coming from? *Doesn't make sense.* He could feel a presence, her presence. *Lorraine.* He didn't want her to be there, not to see her again, not like this. He waited for the usual scene, unable to move, standing still in the corridor that wasn't really a corridor. The walls that weren't really walls, *they only exist in your mind. Yeah? Keep telling yourself that. Keep telling yourself that when her nails are around your neck, and down your chest, your groin... digging and clawing, and feasting. Coldness, burrowing into your heart like ice fire. Yeah, bring it on, bitch.* He could hear approaching footsteps, like high heels on hard flooring. That sparked alarm bells in the back of his mind; something felt very wrong. He had never heard her footsteps before, she had always been barefoot. *Never been able to hear her coming. Come on, where are you, you cold hard bitch? You decaying, skinny, hungry whore, where the fuck are you? Come out, come out, wherever you are...* He could feel his heart racing in his chest. Pounding like it had been right before... the pain was still there, alongside it...the panic, the dread in his gut. Something terrible had happened. *Marcella.* No-one appeared in the distance. No dashing white figure, trailing behind the ripped fabric of her dress. No hand behind him, either. No cold touch. The footsteps had stopped. He listened, waiting, helplessly waiting. Then he felt a sort of warmth around him. It was gradual, slowly spreading around him like a comfort blanket, and it took that warmth for him to realise he had been cold. He could feel another presence now, less malign. He opened his mouth to call out. *Hello?* But he realised for some reason he could not speak. He could smell a familiar scent. It reminded him of someone, momentarily confusing him even further. Then it suddenly came back to him like a rush to the head. *Marcella.* Then he heard her voice. "Stanley? Stanley, I'm here," she said, her voice velvety smooth running through his mind. It calmed him, soothed him like cool rain. Suddenly there she was, standing in front of him, but she was dressed differently. She looked demure in green halter top that exposed her pale skin, and a long grey patterned skirt. He'd only ever seen her wear black. She looked over her shoulder. "His lids... they blinked," she said, seemingly talking to someone he couldn't quite see – all he could make out was an expanse of corridor. Again, he tried to talk to her, but no sound came out. *Is it you? Is it really you?*

"Are you sure he can hear me...? Alright, alright." She turned back to him.

"Stanley? Can you hear me? God... I hope you can hear me. You've been like this for weeks now. I've been waiting for you to wake up. Please, wake up."

It was then he realised he was in a sleep he could not wake up from.

"I want you to know that I'm okay. And I waited for

you... please, please know that I waited," she looked sad now, her voice starting to break up as she talked. Then, for a while, she just looked at him, her eyes wide and wet with tears. He couldn't move, paralysed to the spot. He wanted to go to her, to hold her and tell her everything would be okay. Instead he was immobilised. "I can't wait forever, Stanley. I have to go back to Russia. I'm so sorry," she spoke each word with meaning, and he felt each one like a dagger in his heart.

He wanted to tell her no. To stop her. *No, don't leave. I love... My God. Look at how beautiful... Did I never tell you? Did I never see it before now? Maybe I did, but it blinds and it darkens, doesn't it?*

"I love you - ya tebya lyublyu," she said, in her velvety Russian tongue. Then the warmth began to fade, and with it, she was too. He watched as she slowly evaporated from his view, from his world as it existed right then and there. Eventually, she was gone.

51

"Go to Heaven for the climate, Hell for the company." – Mark Twain

He had no idea how long he'd been walking for, but he was determined to find his way out of the maze. The corridors all looked the same, the floors immaculate and unmarked. No way to tell whether he'd been there before or whether each turn was new. All he knew was that he wanted to find her, to stop her from leaving, *But how?* How could he leave his own subconscious? There had to be a way. They stretched out in front of him in a maddening eternity of blue. *Always that blue, why does it have to be that colour?*

He never grew tired, or stopped to check behind him. The sight of the endlessness was enough to drive him insane if he dared himself to do that. *Don't turn back, just keep going.* He was aware of a vague feeling of thirst, of craving liquid. His throat was dry. His head was throbbing less. In fact, he couldn't feel it at all. He wondered if that meant he was going toward reality, or away from it. It didn't make any sense.

Up ahead, a door stood out from the wall. It was white, and seemed entirely out of place. He walked towards it, relieved to see what was at least, a break from all the blue. He reached for the handle, but it gripped awkwardly. He tried to turn it, but it wouldn't budge. He forced it open. Inside was a small room, square. Stanley recoiled at the sight of himself in a mirror placed on the wall directly opposite the door. For a second, he'd thought it was McAvoy. He looked rough, unshaven. His long-ish dark hair looked lank, unwashed. His eyes looked lost and haunted in the strange light. The lights flickered, and he looked up just as something small and hard landed on the floor in front of him. He bent down to examine it, but already he knew what it was. The frog stared up at him with menacing eyes. Or so he imagined. But really, the frog looked familiar to him now, almost like an old friend. It'd always been on his side in the past... or had it really? The mystery of the Argos frog still bothered him. Another frog dropped onto the hard surface of the floor. Then another, and another. One hit him on the back.

Standing up and pressing himself back against the wall, he watched the as the rate of the dropping frogs started to speed up until it was almost like a rainfall. He crouched, shielding himself with his hands as the sound of the frogs echoed off the wall like giant pieces of hail. Then, as soon as it had started, it was over. He stood, waiting for just more one frog to drop. *Just one more, one more frog, come on, I dare you, you motherfuckers.* No frog fell. They did however seem to be staring at him. He imagined all of them staring with one, conscious mind, looking directly into his soul. They were everywhere, touching his shoes as he tried not to step on them. And he didn't want to step on them, as something seemed to be occurring within the frogs. They were starting to look more real somehow - less carved from jade, more soft and... Was it his imagination, or were they moving? Gradually he began to hear them, whether it was in his mind or in the room it was at first difficult to tell. With horror, he realised they were growing, too.

He felt for the door behind him but his hands encountered nothing but smooth wall. The frogs were now almost the same size as his fist, and yes, they were breathing, and croaking. *Don't toads croak? Not frogs, surely they sound more... what's the word? What do they sound like? Does it matter?* Their noises continued to grow louder, and then the first one jumped. It jumped high in the air, catching him off-guard. The frogs were still expanding in mass, as one-by-one they started to jump into the air before falling back to the ground again. There was nowhere for Stanley to hide, and this time crouching would only make things worse. It was then he noticed with horror that one of the frogs had teeth. It snapped at him as he tried to bat it way with his hand. Then another tried the same thing. In fact, they all had teeth and they were now the size of two fists. But amongst the growing frogs, something else seemed to be taking place in the middle of the floor. He couldn't quite make out the shape or the movement, due to the sheer amount of frogs that were taking up space there, but something was most definitely going on.

Suddenly a hand rose out of the frogs, then an arm, then another hand. Someone was pulling themselves up from underneath the green shiny froggy carpet. A flash of dull blonde hair, then a face, angry as the day Stanley had confronted him in the office; it was the Duke. The frogs seemed to be clearing the way for him now, as he pulled himself up and then to a standing position.

"Well, well," the Duke snarled.

"What are you doing here? And where am I?" Stanley asked, confusedly.

"In your own mind, Stanley... this is all down to you," the Duke replied as Stanley batted away another frog with teeth.

"Well, I want out."

Duke Ford laughed, before brushing off his brocade jacket.

"You can't leave your own mind, Stanley!"

"That's what I'm afraid of..." Stanley replied, unsurely, his eyes drawn to the Duke's clean hands and perfectly manicured fingernails. They almost seemed to glow evilly against the green of the frogs. Stanley stared, dumbfounded. The Duke noticed. "Just what are you staring at?" he asked, irritated.

"I-I was just wondering..." Stanley heard himself muttering. The Duke had parted the sea of frogs now, and a moderately-sized pathway extended from the Duke to Stanley.

"Yes?" The Duke asked.

"You didn't really get those frogs from Argos, did you?"

"No, you're absolutely right there."

"Where did you...?"

"The devil."

"The...?"

The Duke threw his head back and laughed, a loud and maniacal laugh that almost threw Stanley backwards as he struggling to maintain balance amongst the frogs. They had stopped jumping, but were moving all around him, touching his legs. He was all too aware of their teeth. He couldn't breathe; the room seemed to be closing in around him and the frogs, yet the Duke just stood there, laughing. It was getting eerily high-pitched, and it made everything seem fuzzy. Then the Duke was falling forward, stumbling forward, towards Stanley and Stanley was fumbling for the door, yet still all he could feel was the smooth blue wall. Then he found the handle, and turned, just as the Duke was reached out for him with those perfectly manicured hands.

Just then, Stanley saw the family resemblance better than ever. The Duke seemed to be merging into Captain Consul-McBeard, but minus the beard. A pirate's hand raised up through the frogs, and Ford (one of the Ford's, it was getting harder to tell which, whether or not Ford had merged into his brother) laughed harder than ever. It was somehow horrible, as Ford - it could have been either one of them, by now – reached for the hat, to reveal a pointed hook underneath. Instead of grabbing for the hat, Ford took the hook and raised it up to his eye, point first. Stanley turned away at the crucial moment.

Then he was suddenly falling backwards through the door, hitting the floor hard before scrambling to his feet. He turned and ran through the corridors, unable to turn back. He batted away a frog that was hanging onto his jeans by its teeth. His hair felt itchy; he ran his hands through it, paranoid, checking for more frogs. There were none. He ran for what seemed like miles, through the corridors and nothingness of the blue, until all he could focus on was the blue. Everything was blue. He finally forced himself to stop when a feeling of familiarity came over him. It was a feeling he recognised, as he'd had it many times before. She was there. *Lorraine. No. Please, no. Let me go. Just let me...* But the figure dashed across the hallway in front of him, the same way it always had done. The feeling of dread was back in his gut, and he looked down at his still bare feet. He had come this far, couldn't back out now. Marcella was... *Marcella is dead. No. That's not true. Somehow she... she's okay. But is she? Is she really?* Then somehow, he found the strength to run, and before he could even think about it he was finding the blue door as her faraway yet high-pitched moan cut through the air. He couldn't hear the background noise anymore – all was calm and quiet, the air pregnant with her malice, her intent. He could smell an unusual scent, like flowers. It was fresh and somehow real, though the scent wasn't familiar to this particular dream. He was sure Lorraine would not smell of flowers, if he could smell her at all. She was behind the door, scraping the way he always imagined her to be, but this time no sight could satisfy her hunger, no touch could take away her coldness. *Evil, in its purest form,* he thought. He reached for the door, knowing as it yielded, that the first thing he saw would be her eyes. She stood before him, the same as she always had, yet she was so very still; So very dead. Her dress was ripped and the crust around her smudged lips made her look maddened and pervasive. He wanted to look away from her glare, from that evil smile, but he couldn't. She was the thing in the mirror, the thing on the other side that your mother told you didn't exist. *Well she was wrong, because look at it. Look at her.*

"What do you want?" He had spoken the words before he even knew he could talk.

"I want you. You're mine... you did this to me," she spoke, her cracked vocal chords piercing the air in an almost painful tone. Then she laughed; a sickly, maddening laugh.

"No..."

"Oh yes. You did this. And now I've come for you, baby." She moved forward, her skeletal ribs showing through her ripped and ruined dress. It hung open, exposing her miniscule, starved body. But she was hungry now. Oh so very hungry. Her arms reached out for him, as she stumbled unnaturally forward. He did not reach out to catch her, but somehow she managed to stabilise herself without his help.

"You did this to yourself! Not me – you," he spoke the words calmly, and as he saw her expression change to one of surprise, he realised he was not scared of her anymore.

"What?"

"You did this. You killed yourself. I'm sorry that you did. But you... this *thing,* is not you, Lorraine, not really. You're just a part of me. Something I have to let go of." She took another step forward, her foot leaning back unnaturally on the cold hard floor. This time she did not stay upright, and she let out a surprised cry as she fell to the floor.

"You will not do this!"

She crawled across the floor, closer with each unnatural movement, her face looking painfully thin. Her mouth peeled back in a grimace, and he realised it was tearing the flesh in the process. White bone was exposed against dark decaying gums. The teeth were sharp, like something out of a horror movie. He took a step back, trying to distance himself from the thing that had once been Lorraine.

"No, you don't understand, you don't exist. You can't hurt me."

"No!" she cried. She reached out with one jagged clawed hand, tried to grasp at the leg of his jeans, and failed. It dropped to the floor, and he heard the bones crack. The thing screeched out in what could have been anger or agony. Rage filled its eyes. He took another step back as somehow, the thing began to pick itself up from the floor with one working hand. The other drooped at its side. He watched with amazement as it stood, and took another step forward, teeth bared. As it stretched up, the skin around its ribs burst open and he saw the blackness of decaying flesh exposing white bone. Some of its innards dropped to the floor, and in the black mass there was life; maggots crawled and twisted around.

"Look at you... you're dead. Now you have to rest."

It tried to speak, but when it opened its mouth wider, the sharpened teeth began to drop from the dead gums.

"I'm sorry. I need to move on."

The thing shrieked again, a terrible shriek, and he noticed its body was beginning to fall apart, to disintegrate into nothing. Its eyes began to melt down its face, and the skin was slowly falling away, exposing more bone and decay, until finally, she/it was no more. He stared down at the thing that had once been Lorraine, before carefully stepping over it, towards the door on the other side. He hoped it was the right one.

52

"Other men said they have seen angels, but I have seen thee, and thou art enough." - G. Moore

At first there was nothing, then a room of bright white, so bright it hurt his eyes. He awoke with a groan, blinking and at first only registering the colour, or lack of. At least there was no blue. *Never again, blue.* Then feelings began to come back to him. Pain. His throat was dry, it hurt to swallow. Then he realised why; the tubes. He was in hospital. A hand reached out and squeezed his.

"Stanley? Stanley! He's awake, come quickly!"

Granny Hobbes? He tried to speak but something was blocking the words. It felt unnatural, but in his sleepy state, he couldn't figure out why. *Tubes... why tubes?* Instead he simply blinked, imagining the almost humorous look of confusion on his face, like in a cartoon. He turned his head, and his vision focused on his beloved grandmother. She looked tired, restless, but apart from that, well. Her bright red cardigan made her stand out against the white in an almost comforting way.

"I'm here, I'm here, child. Don't worry about a thing, you're here and you're okay," she said, turning to someone else.

"Can you take this damn tube out now? Let him speak."

A nurse came into view, and he realised many other people stood in the background. There was noise, and bleeping, and voices. He let the nurse remove the tube from his throat, and he gasped a large intake of air.

"Do you know where you are?" she asked, her voice bringing him slowly back to the world of the living.

"Hospital? Throat hurts. What happened?" he asked, uncertainly.

"You fell. You had a sharp blow to the head," Winnie explained, calmly. One name came into his head, and the memories came flooding back.

"McAvoy?"

"Arrested; in police custody, last time I checked."

"Oh God..."

He was beginning to remember what happened...the phone call to Gill. The empty theatre, reaching out in the darkness for... *Marcella.*

"Marcella! Where is she?" he blurted out. She had been there, in his dream. She had spoken to him, said that she... The look on Winnie Hobbes' face was a sad one, and his heart sank with the thought that it had been just a dream, after all. Surely not...

"I'm sorry, Stanley," she said, reaching out for his hand. He didn't register her touch, her warmth lost in translation to his skin.

"No..."

"I'm afraid she's gone... back to Russia. She couldn't wait any longer," Winnie explained. A cool wave of relief washed over him, and he took in a deep breath.

"Wait - to Russia?"

Winnie nodded. "Yes, but she was here. She came here every day, well, as much as the staff would allow, anyway."

He remembered her telling him now, in the dream that hadn't really been a dream at all. She had really been there, talking to him. She had really waited. He wondered if she had really looked like that. He raised his hand to his face and felt the stubble on his chin. It'd obviously been a little while since he'd had a shave.

"Ugh... how long have I been out?"

"Six weeks, Stanley."

"Oh God; no wonder I feel..."

"Out of it? You're quite right to feel that way, bet it feels like you're back from the dead, to be sure."

To his left, a large cluster of balloons stood by his bedside, obviously left by Gill. Cards and flowers lined the table. So that's what the floral smell had come from, in the dream. *Back from the dead.*

Stanley smiled, because in a way, he was, and it was nice; calming to hear another Irish accent, the soothing voice of his grandmother. Winnie smiled too.

53

"Each friend represents a world in us, a world possibly not born until they arrive, and it is only by this meeting that a new world is born." - Anais Nin

"Are you sure you're doing the right thing?" Gill asked, playing with the balloons as she watched him pack his bag. He was sat on the bed, still slightly weak from his hospital stay, but strengthened by the presence of his friend.

"Of course I'm sure. Sure as sure as I can be, to be sure," he replied, over-exaggerating his accent, which always made her laugh; but not this time.

"Stanley..."

He stood up, and she delicately placed down the jumper she had bought him only that day. It was getting chillier outside now. He held her in his arms, tight and she reciprocated, it was a proper hug between two good friends. Somewhere in that hug, she managed to smile beneath the tears.

"I have to go after her, Gill," he reminded her.

"I know, Stanley. I know. Can you believe it about the Duke?"

"Yeah, I can believe every word of it. Who would have thought? To be so ashamed of your own brother you actually have to murder him. That 'women in Egypt' joke probably had a lot to answer for..." Stanley shrugged.

"It was the straw that broke the camel's back, most likely," Gill replied.

"Really? According to McBeard – rest in peace – I thought it was the dildo?"

"Well, yes. I suppose we'll probably never know what happened in Ford's warped head. He was behind it all along.

When Bogleur died, I suppose he decided to take matters into his own hands, and not in a smart way. Almost succeeded in bringing down the entire festival, didn't he?"

A casual silence overtook the pair as they pondered the situation. Another mystery solved, although that wouldn't bring McBeard back. Or Bogleur, for that matter. Even if he was corrupt and liked to indulge in pterodactyl porn while dressed as a donkey, he still didn't deserve to end up dead. After all, although Bogleur had been corrupt, he hadn't actually planned to kill anyone. When he'd failed to accept a bribe from Ford to put a stop to McBeard's act... well, he'd decided to remedy the situation himself. And the rest was history.

"Looks like Clive saved the day, though. Finding that file in Rory's office... pity Rory absconded before anyone had the chance to blow the whistle on him. They reckon he made it back to the office to delete all his files right after he thwacked you on the head and knocked you into that coma," Gill said.

"That's when he realised the file was gone. Of course, after that he somehow managed time for a quick vodka or five, before using the rest to set fire to the office."

"You know, I couldn't believe it was actually him that... Well, he was mates with the Duke at Uni. Maybe he didn't have much choice."

Gill nodded.

"Now I just feel numb, like it all happened to someone else," finished Stanley.

"I couldn't believe it, either. Editor of the biggest daily paper in Edinburgh and everything; probably in Mexico or somewhere by now. And who would have thought Bogleur would be so two-faced? It's disgusting... one attitude for the public, another for behind closed doors," Gill said.

"Luckily, most of the acts still got to perform," Stanley replied. It had been all over the news. The scandal; fortunately he'd been safely tucked up in hospital, so the 'exclusive' that would never be an exclusive, never really came out...which was a pity. The Edinburgh Times was now under full investigation as a result of the fall-out. The rest of the press were having a field day over it. Stanley felt a bit used, what with being an accessory for crime and all. He'd never done anything illegal in his life.

"Yeah, as MJK would say, censorship is a cancer," Gill said, thoughtfully.

"This MJK sounds like a wise man," Stanley replied.

Gill was playing with the balloons again. "Did you see Fair's card?"

"Yes... I think I still have it here, somewhere," he said, reaching over to the windowsill.

It read:

Dear Stanley,

I hope you are doing okay in hospital. It has been an odd few weeks without you in the office. I realised I never properly thanked you for what you did. So, thank you. And don't forget to take care of those 'caterpillars' when you get back home.

Much love,

   Fair.

"Sweet, isn't it?"

"Yeah, it made me smile," Stanley replied.

"You know her and Clive are dating now?"

"You're kidding, right?" Stanley was shocked; that was quite a revelation.

"No, it's the talk of the whole office," Gill stated, knowingly enough to make him well aware he was out of the loop. Not that he had ever really been *in* the loop, but that was another matter.

"Wow. Never thought I'd see that coming... although now you've said, it kind of makes sense, in an odd sort of way."

Gill nodded, and she was lost in thought again. She didn't want to say goodbye to him.

"Will you take good care of Jasper for me?" Stanley asked, breaking her thought bubble.

"Of course I will; me and Jasper are best buds by now. He misses you, by the way. Told me to send his love your way," Gill smiled.

"And his fleas, no doubt," he laughed.

"Yes, there is that," Gill replied.

Another silence descended upon the pair.

"Wait? Do you think we've covered everything?" asked Stanley.

"Almost... I mean, just about. But then, there's always the epilogue for that."

Outside, the September sun shone brightly, making him realise he had the chance to start all over again... they both did.

Epilogue

"If it's True Love, none of the rules matter." – Elizabeth Wurzel

Roughly a year later, Princes St. Gardens:

An August summer's day, just like any other, played out upon the cool grass. It was that time of year again, and the festival goers had descended on the city in a colourful array of diversity and hopeful spirit. Along with the hotdogs, he could smell it in the air; it was the Fringe Festival. Stanley casually flipped through the programme he held in his hands, reading out shows in an air that made him sound like he knew a thing or two about culture. He really didn't. But he was working on it. He rolled over on the grass, savouring the sunshine on his face. The programme shined colourfully in the light.

"So, what shall we see next, Anita and the Bear Trail? The Three Mouseketeers, perhaps? What about Naked Jelly Bean Tights? Actually no, that one sounds a bit..."

Marcella looked up from her own programme, and gave him that smile that he'd fallen in love with. It was hard to believe it was almost a year ago since they'd met. She licked her ice cream thoughtfully, as if she was really savouring every cool creamy taste sensation.

"How about The Paranoid Android, at the Underbelly? It's a..."

"You're an Underbelly convert now, huh? Let me guess - Star Trek theme, by any chance?"

"No actually, it's a Radiohead parody," she grinned.

"And that's why I love you."

The End

Other Titles from Cauliay Publishing

Kilts, Confetti & Conspiracy *By* Bill Shackleton

Child Of The Storm *By* Douglas Davidson

Buildings In A House Of Fire *By* Graham Tiler

Tatterdemalion *By* Ray Succre

From The Holocaust To the Highlands *By* Walter Kress

To Save My father's Soul *By* Michael William Molden

Love, Cry and Wonder Why *By* Bernard Briggs

A Seal Snorts Out The Moon *By* Colin Stewart Jones

The Haunted North *By* Graeme Milne

Revolutionaries *By* Jack Blade

Michael *By* Sandra Rowell

Poets Centre Stage (*Vol One*) *By* Various poets

The Fire House *By* Michael William Molden

The Upside Down Social World *By* Jennifer Morrison

The Strawberry Garden *By* Michael William Molden

Poets Centre Stage (*Vol Two*) *By* Various Poets

Havers & Blethers *By* The Red Book Writers

Amphisbaena *By* Ray Succre

The Ark *By* Andrew Powell

The trouble With Pheep Ahrrf *By* Coffeestayne

The Diaries of Belfour, Ellah, Rainals Co *By* Gerald Davison

Underway, Looking Aft *By* Amy Shouse

Silence Of The Night *By* Sandra Rowell

The Bubble *By* Andrew Powell

Minor Variations and Change *By* Graham Tiler

The Darkness of Dreams *By* Pamela Gaull

Spoils of the Eagle *By* Alan James Barker

When I followed The Elephant *By* Tony R. Rodriguez

Calvi Sinners *By* Roberta Vassallo

Titles Coming Soon

The Psychic Biker Meets The Extreme Ghost Hunter
By Paul Green and Stephen Lambert

The Crownless King *By* Phil Williams

The Ascent of Isaac Steward *By* Mike French